"Why should I experience poverty?"

"Forgotten your own ambition," Mac drawled, "to marry a poor man?"

"So that's what you're up to!" Dayle's temper was soaring. "Let me tell you something...you'd be the very last person I'd consider!"

"Oh no," he contradicted her. "You vowed you'd marry the *first* poor man who asked you."

"Well, find yourself another heiress." Her voice broke on a half sob. "If you kept me here for the next fifty years, I still wouldn't marry you!"

"In fifty years," he said gravely, "I doubt if I'd fancy you."

Dayle was literally shaking with anger...and fear. She knew she was not entirely immune to him. If he tried to sway her by employing his undeniably powerful masculinity, she wouldn't stand a chance.

Books by Annabel Murray

HARLEQUIN ROMANCES

2549—ROOTS OF HEAVEN
2558—KEEGAN'S KINGDOM
2596—THE CHRYSANTHEMUM AND THE SWORD
2612—VILLA OF VENGEANCE
2625—DEAR GREEN ISLE

These books may be available at your local bookseller.

For a free catalog listing all titles currently available,
send your name and address to:

Harlequin Reader Service
P.O. Box 52040, Phoenix, AZ · 85072-2040
Canadian address: Stratford, Ontario N5A 6W2

Dear
Green Isle

Annabel Murray

Harlequin Books

TORONTO • NEW YORK • LONDON
AMSTERDAM • PARIS • SYDNEY • HAMBURG
STOCKHOLM • ATHENS • TOKYO • MILAN

Original hardcover edition published in 1984
by Mills & Boon Limited

ISBN 0-373-02625-0

Harlequin Romance first edition June 1984

This book is for Tom, my husband,
who encouraged me to be a person
in my own right.

———————————————◆·◆———————————————

CHAPTER ONE

'ANOTHER hectic day over, Dayle?' Jenny Spencer greeted her friend, leaning as she did so on the half-door of Major's stable. 'You through for the evening?'

Dayle Abercrombie nodded her silvery-fair head and with a brisk slap of farewell on Major's glistening flanks, she left the Suffolk Punch's stall, joining Jenny in the stable yard.

'Yes, that's it; pigs fed, cows milked and the horses mucked out. Phew, could *I* use a bath!'

'I must say you *do* pong a bit, old thing.' Jenny tucked a companionable arm through Dayle's as they strolled across the parkland to the cottage they shared, just inside the boundary of Barnet Country Park. 'It's almost as bad as the manure I've been forking over.' She laughed. 'Who'd have thought, a year ago, that we'd ever have to work for our living?'

'Who indeed!' Dayle agreed, blue eyes sombre.

'Mind you,' Jenny reminded her drily, '*You* don't *need* to work.'

'Not for financial reasons perhaps, but for the sake of my pride . . .'

'Pride!' Jenny snorted. 'If it weren't for pride, you'd be living "happily ever after", now.'

Tired, but with a consciousness of a day's work well done, the two girls entered their cottage, took it in turn to shower then sat down to a meal, cooked to perfection in their pre-set oven.

'You're a fantastic cook, Dayle,' Jenny sighed, half an hour later, as they rose to clear the table. 'No . . .' as Dayle showed signs of wanting to remain in the tiny kitchen. 'You did the cooking, my turn to wash up.'

Dayle flinched; the words brought back memories she had tried to erase.

'I'd rather help, honestly,' she said now. 'You know how I hate having nothing to do.'

Jenny paused, elbow-deep in soapsuds, to look at her friend.

'How long do you think you can go on like this? You never let up for a minute. I think you're afraid you might find yourself with time to think!'

It didn't take too much perception on Jenny's part to recognise *that* fact, Dayle thought later, long after the two girls were in their respective beds. Her friend knew, for she had confided fully in her, that there was much Dayle wished to forget.

Dayle had believed that driving her body to its physical limits would achieve that end; and in one sense it had succeeded, since most nights exhaustion claimed her, ensuring a deep and dreamless sleep. But by day the remedy was not as efficacious. Labouring with the body did not occupy the mind, which was still at liberty to roam in the forbidden pastures of painful memory.

Tonight, Jenny's comment that Dayle did not really need to work had started off one of those trains of thought which, once embarked upon, were inescapable. Little more than a year ago their lives had been very different, both hers and Jenny's. They had been friends right through schooldays and beyond. Both daughters of wealthy men, they had led lives of pampered luxury, sharing the same pursuits and interests. But Jenny's father had lost his fortune through a series of unwise investments and Jenny had joined the ranks of those who had to earn a living.

So far as Dayle knew, her own father was as wealthy as ever. But it was two or three months since she had returned briefly to her home, only to storm out again. vowing nevermore to set foot there, never to accept a penny of her father's money.

How she had changed, Dayle marvelled, thinking about her present lifestyle. But she knew too there had been an even greater alteration in her as a person. She supposed the process had begun, however imperceptibly, on that June evening last year when she had issued her declaration of independence. She and her father had not often disagreed . . . she was too indulged for that . . . except over one particular subject . . .

'Do you ever take *anyone's* advice?' Angus Abercrombie had roared the question at his tall, glamorous daughter.

Usually cool and self-contained, the only person who could make Dayle lose her temper was her father, probably because they were so alike in temperament . . . though neither of them would ever have admitted it.

'Not when it's the kind of advice *you're* always giving me,' she retorted. 'And there's no need to shout!' The blue eyes, so like her father's, were equally fiery.

Angus glared at her in exasperated frustration, running a large hand through his thick thatch of grey hair. Exceedingly vocal in the boardroom, he found himself uncharacteristically at a loss for words in the face of his daughter's stubborn resistance, her refusal to accept that in this matter he knew best.

'You could at least meet the fellow . . . see what you think of him,' he said at last, endeavouring to moderate his tone.

Dayle tilted a round, determined chin, her full, soft lips setting into firm lines.

'So far I've met at least a dozen candidates for the post of your son-in-law . . . and all cast in the same mould. Do you select your Boards in a job lot from Burton's window?' she scoffed. 'Tailor's dummies, the lot of them!'

'At least they've more backbone than those friends of yours who lounge about down at the yacht club!'

This subject was a perennial bone of contention between Dayle Abercrombie and her father. An exceedingly rich, self-made man, with a seat on the board of a dozen companies, Angus was determined that his only . . . and otherwise much indulged daughter . . . was going to marry a man of equal wealth, and one, moreover, with the ability and acumen to manage the fortune that someday would be hers; and he regularly presented the latest hand-picked aspirant for her inspection.

'They all look the same,' she reiterated, 'if it weren't for the occasional variation in colour of hair and eyes . . .'

'All right! All right!' her father said testily, 'you've made your point. But this one's different, I promise you.'

'Is he on one of your wretched boards?' Dayle asked.

'Yes, he . . .'

'Is he rich?'

'Of course, I . . .'

'Efficient, capable?'

'Yes, yes, otherwise he wouldn't be . . .'

'Then where's the difference?' she demanded triumphantly.

'Well, for one thing, he's a Scot . . . like myself,' Angus added with some pride. He invariably boasted that his hard-headedness was solely attributable to his ancestry.

Dayle gave the irreverent shout of laughter this remark always produced.

'A lifelong exile too, I suppose?'

'Impertinent baggage,' Angus rumbled. 'So what if I've never been north of Carlisle? My father was from Edinburgh and my

great-great-grandad on my mother's side was a Shetland
Islander, and it's what's in the blood that counts; and I'll go to
Scotland, aye . . . and to Shetland, when I've time . . . to find my
roots.'

For as long as she could remember, this had been her father's
cry whenever he waxed nostalgic about his ancestry. When
Dayle had been younger she had believed he would do as he
planned, had shared his enthusiasm for seeking out the past; but
nowadays she did not place much faith in his ever achieving his
ambition; the City occupied too much of his time. Of course, she
would still like to see the places from which her ancestors came,
as long as she didn't have to live there. This was her scene . . . the
residential area within easy commuting distance of London and
the various clubs to which she belonged.

'Just *meet* Callum,' Angus wheedled now. 'You might even like
him. He's a real charmer. Every woman he meets falls for him
like a ton of bricks.'

He couldn't have chosen a recommendation more likely to
harden his daughter's resolve. If there was one type of man she
detested, it was the kind who had every woman at his feet. Any
man who wanted to gain *her* respect would have to pursue her,
not the other way around.

'He sounds quite insufferable,' she said coldly, 'and what a
ridiculous name . . . Callum. I wonder he doesn't get it changed
by deed poll. It makes him sound like a monster in *The Tempest*. I
shall call him Caliban.'

It was only since she attained her majority that Angus Abercrombie had realised just how much he had spoilt his motherless
daughter. With the money to gratify her every whim, he had
done just that, determined that she should never have to endure
the hardships he had known in his youth. Now nineteen, tall,
proud, svelte, she was coolly self-possessed, a typically poised
product of the private finishing school in Switzerland, with every
accomplishment except domestic skills; and sometimes Angus
wondered uneasily if it wouldn't have been wiser to give her a
more practical education, to expose her to the more prosaic side
of life. What would his late wife have said, he mused guiltily, to
know that her daughter couldn't even boil an egg? His Eileen
had worked hard in the early days of their marriage, her loyalty
and support making a secure foundation for his struggle to the
top.

Still, he *was* at the top, he reminded himself, and his daughter didn't need to know how to boil an egg, or to perform any other such mundane chore. A rich man's daughter, she would be a rich man's wife, if he had his way, with servants continuing to supply her every need. The stifling of his own momentary guilt and his determination to ensure her future security made him speak more forcibly than he might have done, considering his daughter's stubborn streak.

'You'll meet young Callum, and what's more, you'll be civil to him. I've invited him for dinner a fortnight tomorrow, along with a few other folk. You've had fair warning, so no tricks . . . like pleading a previous engagement.'

'Since I'm your hostess, I shall of course be courteous to any guest you invite here,' said Dayle, her sweet, husky voice very controlled, a sure sign that she was perilously close to losing her temper. 'But do warn Caliban not to get too excited.'

'What d'you mean?' Angus enquired suspiciously.

'I mean that, while he may be on your short list of prospective husbands, he is emphatically *not* on mine.'

'Damn it!' Angus exploded. 'What can you possibly have against him, when you haven't even met him?'

'A rich womaniser?' Her tone was satirical, 'One who's prepared to suck up to the boss in order to meet his daughter? Shall I tell you something, Daddy? Rather than marry one of your stereotyped boardroom élite, I'll accept the first penniless man that asks me . . . and don't think that's an idle threat. I mean it!'

On this devastating exit line she swept out of her father's study, leaving Angus Abercrombie with considerable and unpleasant food for thought. He knew only too well that Dayle, once she took a notion into her head, or issued a statement of that nature, was quite capable of carrying it through, with what he termed pigheaded disregard for consequences . . . not realising that his daughter had inherited the stubborn determination which had carried him up in the world.

She'd do it too. Dayle vowed, unconsciously echoing her father's thoughts, as she ran up the stairs and entered her own second-floor sitting room, decorated and furnished to her own taste . . . though not by her. She had merely directed the operations of the expensive firm employed by Angus to do the work.

Still brooding on her father's irritating attempts at match making, she draped her slender length on an iron-framed,

Victorian chaise-longue, upholstered in palest green, and looke
around her with complacence, while meditating on her lates
verbal battle with Angus.

Wallpaper and paint in delicate, harmonising shades of gre
and green were matched by the heavy brocade curtains, heavil
encrusted with embroidery, which framed the double-glaze
windows, giving a beautiful view over the surrounding country
side and, more immediately, the velvety lawns with their shad
ing of tall trees.

Rich men were all the same, she thought. They had only on
aim in life . . . to increase their wealth, to form alliances witl
others of equal financial stature. It did not seem inconsistent t
her that, for her part, she should enjoy the possession of thi
wealth. How much more worthwhile it would be, she muse
romantically, to bestow her hand and fortune on a really poo
man and witness his grateful delight. She would buy him a hous
and plan the whole décor . . . not just one room.

Because of her father's conscientious care, Dayle had no
encountered any impecunious young men; thus it had neve
occurred to her that without his concern she would be the targe
for many an unscrupulous fortune-hunter, that the type of ma
who would be willing to marry her solely for her money woul
not be worthy of her regard . . . an accusation she was always to
ready to level against the men her father presented to her.

Boundlessly energetic, Dayle could not sit still, nor endure he
own company for long. The day stretched ahead of her, to spen
in whatever occupation she pleased, with whom she pleased . .
within a circle of approved acquaintances. What should it be
The riding stable, where her own mare was at livery, the tenni
club, the yacht club . . . or shopping?

She moved into the adjoining bedroom and riffled through th
enormous wardrobe, where dresses by Mary Quant an
Emanuel brushed against gowns by Balmain, Cardin an
Givenchy. In her red Fiat sports car she could be in London i
under an hour. But it was too hot, she decided, for trying o
clothes; besides, there was nothing she really wanted. A visit t
the hairdresser, perhaps? If allowed to grow, her hair swiftl
became unmanageable. She studied her reflection in the full
length mirror. But the thick silver cap of hair, with its short
casual, expensive cut, needed no attention.

Sometimes, nowadays, Dayle heaved a nostalgic sigh for tha

short, easily managed style. Her wages didn't run to expensive hairdressing salons and her hair, now long and heavy, was generally scraped back and secured by a ribbon at the nape of her neck. Nor were there any model dresses in her present wardrobe; jeans and T-shirts were the order of the day, relieved occasionally in the evening by a cotton dress or blouse and skirt. What a lot she'd learnt in a year . . . what a little monster she'd been in those days, only she hadn't realised it then . . .

She didn't blame all these young men for being so willing to fall in with her father's wishes, for being so eager to marry her, Dayle had conceded charitably that evening a year ago. Knowing of her future prospects as her father's sole heir, seeing her against the expensive, tasteful elegance of this house, one could under- stand their ambition . . . especially with the added bonus of her good looks. Complacently she turned her head before the mirror, studying the high cheekbones . . . an inheritance from her mother . . . curving downwards to a round, determined chin, the short, straight nose, the full mouth with its natural, inviting pout. Dayle didn't feel that it was conceited to recognise her own beauty. So many people, men in particular, had told her she was lovely that she now took it for granted, expecting and generally receiving the homage due to her. This new man . . . what was his name? . . . Callum . . . would, of course, be no exception. He would be just as predictably boring as the rest, ingratiating, anxious to please, uttering platitudes . . . in fact, another stuffed shirt.

Finally Dayle decided to drift down to the Yacht Club. There would be other young people there, similarly circumstanced . . . teenage sons and daughters of rich men, with nothing to do but indulge themselves, spending their father's money. Dayle had a splendid seat on a horse and played a punishing game of tennis, but admitted frankly to being useless in a boat. The slightest motion made her feel sick. However, she knew she looked delightful in white slacks and sweatshirt, with the club's dark blue anchor motif and a cap at a jaunty angle on her neat, elegant head.

She was greeted with flattering delight by the half dozen or so boys lounging about in the club room, slightly less enthusiasm being shown by their girl-friends. Somehow they always felt their own not inconsiderable charms diminished when Dayle put in an appearance. Amongst the girls, only Jenny Spencer greeted her with genuine warmth. Jenny was a friend of long standing. They had been through school and finishing school together and recently they had joined a young ornithologist society; and despite being two very sophisticated young women kept up their interest in bird-watching. Besides, Jenny's own beauty could stand comparison with Dayle's. She was as dark and voluptuous as Dayle was blonde and svelte.

'Hallo, old thing! How's life treating you today?'

Dayle's mouth formed into an exaggeration of its normal delicious pout and as one man the boys leant forward, eager to hear her answer.

'Hideously! The revered parent is trotting another horse out of the boardroom stable for inspection!'

'Oh! Any good?' Jenny enquired interestedly. More practical than her friend, she was always telling Dayle she was a fool to pass up all these handsome, eligible men.

Dayle shrugged.

'I haven't met him yet. The big day's a fortnight off. But he sounds just like the rest. You know Daddy's idea of the perfect husband!'

'I suppose you jibbed as usual?'

'Well, natch! So would any self-respecting woman. I mean to choose my own husband. In fact I told the revered P. so. I gave him quite a jolt, I fancy . . . told him I'd marry the first penniless man who proposed.'

'You didn't? Oh, how priceless!' Jenny squealed with delighted laughter. 'Hey, listen to this, gang! Listen to what our Dayle's done now!'

The story was repeated for general edification, with varying reactions. The boys, thinking it all a bit of a lark, egging Dayle on, the girls, slightly shocked, yet envious of her daring spirit . . . opposing her father's wishes.

'Suppose he cuts you off with a shilling?' one of them ventured.

Dayle tossed her elegant head.

'He won't,' she said confidently.

The rest of the morning passed pleasantly, in the invention and relation of more and more exaggerated versions of what Dayle's future life might be, married to a penniless husband, and when she returned home, it was in a glow of satisfaction at her own popularity and with the determination to carry out her wilful plan even more firmly fixed.

To her surprise, in the days that followed her father made very little reference to the subject of the forthcoming dinner party. Usually when he was producing yet another eligible man for her inspection he was anxious for days beforehand that everything should be meticulously planned, to the very last detail . . . even to the extent of suggesting to Dayle what she should wear . . . advice that on principle she rarely followed. But apart from enquiring whether the date was in her diary, the menu planned and the staff advised, he appeared strangely casual about the whole affair . . . almost, she thought, as if he had more important things on his mind; and since the subject of bestowing her hand in a suitable marriage generally took precedence over everything else, she was not a little piqued.

Normally wholly concerned with her own interests, even Dayle finally noticed her father's increasing preoccupation, the fact that he seemed unduly anxious about something or other. Once or twice, looking up to speak to him, she had caught him with a worried frown creasing his broad forehead. But to all her enquiries Angus repeatedly assured her that nothing was amiss.

This in itself was strange, for Dayle was accustomed to hear her father relating the numerous aggravations of his working day. He had given up long ago trying to instruct her in the running of his various business interests. Dayle simply found the subject boring. As long as the firms concerned continued to afford her the lifestyle to which she was accustomed, she was quite content that others should shoulder the burdens. But now a niggling little worry crept into a corner of her mind. Under her nonchalant manner was a very real affection for Angus, but there was also a strong streak of self-interest. Was her father experiencing financial problems? It was all very well to declare, in a fit of temper, that she wouldn't marry a rich man. But she had no objection whatsoever to being a rich woman . . .

It was amazing what you could learn to do without, Dayle thought, turning restlessly on the single bed, watching the moonlight stream through the cottage window. She never slept with her curtains closed now . . . not since she had slept in a certain room which boasted no curtains at all. Someone . . . she refused even to think his name . . . had once accused her of being a parasite. He wouldn't be able to level that charge at her these days. But a year ago . . .

Then Dayle's only concern had been for her father's business interests, for possible effects upon herself. She had even begun to

visualise scenes in which her father told her they were penniless
to imagine the humiliation of having to resign from all her clubs
having to buy her clothes at chain stores. What would happen to
the elegant dinners over which she presided . . . so much a part of
the Abercrombies' way of life? the visits to the opera, the ballet
. . . holidays in the South of France. At nineteen, Dayle had
visited more countries than many people saw in a lifetime.

Watching Angus more closely, she noticed that he was taking
an unnaturally keen interest in his mail. Normally, the day's
letters were thrown in a huge pile on to the massive mahogany
desk in his study, to be sorted through each evening at his
leisure. But now, before leaving the house, he shuffled carefully
through his correspondence and almost daily he removed one
particular envelope and thrust it into the breast pocket of his
jacket.

It was always the same sort of envelope, the keen-eyed Dayle
observed. She would have suspected that her father was con-
ducting a clandestine correspondence with some woman, but for
the dingy, rather crumpled appearance of the letters. This ritual
had gone on for over a week when, one morning, Angus Abercrombie sorted his mail with less than his usual care; Dayle
recognised the familiar envelope, but, for her own reasons, she
deliberately did not draw his attention to it.

As soon as she heard her father's Rolls draw away, she
abstracted the letter and took it up to her room. She had a
Teasmade at her bedside and it was the work of a moment to
steam open the cheap, poorly sealed envelope. She didn't know
what it was she expected to discover, but it was certainly not the
message which revealed itself to her startled gaze; for it concerned herself, and in a most unpleasant context. Once more she
perused the words on the soiled piece of paper. They were
printed crudely, by an illiterate hand, if the spelling was anything to go by.

'Your a ritch man, Abercromby. So pay up if you dont won
your dauter to disapear, or something worse to happen to
you.'

Dayle's first reaction was one of disbelief. This couldn't be
happening . . . not to the *Abercrombies*! It was the sort of thing
that happened to other people . . . to politicians, film stars,
millionaires.

Then, with a cold, nauseous feeling, she realised that her father probably was a millionaire and that unless this letter was some kind of sick joke, it *was* happening.

What had been in the earlier notes? What had her father done about them? Had any money changed hands . . . or had he turned the matter over to the police? Should she tackle him about it? She realised that she had placed herself in an invidious position. Indulgent as her father was, he would be furious if she admitted to opening his mail. But how could she exist in this state of uncertainty, not knowing if she was in danger every time she left the house . . . and what *was* the alternative, the implied threat to her father?

All her instincts prompted her to phone one of her friends, someone . . . anyone . . . just to talk about the horror of what she had discovered. But pride revolted against baring her soul in this fashion . . . she, Dayle Abercrombie, who had a reputation for poise and total self-control. Nevertheless, she was not accustomed to feeling uncertain and insecure and she didn't like it. She resealed the envelope and went slowly down-stairs to replace it in the study.

Now it was her turn to be preoccupied, and dinner that evening was an unusually silent meal, father and daughter each absorbed in their own thoughts. Over coffee, as she eyed him surreptitiously, Angus seemed suddenly to reach a decision.

'Dayle!'

'Yes, Daddy?' She was instantly alert. Somehow she sensed that this was more than a conventional opening gambit.

'I've been a bit worried lately. I've tried not to let it show, but . . .'

Dayle smiled wryly. In that case, Angus was a very poor actor.

'I have noticed, actually. Do you want to talk about it?' She held her breath, praying that he would bring the matter that occupied both their minds out into the open, so that they could discuss it. Somehow she felt that to talk about it would dispel some of the anxiety she felt. Despite her vaunted sophistication, she still retained a childlike faith in her father's ability to solve every problem.

Angus hesitated, then shook his head.

'No . . . no, perhaps it'll sort itself out. But, Dayle, whatever happens, remember I always have your interests at heart. You've always come first, and you always will. Just . . . just take care of yourself, eh?'

Her heart contracted, and for the first time in her life that she could remember, she actually felt guilty. The poor darling didn't want her to know about the threats. He would be terribly upset if he found out that she'd opened that horrid letter. Was he going to pay this horrible person . . . or persons? She hated the thought of someone bleeding her father for money. He might be fabulously rich, but he had worked hard for his wealth; and she didn't like the idea of it going to someone who had probably never done an honest day's work in his life. It didn't occur to her that her threatened intention to marry a poor man would have virtually the same effect.

'You take care too, Daddy,' she said huskily.

She felt extremely nervous next day. True, the servants were about and surely no one would attempt to abduct her in broad daylight, from her own home? But she certainly wasn't going to risk leaving the house. Even shopping held out no charms for her, and she hung around all day, boredom and irritability mingling with her fear.

'Been anywhere nice today?' Angus asked, when he returned that evening, showing surprise when she admitted that she had not. 'I suppose you haven't noticed any strangers hanging about?' he enquired casually, 'in the street, I mean?'

A frisson of fear zipped along Dene's spine.

'No—no . . . why do you ask?'

'Oh, just checking.' His tone was too airy. 'There've been a few burglaries in the area lately. Can't be too careful.'

This verbal fencing was very wearing on the nerves, Dayle thought. She wished either that Angus would come right out with it and tell her about the threats, so that she could ask what action he was taking . . . or that she hadn't read the wretched letter.

Two or three days passed; there had been no more crumpled brown envelopes in the mail. Dayle felt sure she would have noticed. Insensibly she relaxed, as she began to think that somehow the incident must be over, the problem resolved by her father. Certainly Angus appeared more at ease, more his old self, laughing and joking with her at meal times.

It was a shock to realise that, in two days' time, they were supposed to be entertaining and that she had done very little in the way of preparation. She had been too engrossed with the matter of the letters. It was such a relief to feel safe again that Dayle exerted herself more than she would otherwise have done, driving the well-trained staff nearly demented with her demands, her constant supervision. Only their impeccable manners and fear of losing their positions in a wealthy household restrained them from irritable rebellion.

Thus, on the evening of the momentous dinner, Dayle knew that her father would not have occasion to be ashamed, either of her, or of the meal she had ordered for his guests.

'Everything ready for tonight?' Angus had asked that morning as he left the house. 'Callum is looking forward to meeting you.'

'Really?' Dayle, her calm restored, was her old supercilious self. 'I can't think why. It won't do him any good.'

She had planned that pre-dinner drinks should be served in the drawing room, an eighty by twenty-five-foot apartment that ran half the full length of the rear of the house. The room looked delightful on this mild summer evening, she thought, the large sliding windows open to the garden, so that the sunlight might play on cream and grey paintwork, bringing out the jewel colours in the Afghan rugs that scattered the dark oak floors.

The room was totally free from clutter, having a sitting area at each end, so that two totally different conversations could take place without one disrupting the other. One end wall held white floor-to-ceiling shelves, with a museum of Angus's favourite possessions . . . a few antiquarian books in leather bindings, glass paperweights and a collection of chess pieces in various materials, ranging from plain wood to jade and ivory.

The house being fully centrally heated, there was no fireplace, and as a focal point Dayle always arranged an enormous display of flowers in an antique copper container of vast size and uncertain purpose. Tonight the flowers she had chosen were tall, straight spikes of delphinium, varying in shade from white to light blue, through to purple.

Since she had gone to such pains over the meal and the house, she felt that she too might as well appear to advantage. She was not in the least interested in impressing this Callum person . . . or Caliban, as she still referred to him in her father's presence . . . but at least he should see and regret the unattainable; she had no objection to this opportunity to deflate his pretensions, to bestow yet another set-down to one of the 'tailors' dummies.'

With her healthy tan and natural, glowing colour, she had little need of cosmetics, other than eyeshadow and lipstick, but it was a daring, rather outré outfit that she chose to wear. Knowing that the other female guests were likely to be fifty-plus and dowdily dressed . . . Angus always made sure on these occasions that no one should outshine his daughter . . . she took a perverse delight in imagining the pursed lips and disapproving glances.

The orange and gold jumpsuit in glitter-striped silk georgette clung seductively to her full, taut breasts above the narrow waist. Dangling gold earrings in an elongated leaf design drew attention to magnificently chiselled cheekbones, the casual elegance of the short blonde hair. Perilously high-heeled slippers, adding another four inches to her five feet seven, completed the ensemble, and before leaving the bedroom she clasped on a heavy bracelet, jangling with gold charms, and sprayed on an expensive scent.

'Eat your heart out, Caliban,' she pronounced aloud, as she regarded the total effect in the full-length mirror of her wardrobe.

It was incredible to think that, once, *that* lifestyle had completely satisfied her . . . the days spent in occupations that could really only be described as hobbies . . . nothing more irksome demanded of her as her father's daughter than the overseeing of his household staff, menus arranged in consultation with the French Chef and a little flower arranging . . .

Once she had been the proud possessor of long, tapering, faultlessly manicured nails, setting off slim, dainty hands which had never known what it was to be soiled. These days her nails, for practical reasons, were cut ruthlessly short and there was no point in applying nail varnish, which would soon be cracked and flaking; and as to dirtying her hands . . . she could imagine the goodnatured teasing she would receive from her workmates at the Country Park, if she had donned white cotton gloves here . . . as she had once done, just for flower arranging. Even heavy duty gardening gloves could not exclude the grime which somehow found access to her once soft white flesh. In fact, she scarcely ever remembered to wear any protection on her hands, except when it was her turn to work in the walled garden of the estate, weeding amongst the viciously thorned rose bushes. No one could call her hands 'useless adornments' now . . . strong, tanned and, despite her intermittent efforts to improve them, inclined to be calloused. Looking back at that almost dreamlike figure in its elegant georgette jumpsuit, waiting for her father's guests to arrive, it was nearly impossible to believe that she was the same girl . . .

Dayle had always prided herself on punctuality, and she had been in position exactly five minutes before the guests were due to arrive. Doubtless, she thought with cynical amusement, the Callum person would arrive first, eager to ingratiate himself with his senior director's daughter.

After the appointed hour had come and gone, Dayle began to consult her watch, impatiently at first, then with growing annoyance. This really was too bad. No sign of any of the guests; her father had not yet put in an appearance and, worst of all, the maid deputed to hand round the tray of drinks was not yet on duty in the drawing room.

Dayle was moving across the room, intent on ringing the bell which would summon the dilatory servant, when a sound from the open window behind her caused her to turn. A man stood just inside the room, hands behind him, his back to the sunlight outside, so that his face was in shadow. Though Dayle could not make out his features, it was obvious from his clothes that he was no dinner guest. Tall and broad-shouldered, he was dressed in faded denims and a short-sleeved shirt, both items of clothing having definitely seen better days. His bare feet were encased in scuffed, open sandals.

'Yes? What is it?' Dayle raised haughty eyebrows at this incongruous apparition.

'Miss Abercrombie?' he asked. 'Miss *Dayle* Abercrombie?' His voice was deep, pleasant, with just the faintest trace of an accent, which she could not place.

She nodded her head in cold acknowledgement.

'The back door is at the side of the house, if you're delivering something.'

'Oh, I'm not delivering,' he said easily. 'I'm collecting.'

Then, before she could fathom his intention, he had moved in on her, with surprising swiftness for a man of his size, one arm going around her shoulders, while his free hand clapped a wad of material over her nose, material which smelt abominably, which made . . . her . . . feel . . . strange . . . very strange, she thought confusedly, as she began to crumple into the stranger's hard embrace.

CHAPTER TWO

It was a long way back from wherever she had been. Dayle struggled to hasten her returning consciousness. She was aware of a dull, throbbing headache, dry mouth and a feeling of nausea. She must have fainted? But no. It was more than that. Now, with a panicky sensation in her throat, she remembered the man and the evil-smelling cloth in his hand. Wherever she was, it was dark and stuffy and she couldn't move . . . something was restraining her, and her face felt stiff and strange.

Experimentally, she tried to shift a hand . . . useless . . . what had he done to her?

As her brain slowly cleared, shaking off the after-effects of chloroform, for she was certain that was what he had used, realisation dawned. She could not move because she was bound hand and foot, and gagged, lying beneath a heavy covering of some kind . . . a car blanket probably, since she seemed to be in a moving vehicle . . . one whose springs badly needed attention, for she was being jolted and jarred in a most unpleasant manner.

Fear and indignation mingled, as she interpreted her situation. Those crumpled notes! They had *not* been bluff, nor had her father succeeded in staving off the threat they contained. She had been abducted, in broad daylight, from their own home, only moments before she should have been surrounded in a protective cocoon of her father's guests. If only they had not been late, she thought bitterly.

Fear mounted and with it grew despair, as she realised her complete helplessness. She could not aid herself in any way. She didn't know where she was, who her assailant was, or their eventual destination. The only faint ray of hope was that her father would not allow her to be in this position for long. Once he received the ransom note . . . there was bound to be a note, there always was . . . Angus would pay for her release. Unless . . . unless the sum were too great? If only this man were not *too* greedy! Suppose he asked for an impossible amount? Well, she would tell him, she thought, with a touch of her usual spirit . . .

she would tell him to moderate his demands, when she was able to speak.

She was suddenly anxious for this journey to be over, so that she could face her captor, tell him just what she thought of him . . . find out exactly who he was and what he had in mind. She wondered how long she had been unconscious. Certainly by now her absence would have been discovered, and she could imagine her father's anguish, the chaos that must exist at the house right now, the ruin of her dinner party . . . and after all her hard work! The thought increased her indignation. This was intolerable! She was not going to endure this discomfort a moment longer.

She found that it was possible, with an effort, to drum her feet against what she presumed must be the door panels, and this was confirmed when a deep voice protested:

'Quit damaging my car, or *I'll* damage you!'

It was definitely the same voice, the voice of the man who had abducted her. Moreover, judging by the absence of any other sound, he was alone. Dayle felt a little more hopeful. There might be more chance of outwitting one man. But if he thought she was going to take any notice of his words, he had seriously underestimated her. At least her action had brought some response, and she was going to keep it up until he was forced by sheer irritation to release her from this undignified position; she shuddered at the thought of what its effect must be on the elegant outfit she was wearing. So even though it put intense strain on her stomach muscles, she began to jerk her legs, hammering with her heels, trying to do as much damage as she could to his beastly car. She was young, extremely fit and determined, and she could keep this up, she thought grimly, for as long as necessary.

It didn't take long. After five minutes, in which she could almost sense his rigid self-control, his attempt to ignore the noise she was making, she heard him swearing under his breath. Then the car swerved and braked violently.

Her heart began to beat rapidly as she heard the driver's door open, slam to, heard him striding around the car to the near side. Then the back door was wrenched open and the enveloping blanket dragged away. Dayle blinked. It was daylight and apparently early morning. So she had been unconscious all night. By the time her eyes had focused properly, she had been lifted bodily from the back of the car and placed upright in the front passenger seat, still bound and gagged, and she registered the fact that this man was immensely strong . . . for she was tall and well-proportioned. The door slammed shut and her captor walked around the car and slid back behind the wheel.

Dayle looked around her. They were parked in a small layby on a quiet road . . . not another vehicle, or a pedestrian in sight, nor were there any recognisable landmarks.

'Explanation time, I think.' His voice was quiet and deep, with just that elusive trace of an accent, as he turned sideways in his seat to look at her.

Blue eyes glittered furiously at him, while muffled sounds issued from behind the gag and he raised one large, well-shaped hand, his mouth twisting into a wry smile.

'Oh no, we won't remove that . . . yet. An angry woman is a very talkative woman, and I intend to do all the talking, just for the present.'

His eyes, she noticed were startlingly green and they were appraising her in what she considered to be a very insulting manner from a complete stranger; his appraisal had almost a sexual quality. He was good-looking, she supposed, if you liked that raw, blatant kind of masculinity, his chin square and pugnacious. A scar ran down from the right-hand nostril of a broad, straight nose, to the corner of a large, firm mouth. The thick, slightly over-long hair was a robust chestnut, that just escaped being red. Altogether he exuded an air of ruthlessness, inflexibility and odious self-confidence. Who was he, this hateful creature who had dared to snatch her away like a kidnapped child?

'Of course you're wondering what this is all about?'

Oh no, she wasn't! At least she was one up on him there. He was the despicable creature who had sent her father those threatening letters, only . . . he spoke like an educated man, and those notes had been penned by an illiterate hand. But of course, she thought scornfully, he had disguised his writing, deliberately misspelling some of the words, so that if her father had called in the police, they would be misled.

'I gather you're a reasonably intelligent girl, despite having been spoilt rotten from your cradle.'

Her breast heaved on an indignant gasp. Oh, if only she could speak! It was . . . it was typical of the type of man he must be, to sit there and insult her, when she could not retort in her own defence. 'Reasonably intelligent' indeed! When she had received the best education money could buy . . . 'spoilt rotten'! How dared he! What could he possibly know about her?

'As I don't want you to burst a blood vessel,' he continued conversationally, his eyes still lingering on the flimsy material of her evening suit, where it rose and fell to her agitated breathing, 'I'll tell you that you'll be allowed to have your say, in a moment or two . . . though I've no doubt the first ten minutes will consist of totally illogical insults. But first there are a few facts you'd better know.'

Yes, perhaps he would regret letting her speak, Dayle seethed, when he'd been on the receiving end of her opinion of him! Illogical insults indeed! He deserved every epithet she could imagine. Well, she could wait. It gave her a chance to rehearse the blistering descriptions she intended to apply to him. He would find that she could be very logical indeed and very much to the point. Strangely, now that she could see her adversary, she was not so afraid. The unknown was always the worst: and he was at least an attractive, comparatively young man. He didn't *look* like a villain.

'I'll come straight to the point, which is that your father's wellbeing depends upon your good behaviour. I want you to understand that, because when I untie you, as I intend to shortly, any attempt on your part either to escape, or to attract attention to us . . . screams, shouts, or any other little ploy . . . and I wouldn't give *that* for your father.' He clicked his fingers expressively under her nose.

The hostile expression in the blue eyes turned to one of fear. They'd got her father too? So that was why he hadn't shown up at his own dinner party. But how had they contrived the non-appearance of the rest of the guests . . . the servants . . . and just who were *they*? With whom was this man in league? Surely he couldn't have achieved two abductions single-handed?

'Do you understand what I'm saying?'

Dayle nodded, furious with herself because she could feel her eyes filling with tears. What was going to happen to her? To her father? What did they want of the Abercrombies? *Was* it just money, or something else? For the first time, she wished she had listened to her father when he had talked about the various enterprises with which he was concerned. Was he in possession of some industrial secret that this man and his associates wanted? At that moment, Dayle would have changed places with any other girl in the world . . . the ugliest, the poorest. Good looks, wealth, were not the most important possessions after all, she discovered. Peace of mind was, the knowledge that someone you loved was safe . . . and Dayle *did* love her father. How she regretted all the light hearted jokes at his expense, the casual references to the 'revered parent' . . . her resentment of what she considered interference in her life. Just get me . . . us . . . out of this, she invoked some unseen power, and I'll do whatever Daddy wants. I'll even marry one of his stuffed shirts!

A large hand advanced towards her and she flinched away, expecting a blow. But a long finger flicked away the tears that hung on her lashes and the quiet, deep voice was surprisingly gentle.

'Now, now! There's no need for that. No harm will come to you, or your father, just as long as you do exactly as I tell you . . . right?'

Again she nodded.

His hands moved deftly, unfastening the bonds at her hands and feet first, and for one wild moment she wondered if she could kick him, hurt him sufficiently, so that she could jump from the car. But her limbs were too cramped to be able to move quickly and they were miles from anywhere. She didn't stand a chance . . . and besides, she couldn't risk retaliation upon her father.

The man seemed to hesitate before removing the gag and she guessed he was not looking forward to her use of her only weapon, the tongue-lashing he expected. Strangely enough, now that she was free, all the insults she had rehearsed seemed childish and ineffectual and she could only sit there and glare at him in dumb fury.

'Well! *That's* certainly unexpected,' he drawled. 'I thought all that dammed-up fury would flood over me!'

He was laughing. He was actually daring to laugh at her, because he knew she was helpless, because of the fear of what he might do to Angus Abercrombie.

'You swine!' she hissed. 'Who are you? What do you want? And what have you done with my father?'

'For the moment, you don't need to know the answers to your first two questions. But, as I said, your father is quite safe, while you behave yourself.'

'But where are we? Where are you taking me?' she insisted, 'and how do I know you're speaking the truth about my father?'

'As to where we're going, you must just wait and see, mustn't you? But I'll make a bargain with you. If you behave yourself, I'll stop at the next telephone kiosk and you can speak to your father.'

There was nothing she could do for the moment but agree. But he needn't think she was going to be this complacent for long, Dayle thought simmeringly. Without actually jeopardising her father's safety, she was going to be as much trouble to this man as she could be. She hadn't actually formulated her plan of campaign, but she would work on it as soon as she had spoken to her father. How long would she be allowed to talk to him? Would it be long enough for Angus to tell her what she should do? To tell her just who it was who had abducted her and what were their demands?'

It was about two miles to the nearest phone box.

'If you'll tell me what number to ring . . ' she began.

'Oh no.' The long, well-shaped mouth curved into an ironic smile. 'I'm afraid your freedom is going to be a little more curtailed than that. *I* will dial the number for you.'

'There . . . there's not room for two people in a kiosk,' she protested.'

Actually there was, as she knew very well, but only just . . . and she disliked intensely the thought of being so closely confined with this very large, very masculine man. For she could not deny that, in other circumstances, he would have been intriguingly attractive. He was very different from the kind of man she usually met . . . older and with less of the smooth veneer of civilisation about him.

As she had feared, they were very cramped, and as he dialled his broad shoulders deliberately obscured her view, so that she could not see the number he selected. Dayle waited breathlessly, the ringing tone clearly audible, then there was a click, as someone, somewhere, lifted the receiver. Her captor passed her the handset.

'Hallo! Daddy?'

'Dayle?' The voice was sharp with anxiety. 'Where are you?'

The sound of the beloved voice was too much for her self-control.

'I . . . d—don't know,' she sobbed. 'Oh, Daddy! Are *you* all right? H—he said . . . H—have they hurt you? Who *are* they? And what do they want?'

There was a silence which seemed endless to the waiting girl, and then Angus Abercrombie replied, his voice unusually gruff.

'Yes, *I'm* quite safe. But listen, Dayle . . . it's very important that . . . that you shouldn't antagonise . . . these people. I want you to do whatever this man asks of you . . . *anything*! Do you understand?'

'A—anything?' She choked over the word. Just what did that entail?

'Please, Dayle. I wouldn't ask it of you, unless it were very important.'

'F—for how long? Daddy? When are you going to get me out of this? Is . . . is it money they want, or . . .?'

Abruptly the handset was removed from her tremulous grasp.

'All right, that's enough! You know now that your father's OK. He's told you what you have to do.'

'B—but he *hasn't* . . . not properly.'

She tried to regain possession of the instrument, but he fended her off with one large hand, replacing the receiver with the other. Furiously, she kicked his shins. It wasn't a difficult feat in the enclosed space and Dayle had the satisfaction of hearing him gasp with pain. Then two large, heavy hands settled on her shoulders, their grasp warm through the delicate fabric of the catsuit, and for the first time in her life Dayle was shaken until she felt her head must snap from her neck.

'You have a very short memory!' he said grimly, when he released her. 'Your father just warned you not to antagonise me. You've got off lightly this time, but any more of *that* and you'll be severely punished. From now on, you do exactly as I tell you . . . whatever and whenever!'

As he marched her back to the car, Dayle's mind was a whirl of misery, indignation and fear. What would this man demand of her? Her father had begged her to do anything that was asked of her . . . anything? She shuddered, her fertile imagination immediately visualising the worst . . . the *very* worst. But surely her own father couldn't have meant . . . *that*!

'Wakey, wakey, Dayle!'

Jenny Spencer shook the sleeping girl's arm and Dayle opened heavy eyes, to see her friend, already and washed and dressed, standing over her with a cup of tea.

'Heavens!' She yawned. 'What time is it?'

'Seven-thirty.'

'Oh no!' Dayle sat up and glared at her silent alarm clock. 'That's the first time I've ever forgotten to wind the dratted thing.'

That was what came of allowing herself to dwell upon the

past, she thought, annoyed with herself this morning for last night's self-indulgence.

'Good thing you're in the café today,' Jenny commented. 'At least the hordes don't start arriving till nine-thirty. Animals won't wait for *their* fodder!'

This was one of the things the two girls liked so much about the Country Park. Their duties were worked on a rota system, so that no one had a chance to become bored with a particular task.

Today Jenny would be in the garden shop in a fresh pink overall, selling plants and produce, while Dayle would be tending the large tea urns and selling lemonade, squash, crisps and biscuits to the long streams of schoolchildren, here on educational visits to the park.

Barnet Country Park, once the home of the Earls of Barnet, was now the property of the County Council and comprised a stately home, set in a thousand acres of parkland, open to the public from Easter to October. It was a regular item on school curricula, to make the full day visit . . . and it needed a full day to get around all the features that the Park had to offer . . . the farmyard, with its large variety of animals and birds, the Victorian walled garden, a fascinating survivor of the past . . . and of course, the house itself, now a museum, filled with historical relics of the Earls whose family home it had once been. Dayle knew that she had been very lucky to find a job which she enjoyed so much, and she could have been happy and contented, but for her memories . . .

'It's not like you to oversleep,' Jenny commented over breakfast. She looked anxiously at her friend.

Dayle had never been plump, but since her mysterious disappearance a year ago she had acquired a fine-drawn look, a fragility usually belied by the energy with which she threw herself into her daily tasks. But this morning she looked more drawn than usual, the shadows under her eyes more pronounced.

'Sure you're feeling all right?' Jenny probed delicately.

'I'm fine,' Dayle reassured her. 'Don't fuss, Jen'. It . . . It's just that I didn't sleep too well. I started thinking about . . . about . . . well, you know . . . and it took me ages to drop off.'

Dayle had still been wondering just what concessions her father expected her to make to this man, as the car drew out of the layby. A few miles of country lanes and they joined a motorway.

At last she was able to pinpoint her position. Twenty miles from Aberdeen! It just wasn't possible! Her captor must have driven all night; and what were they doing so far north; where were they going? She longed to know and yet, since that degrading physical punishment in the kiosk, she had vowed that she would not demean herself by questioning this . . . this person, or even speaking to him. For the last few miles her brain had raced through the possibilities open to her, as she calculated her chances of escape, of obtaining help.

As to escape . . . well, he would have to sleep some time. He couldn't watch her every minute of every night and day; and surely they would have to touch a town, some form of civilisation . . . would have to stop for food . . . and other necessities? But . . . and she sighed deeply as her thoughts came full circle . . . any such action on her part would result in retaliation at her father's end. *She* might escape, but presumably this man had only to make a telephone call to some fellow conspirator for Angus to suffer for her rashness.

'Thought it all out, have you?' he asked, maddeningly perceptive. 'Decided it's not worth the risk?'

She drew a deep breath and dug white, even teeth into her bottom lip. She would *not* answer him; he'd soon get tired of trying to take a rise out of someone who refused to be drawn.

'I thought you might like to know where we're going . . . my name? After all, you'll have to call me something. We're going to be together for a long time.'

Dayle knew what she'd *like* to call him . . . only it wasn't the kind of language she was accustomed to using, and what did it matter where they were going; all places were the same to a prisoner. But his remark about being together for a long time was definitely disturbing. It didn't sound as if any satisfactory negotiations had begun for her release. Just how long was a 'long time'?

'My friends call me Mac,' he continued, his voice still even, pleasantly deep and quiet.

She remained stubbornly silent. He was no friend of hers. There was no justice. She knew some really super men who'd been blessed with the most unfortunate voices . . . high-pitched, or squeaky, and here was this . . . this villain with the most beautifully modulated tones she'd ever heard, a sexy sensuous sort of voice . . . or it could be, she amended hastily, if he were a different kind of man.

'Strange how mistaken one can be,' the man who called himself Mac continued conversationally. 'I'd have expected your type to be very talkative . . . a bit gushing and pointless in content, but decidedly with plenty to say for yourself.'

This time Dayle was stung into making a rejoinder.

'But then I don't suppose you get much opportunity of associating with my type,' she said scornfully, her blue eyes deliberately disparaging as they surveyed him, sliding from his burnished head, down over faded shirt and denims to battered sandals. 'We're hardly in the same social sphere, wouldn't you say?' He'd find that she *could* use her tongue, and to some effect, if she chose.

'That's what you think, is it?' he said thoughtfully. Irritatingly, he didn't seem a bit ruffled by her comment, but if they were going to be together for any length of time, as he'd indicated, she swore she'd get under his skin somehow. 'You don't seem particularly interested in our destination . . .'

'I'm not,' she interrupted.

He continued as if she hadn't spoken.

'But you may as well know that we're headed for the Shetlands.'

That *did* rouse her.

'The Shetlands?' she squeaked. 'Whatever for?'

'Oh, I don't think I should reveal everything to you all at once,' he said mockingly. 'Better to give you time to assimilate one piece of information at a time?'

Just as if she were some kind of imbecile! Oh, if she could only demonstrate to him just how superior *was* her intellect! But the Shetlands, she mused . . . that was quite a coincidence. It was only recently that her father had spoken of his family's antecedents, and if it hadn't all been in the dim and distant past, she would have imagined this to be some kind of family vendetta, that she was being taken to the Shetlands by the descendant of some enemy of her father's forebears.

Dayle had only vaguely heard of the Shetlands, not known much about it, until her father's most recent reference had stirred her curiosity. All she had known was that it was up north and that the tiny Shetland ponies came from there. But a trip to their nearest reference library had enlarged her knowledge a little. She knew now that there were more than a hundred of the islands, only twenty being inhabited . . . that with the Atlantic on one side and the North Sea on the other, the Gulf Stream ensured them an equable climate, the winters being mild with long nights enlivened by spectacular displays of the Northern Lights, whereas the cool summers had remarkably short nights in midsummer . . . nights never totally dark, which the Shetlanders themselves called the Simmer Dim. She knew also that the islands owed their first appearance in history to their discovery by Norse seamen. But she had never expected that she would actually go there.

'We'll be in Aberdeen shortly.' the man called Mac interrupted her thoughts. 'We'll be flying from there to the mainland of Shetland. Just remember, will you, we'll be amongst other people for a while . . . behave perfectly naturally, as if we're good friends . . . no tricks, or you know what will happen?'

'Does . . . does my father know where you're taking me?' she ventured. It worried her, this increasing distance between her and all that she was accustomed to. The farther they travelled, the longer it would take for her to return.

'Now would I be likely to reveal that?' Mac was scoffing at her. 'What sort of hold would I have over your father if he knew where you could be found?'

'Will I be able to telephone him again?'

'No.' His reply was uncompromising. 'I can't risk you trying to let him know where you are, or telling him anything else that I don't want known.'

She would not plead with him . . . pride forbade it, even if she had imagined it would be of any use. Dayle strove against the rising tide of misery and despair that threatened to engulf her. But she could not stifle the involuntary sob that escaped her trembling lips, nor disguise the sudden moisture in her large blue eyes.

When her captor spoke again, his voice was gentler, kinder.

'No need to look so tragic. I'm not bad company. If you behave yourself, I dare say we shall get on tolerably well together.'

'Never!' she said vehemently. 'And I warn you, if ever I see a chance for revenge, I shall take it!'

He laughed easily.

'Unlike you, I don't scare very easily.'

'I . . . I'm not . . . sc—scared,' Dayle stammered. 'I . . . I . . . just . . .'

They were driving through heavy traffic now, as they negotiated the approach to Dyce, Aberdeen's airport, but Mac spared her a fleeting glance from those strange green eyes.

'You're terrified,' he said with uncomfortable truth.

It was incredible, that she should ever have been afraid of Mac. But *then* she hadn't learnt to trust him, hadn't succumbed to the quiet charm that overlaid a will of steel. Just then, as they joined the crowds that thronged the airport, she had feared him, and hated him . . . as she hated him now, but for different reasons . . .

It was terrible, being part of a crowd . . . a multitude of people, going about their normal, everyday business, not knowing that one of their number was an unwilling participant; frustrating to know that there were so many people close at hand, yet she was powerless to ask for their help. All she could do, with Mac's strong hand at her elbow, was to accompany him across the sun-warmed tarmac to the plane . . . the plane which was to take her even farther on this journey into the unknown.

'It's only a short flight,' Mac said, as he fastened his safety belt. 'Not nervous, are you?'

'I've probably flown more times than you've had hot dinners,' she told him loftily, brushing aside his hand, as he made to help her with her belt. 'I can manage.'

'Do you ever use little expressions such as "please" and "thank you"?' he asked curiously.

'Not to people like you,' Dayle retorted.

She was accustomed, when she gave people one of her set-downs, for them to remain suitably chastened, but Mac seemed not a whit put out, continuing to talk as if she had merely made some polite observation in reply to one of his.

'The name Shetland derives from the Norse "Hjaltland",' he said conversationally, during take off. 'Meaning "High Land". The largest island in Shetland is called Mainland . . . it's bigger than all the others put together.'

Dayle shrugged to show her total lack of interest. Besides, she could have told *him* the facts he had just recounted. She kept her gaze fastened on the window beside her, though there was nothing to see at present, except bright blue sky and white cloud formations.

'It was originally inhabited by the Picts, until the Viking invasion,' he continued, undeterred by her silence.

'I'm really not the slightest bit interested in your "trave-logue",' she drawled, without turning her head towards him, 'or in anything else you may have to say.'

'A pity,' he commented, 'because there may come a time when you'll be glad of my knowledge.'

'I can't imagine my ever wanting to ask you anything!'

'Very well,' and for the first time there was an edge of irritation to his voice. It was not pronounced enough yet to be termed anger, though Dayle was determined she would succeed in rousing him to a fury before their association was done. 'From now on, if you need to know anything, you'll have to ask . . . politely . . . and perhaps, just perhaps, I'll answer you.'

Dayle's first introduction to Shetland was the sudden and splendid sight of Sumburgh Head, with a savage tideway dancing at its base and beyond it, to the west, the dramatic high cliffs of Fitful Head. A mile or two farther north of the coastline lay the airfield, on a little area of low ground. Besides its normal traffic, the airport was also busy as a North Sea Oil helicopter base.

Without hesitation, Mac led her towards a line of parked cars and opening the passenger door of one of them, indicated that she should get in. The keys were already in the ignition and she surmised, correctly, that this was a hire car. Mac was taking pains to cover his trail, she thought . . . the change from car to aeroplane and now a second vehicle, probably hired under a false name. She doubted in any case if Mac was his real name. He was not likely to leave any such clue as to his identity, once this was over.

In spite of her resolution it was very difficult to subdue her natural curiosity, not to ask where they were headed, how much longer their journey, as they drove out of the airport car park. The road signs were indicating Lerwick and for the moment, she supposed, she must assume that was their destination.

They travelled north, the road keeping to the east of a backbone of low hills. The long peninsula with its ragged projections to east and west was a vista of constantly changing scenery, being pierced in places by long, tranquil, winding inlets of sea, or revealed bays, flanked by awesome cliffs, battered over the years by fierce seas into arches and fissures. Dayle recognised much that she had read about . . . the green-brown hills, scarred with the darkness of peat hags, dotted with sheep, familiar grey-white fleeces intermingled with the distinctive black and brown of the Shetland breed. There was the wilderness of empty moors, ragged beautiful scenery with trees a rare sight. The inhabitants, she knew, were mostly fishermen and crofters, farming on a small scale, with only a few sheep, cattle and crops, because of the unpromising soil.

'We'll stop in Lerwick for supplies,' said Mac, speaking for the first time since their acrimonious interchange on the aeroplane. 'And you'll need to do some shopping.'

Shopping . . . what sort of shopping, and with what? Dayle wondered. You didn't carry money in a figure-hugging evening catsuit.

He jerked his head towards the crumpled outfit, once her pride and joy as an exclusive model.

'You'll need to fit yourself out with a few suitable clothes . . . jeans, T-shirts, sweaters, an anorak and waterproofs for bad weather. I'll provide the money, naturally.'

Apart from her utter distaste for accepting any money provided by him, Dayle couldn't really see the point of all the clothes he had mentioned.

'It's summer,' she protested.

'Shetland is less warm in summer than you're accustomed to. Besides, it won't always be summer.'

CHAPTER THREE

His reply left her gasping, bereft of speech. It was only June now . . . the weather wasn't likely to deteriorate for another three or four months. Was that how long he . . .? She opened her mouth to ask him, then shut it firmly. She wouldn't give him the satisfaction; but she was worried . . . very worried.

'Lerwick,' Mac announced a few moments later. 'It was Cromwell who virtually founded the place. He built the first fort here, to keep Dutch invaders at bay.'

Lerwick, the capital of Shetland, was a place of singular charm, even to Dayle's jaundiced gaze, contained within a small peninsula and overlooking Bressay Sound. On its seaward side, the oldest part of the town, a long, winding, flagstoned street was well supplied with shops, set at odd angles and irregular heights, many of them displaying the work of Shetland knitters. At its north end, the street terminated in quays busy with fishing vessels of many nations and where picturesque warehouses thrust out into the sea. The harbour was alive with men and brightly painted boats; silver-sided fish, which Dayle supposed must be herring, poured out in streams on to the quayside, as hopeful gulls patterned the air on hovering wings. At the south, between old houses, their foundations in the tide, was a minute beach. Ascending from this main shopping thoroughfare, were narrow lanes, where most of the older, surviving houses, separated from each other by only a few feet, could be seen. These steep alleys, with stairs and garden walls gave the town great character, their mellow brick overhung with the leaves of trees that flourished in their shelter.

But Dayle was allowed scant time for sightseeing, even if she had been inclined to show any interest in her surroundings. Her attitude, outwardly, was one of supreme indifference. How different things would have been, though, if she could have come here with her father.

'Lerwick's become a prosperous place with the advent of the North Sea Oil installations,' Mac commented. He did not seem

36

to expect any reply and certainly wasn't getting one. 'Mind you, it hasn't done so badly over the years . . . right up since the eighteenth century, when nearly every private house had its own jetty and storage for smuggled goods. Those old houses down at the south end are called "lodberries". Ships used to unload at their sea doors and the cargoes were brought in by two entrances . . . one official, for the Customs men to inspect, and a second, taken up via a passage in the foundations, leading to houses on the opposite side of the street.'

Dayle found herself being whisked in and out of shops, and despite the shabbiness of his clothes, the wallet which Mac produced from the back pocket of his jeans was bulging with notes, which he peeled off without appreciably lessening the bulk. Dayle wondered cynically whom he had held to ransom for *that* particular wad of money!

Her various packages stowed in the car, she was then forced to accompany him on a tour of the provision stores, and with a sinking heart she realised that, on the evidence before her, they were stocking up for a considerable length of time.

Some time during their shopping expedition, Dayle had realised that she was starving. She hadn't eaten since yesterday lunch time and then it had only been a snack, knowing that there was to be a dinner of several courses during the evening. But she was too proud to confess her need to Mac, as she glanced wistfully sideways into waterside cafés.

It was a relief, therefore, to find that he too was only human; but he did not suggest taking her to a restaurant, where they might eat in comfort. Instead he bought rolls, ready-filled with ham, crisp lettuce and tomatoes, and ate as he drove, indicating that Dayle should help herself.

'I don't suppose you're used to picnic meals,' he said, with a faint touch of irony in his deep voice.

'Actually, I'm very fond of picnics.'

What Dayle did not tell him, though she suspected he could guess for himself, was that, to her, a picnic was a gracious, well-planned affair, with a properly packed basket and ice-box, folding table and chairs, held in sylvan surroundings, to which she and her friends had been conveyed in their fathers' chauffeur-driven limousines. She disliked intensely the feeling that she had crumbs in her clothes and the fresh, crusty rolls were large and unwieldy, very unlike the dainty sandwiches to which she was accustomed. But she had to admit to herself that food had

never tasted better. Principally, of course, because she had never
been so hungry before.

From Lerwick they drove out on to the rugged, empty moors
beyond, the sea never far from sight, as long inlets delved deeply
into the coastline. At one point the land was all but cut in two,
almost forming a separate island, as it narrowed to about a
hundred yards across. The road, cut through rock, hung shelf-
like, with the North Sea on one side and the Atlantic on the
other, and climbed and twisted, to descend rapidly once again to
more, wild, rocky moorland.

The small car swung off the main road, following a minor
highway towards a small settlement on the western coastline.
Was this their final destination at last? Dayle was longing to
stretch cramped limbs, to brush herself free of crumbs, to take a
bath. She had never felt so scruffy or unkempt in her life, her hair
uncombed and without a scrap of eye-shadow or lipstick to
enhance her appearance. The new, stiff denims, which Mac had
insisted she don immediately, felt rough and uncomfortable
against her pampered skin and she looked scornfully at her feet,
sensibly clad in woollen socks and sturdy, reinforced pumps.

But, to her horror, she discovered that this was not the end of
their journey. Mac drove through the small village without
stopping . . . out to the end of a narrow jetty, where a large
fishing boat swayed to the movement of the tide.

'Help me unload the car,' he ordered, as he unlocked the boot.

'I'm not accustomed to carrying heavy loads,' Dayle protested.

'Time you learnt, then,' was the brusque reply, and a carton of
tinned foods was thrust into her unwilling arms. 'Take it to the
edge of the jetty and pass it down to Simon.'

Simon, a burly, elderly man, his face the colour of old mahogany, his bristling eyebrows bleached white with sun and sea
spray, was apparently the skipper of the boat, which, Dayle
noticed with trepidation, was named *Storm Rider*.

Sullenly she trudged backwards and forwards, until the small
car was unloaded of its widely diverse contents . . . sacks of
chicken food, gas cylinders side by side with canned goods and
Dayle's new clothes.

'Into the boat with you,' Mac commanded.

Dayle looked doubtfully down at the lifting, swaying vessel. It
would be difficult to obey with dignity. But she was given no time
for hesitation or protestation. Two strong arms thrust her out

into space over the wavering deck and Simon received her from
Mac, with no more ceremony than that with which they had
shifted the stores aboard, she thought furiously. Impossible to
maintain her poise, being manhandled like that.

'Oh, you . . . you . . . *peasants!*' she stormed.

'Sit down out of the way, and shut up,' Mac told her. 'Simon
needs all his wits about him to negotiate the reefs.'

Dayle sat down abruptly on a neat coil of rope, her hands
clenched. Not for the world would she have admitted it to this
arrogant, dictatorial, unprincipled lout, that she *loathed* boats
. . . hated being on water. She was bound to be sick, she thought,
disgusted by the undignified light in which she must shortly
appear. Not that it mattered what this Mac thought of her. In
fact if she *was* sick, she had a good mind to make sure he was on
the receiving end!

Outside the reef, the blue water was deceptively calm and
Dayle thought perhaps she might make it to whatever island the
two men had in mind as their destination. But as they left the lee
of the mainland, the lift of the Atlantic swell could be felt, the
front of the boat heaving to meet the sky, being suspended, then
falling downwards into a deep trough so that the stern reared up
high. The whole process was repeated on the next swell. The sea
was running high, with white-capped waves from shore to shore,
but due entirely to Simon's skill they were moving safely between and over the threatening ridges.

'All right?' Mac asked her casually.

'Of course,' she told him stiffly.

But the movement of the boat, the smell of the engine fuel, the
all-pervading reek of fish soon caused Dayle's stomach to heave,
and within minutes of leaving the shore she was retching miserably over the side of the boat, feeling too ill to carry out her
intended revenge and glad rather than otherwise of strong hands
that supported her in her paroxysms of sickness.

She was too limp to care or to take an interest, when Simon
sang out:

'Haa island dead ahead!'

The hands stopped their comforting ministrations, leaving
her to fend for herself and Dayle sat, bent over in a shivering
huddle, as their purchases were transferred to the fishing boat's
dinghy and Mac rowed swiftly to the shore, deftly negotiating
the foaming currents. She was still in the same place, totally
immobile, when he returned, having unloaded the dinghy.

'You next,' he told Dayle, and she was bundled into the dinghy, again with scant ceremony.

This time it was Simon who took the oars to row them across. The little boat slid alongside a rocky promontory and with Mac's help she stepped on to a ledge. Swiftly he followed her and she turned to see Simon rowing steadily away. He was leaving them. They were all alone on this island which, at first glance, seemed scarcely larger than the grounds of her father's house.

'He . . . he's taking the dinghy!'

'Of course. He needs it.'

'But . . . but how do *we* get off the island?'

'We don't . . . at least, not for some considerable time.'

Dayle stared at him aghast. Haa Island was not so far from Main Island in terms of sea distance, but without transport it might as well be the other side of the ocean.

'That means we're all alone here . . . j—just you and me.'

'It scarcely needs vast mathematical expertise to deduce that,' he agreed with hateful sarcasm.

'It . . . it's not right, me being all alone here with you.'

'Afraid for your reputation?' he asked interestedly. 'You don't seriously imagine I have designs upon your person . . . a spoilt, useless, mannerless brat?'

'How would I know?' she snapped. 'Somehow you've forced my father's hand, so that he's told me to do anything you ask . . . *anything*,' she repeated, 'how do I know what that involves?'

'You don't, do you?' he said pleasantly, 'you'll just have to wait and see.'

'If . . . if I thought you intended to lay so much as a finger on me, I'd . . . I'd throw myself down there first!' She gestured towards the restless, boiling sea below them.

'Really?' Mac managed to sound lightly incredulous instead of suitably impressed. 'How dramatic! I wonder if I'll ever have occasion to remind you of that threat? But come on, we've wasted enough time. We have to get these supplies up to the cottage and it'll take us two or three trips.'

'It will take *you* four or five,' she informed him coldy. 'Because *I* don't intend to carry a thing!'

She turned away with the intention of marching on ahead. Now that she was on dry land, her hauteur, her self-assurance had returned. She had almost forgotten the pathetic, nausea racked self of a few moments since. But a couple of swift strides brought Mac level with her and she was forcibly dragged back towards the pile of stores.

'While we're on this island you'll pull your weight, my girl! I don't carry passengers.'

'Then you shouldn't have brought me here. I didn't ask to come to this beastly place.'

'Oh well,' he said with aggravating cheerfulness, 'let's look on the bright side. In a few months you may even come to love it.'

As he spoke, he thrust a carton into her hands and piled sundry other small packages on top, turned her around and with a sharp slap on her denimed behind, set her on her way. Fuming, Dayle strode on ahead, not knowing where she was supposed to be going . . . not caring. 'In a few months' he'd said. He wouldn't . . . he *couldn't* keep her here that long; and how dared he treat her like this? Just because he had kidnapped her, because his accomplices were holding her father somewhere as surety for *her* good behaviour . . . or the other way around . . . she was a little confused, he didn't have to treat her as a beast of burden or with such . . . such familiarity! Many men had hinted that they found Dayle good to look at in tightly fitting trousers, but not one of them had ever attempted such a . . . a liberty!

As Dayle climbed the steep pathway, she was in no mood to appreciate the beauties of nature, but even so, she could not help taking in the attributes of her island prison. The hillside on either side of the rough track was a mass of flowers . . . primroses, violets, bluebells, while heather and bracken clothed the hilltops and pink thrift nestled between rocks on the cliffside. As she climbed higher, she passed through meadowy areas, carpeted with buttercups and daisies, birdsfoot trefoil.

Mac caught her up, moving smoothly, effortlessly, though his burden was greater than hers.

'Pretty, isn't it? We get spring and summer together here . . . all the flowers bloom at once. The season begins late and ends early. There's the cottage,' he continued, 'your home for the next few months.'

She stopped then, facing him squarely.

'You keep on saying "months". What makes you think it's going to be that long? My father won't let you keep me here that long. If you ask for money, he'll pay it. He . . .'

'There are other things in life besides money,' he said obscurely. 'Come on, we've got to get this lot unpacked, then you can cook me a meal.'

Dayle did not move, gaping at him open-mouthed.

'Me? Cook . . . for you? I . . .'

She was about to tell him she had never cooked a meal in her life, hadn't the faintest idea where to begin. But pride forbade such a disclosure. He must already think her pretty feeble, after her degrading illness on the boat.

'I've no intention of cooking for you,' she ended flatly.

'Then you'll go hungry yourself,' he informed her pleasantly, 'because if I do the cooking, I shall only prepare my own. I'm your guardian, Miss Abercrombie, not your servant.'

So saying, he stepped around her and led the way, leaving Dayle with no alternative but to follow, for once in her life entirely at a loss for words. She, who had always prided herself on her maturity, who had always had the last word in any altercation, now felt like an angry child, baffled by an adult's superior argument.

The cottage was set on a sheltered shelf of a small hill, on the opposite side of the island to their landfall and overlooking a curving beach some four or five hundred yards along. The dwelling was low-built, small and austere-looking, nestling in the hillside, as though it had grown there, its appearance enlivened only by the wild roses just in bud and honeysuckle about to flower, which festooned its walls.

'Not bad, is it?' said Mac with evident pride. 'A year ago, it was in terrible condition . . . rotten woodwork, broken windows, the walls reduced to bare brick. I had to completely re-render them. It was hard work.'

'*You* . . . working?' Dayle sneered. 'I thought you lived off other people's money . . . *ransom* money!'

'There's still plenty that needs doing,' he continued, ignoring her interruption. 'Plenty of work for another pair of hands.'

'Well, they won't be my hands,' she retorted.

He looked at them, clasped around their burden.

'They are rather useless adornments,' he agreed, 'but we'll soon alter that.'

The central door was not locked.

'No point really,' Mac explained. 'No one else ever comes here, except the occasional birdwatcher. The former inhabitants deserted the island over a hundred years ago. There are a few ruins left, over that hill,' he nodded towards the north, 'but you'll have time for exploring.'

There was a room on either side of the door, one furnished

rather sparsely as a living room, the other a primitive kitchen. In both rooms, Dayle noticed, there was no electricity, the sole source of illumination apparently the large oil lamps. From the doorway, stairs ascended steeply.

'Bedrooms . . . two of them, you'll be glad to hear.' Mac moved into the kitchen, dumping his load in the middle of the floor. 'You'll find plenty of cupboard space for the stores. Running water has to be fetched from the spring in that bucket and when the weather turns bad we use wood and peat for fires. But there's Calor gas for cooking.'

Dayle had never seen a Calor gas stove before, let alone used one. She felt an infantile desire to throw herself down on the floor and scream and kick and have hysterics, as she had done as a small child, when something had been beyond her capabilities. It was ridiculous to expect her to live like this! She just couldn't do it. But she had an idea that such histrionics would receive scant sympathy from Mac. Setting her teeth, she unpacked the tinned and packet goods, stowing them away in the cupboards indicated, then, disconsolately, she drifted into the tiny living room, which looked as if it had been furnished over the years with other people's discards. The floor was dusty, the upholstery looked water-stained, as though at some time the floral suite had been dropped in the sea; and there were no curtains at the small windows. When she commented on this, Mac smiled wryly.

'I've never found much need for privacy. The only creature likely to stare in through that window is a sheep, or the cow, when she gets loose, as she frequently does. Oh, that reminds me . . you'll have to learn to milk her.'

Despite the unhappiness that always swamped her whenever she thought back to those days on Haa Island . . . days which in retrospect had taken on the aspect of an idyll . . . Dayle could not restrain a small smile, especially when at milking time, she recalled her horror of Mac's pronouncement. It had never occurred to her that people still actually milked cows by hand. Some of her father's friends were farmers . . . wealthy farmers, naturally, with enormous milking parlours where everything was done by machinery, the only human involvement with the cow being the attachment of the milking cups. Nowadays, when it was her turn to work in the Park's Home Farm, she milked half a dozen cows twice a day and thought nothing of it. But then she had rebelled violently, staring at Mac wildly, her icy control

broken. This was the last straw. She was quite at home wit
horses . . . but cows!

'I'll see *you* in hell first!' she shouted. 'You can milk your ow
damned cow! I . . .I'm . . .' her voice broke and she felt a longin
to be alone, to shed her tears of frustration and misery in privat
. . . 'I'm going to bed.' She whirled on her heel and started for th
stairs.

Mac had been seated, but his reactions were surprisingl
swift; and once again she found her flight halted by those larg
hands.

'Oh no, you don't, my girl! I'm hungry, if you're not. We'll ea
first, and then I'll show you where the bed linen is kept and yo
can make our beds up.' He propelled her over the threshold o
the kitchen. 'Since you're so tired,' he said considerately, 'a
couple of boiled eggs will do for now. Call me when they're
ready.'

Dayle stood in the kitchen and stared at the Calor gas stove
How on earth did the beastly thing work? She had a distinc
premonition that any attempt on her part to light it would resul
in the cottage blowing up or at the very least catching fire. Again
she felt her lips begin to quiver. What was she *doing* here? In les
than forty-eight hours her whole life had been turned upside
down, by one man . . . a complete stranger. She had never felt so
helpless in all her nineteen years. There had always been
someone to cushion life's difficulties. In adult life at least, she
had never been faced with something she could not do. She
dreaded the look of scorn on Mac's face, but unless she wanted to
see anger there instead, because his supper was not ready, she
had to admit her shortcomings.

Hesitantly she moved back into the living room.

'I . . . I don't know how to light the stove,' she said stiffly. She
was not going to apologise for the fact.

Mac shook his coppery head, his expression indicative of
sorrow rather than annoyance.

'Your education *has* been sadly lacking,' he observed.

'Education? At lighting primitive contraptions like that? My
father had rather higher things in mind when he considered my
education. It's not the sort of thing someone in my position
expects to have to do.'

He looked down at her, the fascinating green eyes scornful.

'A helpless woman is incomplete . . . only half alive. My sisters could run a house single-handed by the time they were thirteen and fifteen respectively.'

Comparisons were odious to Dayle, and to be contrasted with *his* sisters and found wanting . . .

'Well, of course people from an inferior walk of life . . .' she began.

His lips tightened, the eyes now flashing green fire.

'Just one of my sisters would be worth half a dozen of you! But perhaps you'll be halfway useful to someone before you leave here.'

He thrust past her into the kitchen and set the single burner going.

Alone again, Dayle filled a saucepan from the large bucket, which Mac had told her contained the spring water, and placed four eggs in the container. How long did one cook an egg, she wondered, and did you allow longer for four of them? Anxiously she brooded over the saucepan. Nothing seemed to be happening, the water was not even hot yet.

'I'll have three slices of bread and butter with mine,' the deep voice announced from the other room. 'We may as well make the most of the fresh bread. When that runs out you'll have to bake more.'

Dayle felt a strong impulse to scream. If Mac had been standing anywhere near her, she felt she could cheerfully have fallen upon him with just her bare fists, certain that in her present mood she was capable of inflicting the injury she desired. He had abducted her, insulted her, belittled her . . . now he was making a menial of her . . . and it seemed to matter not a jot to him that she must be one of the most attractive women he had ever encountered. He was blind, unfeeling, prejudiced . . . Lips set, she sliced the bread, imperilling her fingers. The slices were ragged and uneven, wavering from paper-thin to doorstep-thick in one slice, but eventually she managed it. This task had taken so much of her time and attention that she had completely forgotten about the saucepan and its contents. Returning to the stove, she was horrified to see that the water was boiling fiercely and that all but one of the eggs had cracked and the white part had seeped out, solidifying around the outside of the shell. Hastily she grabbed a large ladle and scooped the eggs out of the water, brushing the telltale traces of coagulated albumen away, and put the eggs on the plates she had discovered; there seemed to be no eggcups. Carefully she carried the plates to the table, the eggs rolling wildly as her hands trembled with fatigue.

'The eggs are cooked,' she announced coldly from the door-way.

Mac strolled through and took his place at the table. Gravely he inspected the contents of his plate and she thought, but she couldn't be sure, that his mouth twitched slightly. If he dared . . . if he so much as *dared* to make one of his sarcastic comments, she'd break his plate over his head! He took a knife, tentatively cutting off the top of one of the eggs.

Dayle followed suit. They ate in silence. Dayle's egg re-sembled the consistency of rather tough rubber and she sus-pected that Mac's was in a similar state; but she was not going to admit that she found her own cooking most unpalatable.

Suspiciously she watched as he examined the slices of bread and gloated when he began to cough rather excessively. She hoped his food choked him.

The pungent smell of burning, however, drew his attention from the unappetising fare and he leapt up with a smothered oath.

'You're supposed to turn the gas out when you've finished cooking. You're lucky you haven't burnt the bottom out of this pan—it's boiled dry! As it is you're going to have quite a job scouring off this mess.'

That did it! Already she had broken two nails, had nicked the soft flesh of one finger with the bread knife, and now he expected her to completely ruin her hands by *scouring out a pan*! Dayle jumped up from the table, tears streaming down her lovely face, her sweetly husky voice choking over the words.

'I won't! I won't! I won't! I'm *not* a skivvy. I'm *not* going to slave for you! *You* brought me here . . . *you* wanted me here . . . *you* can do all these horrible jobs! I d—didn't ask you to come here to this godforsaken place. I'm tired, I'm dirty, I've been seasick. I haven't had a decent meal for nearly two days and . . . and I . . . w—want to go home . . .' She ended on a despairing wail, like a frightened child; and saw the mocking look in his startlingly green eyes change to something else, something that looked like . . . compassion? But the look was gone so quickly that she thought she must have imagined it.

'Very well,' he said, matter-of-factly, 'perhaps you *have* had enough for today.'

'For today?' Her voice became hysterical. 'For today, tomor-row, next week . . . for the next hundred years!'

'Now you're exaggerating,' he said repressively, 'a typical female reaction. Don't try me too far. I'll let you off the chores for tonight.' He smiled. 'You can do them in the morning—they'll keep. Let's go up and I suppose I'll have to show you how to make the beds up?'

It was an effort to drag herself up the steep stairs. Dayle was used to a busy, even an athletic life, but she had never felt this drained and weary before. She was horribly conscious too of the man behind her . . . a complete stranger, and here they were, going upstairs to the bedrooms. Never mind that he was the captor and she his hostage, or that the beds weren't even made up. It was the thought . . . it suggested an intimacy that appalled her, and her father's words crept back to haunt her . . . 'do whatever he asks of you.'

An appraising look around the rooms confirmed her worst fears. The doors fastened with a single old-fashioned latch. There were no keyholes, no bolts. If possible, the rooms were even more spartanly furnished than those downstairs. Alcoves in one wall boasted a rail and a few bent wire hangers for clothes. There were no curtains or floor coverings and there were *camp beds*! Dayle had never slept in a camp bed in her life. A cupboard on the tiny landing between the two rooms yielded up sheets, blankets and pillows.

'Good thing it's summer,' Mac said cheerfully. 'They don't seem to be damp. In winter we have to keep them downstairs by the fire.'

He showed her how to contrive a neatly folded cocoon out of the sheets and blankets, and Dayle was relieved that he didn't ask her to try her hand at it . . . though no doubt he would, in time, she thought bitterly.

'Which room would you like?'

She raised incredulous eyebrows at him. He said it as if this were a five-star hotel and she had the choice between two expensive suites. She shrugged.

'Surely it's immaterial. They're both as bad as each other.'

'Suit yourself. In one of them the window panes rattle when the wind gets up and in the other the roof leaks. I haven't had time to do much since I . . .' He stopped abruptly, but Dayle was too tired to care what it was he had left unsaid.

'I'll have this one, then.' She indicated the door to the right of the stairs.

'Goodnight, then,' he said, as she crossed the threshold.

Dayle, fastening the latch, did not bother to answer him. She
was looking around the room fruitlessly, for something to place
against the door.

As she surveyed her primitive sleeping arrangements, it
dawned on her that their shopping list had not included sleep-
wear. Her nose wrinkled fastidiously. Was she expected to sleep
in her clothes, or her lingerie? Or with nothing on at all? Of
course it wasn't something that would occur to her captor. He
looked the sort who would quite happily sleep totally naked. She
felt a hot tide of embarrassment covering her at the thought; and
suppose she had to get up in the night, to go to the . . . Her
discomfort grew, as she realised she didn't even know where it
was. Purposefully she flung open her door, crossing the gap to
Mac's in one step. She rapped with her knuckles on the wooden
panels.

The door opened immediately and she moved backwards
hastily at the sight of him. Fool! She should have realised that he
might have begun to undress. Fortunately he had not yet
discarded his trousers, but his feet were bare . . . and his upper
torso. She had realised that he was broad and well made, but she
was not prepared for the effect upon her of his muscular chest
with its down of reddish hair. She could almost feel the warmth
exuding from all that naked flesh. She dragged her fascinated
gaze away from the sight, meeting his eyes, in which lurked a
gleam of mockery as if he recognised her discomfiture and it
cause.

'What! Lonely already?' he asked.

Dayle was horrified at this interpretation. Surely he didn't
think . . . Oh, he *couldn't* . . . the conceit of him!

'You didn't tell me where the . . . the bathroom is.'

'We don't have such refinements . . . just a dip in the spring in
summer and a tin bath in front of the fire in winter.' He was
deliberately misunderstanding her. She was sure of it.

'I . . . I didn't mean that, and you know it!'

'Oh! I *see*!' He spoke as one suddenly enlightened, infuriating
her still more by his hypocrisy. 'It's outside, around the back . .
a lean-to against the rear wall. Would you like me to come down
and show you?'

'No!' she snapped. 'That won't be necessary. I just asked, in
case . . . in case . . .' Flushing still more deeply, she retreated into
her own room and slammed the door in his grinning face.

Dayle settled for sleeping in her underwear. She undressed

with only the moonlight flooding through the uncurtained window for illumination. Somehow she wriggled her way into the blanket cocoon Mac had contrived; but now that her body had the ease it craved, she could not relax. Her brain was over-active. On her own, all the fear and despair of the day crept back to torment her. Mac was domineering, intensely irritating and an unprincipled crook . . . he must be . . . but at least he was company, and her anger at his peremptory commands had for the most part kept other, weaker emotions at bay.

As she shifted restlessly in her far from comfortable bed, she found the tears of exhaustion and misery sliding down her cheeks, dampening the rough material of her pillowcase. If only she could put the clock back! Just two weeks ago she had been defying her father, denying his right to arrange her life. If she had known then what she knew now . . . or so she persuaded herself . . . she would have agreed to marry his Callum person, sight unseen. Even that couldn't have been as bad as her present situation.

It was amazing how one could adjust to circumstances, given no alternative, Dayle thought, as she filled up the urns in the small but well-fitted café kitchen and gave the serving area a wipe over. Not that it would stay clean for long, once grubby little hands had rested on it, tipped over their orange juice and the girl she was working with today, naturally accident-prone, had over-filled the paper cups with the dark brown tea.

She had often mused on the subject of adjustment . . . then, and since. Who would ever have thought that the time would come when she would look back on her experiences on Haa Island with nostalgia and gratitude for all that she had learnt there.

She would never have been able to perform even such simple tasks as serving tea, or preparing piles of sandwiches, she thought . . . let alone the agricultural and horticultural skills that were required of her here. Of course, she conceded, she would never have needed any of these accomplishments, if Mac had not abducted her. Most probably she would have gone on in the belief that such mundane things were the province of servants, their performance necessary, but a complete mystery.

If he had not removed her from her accustomed surroundings, that day in June a year ago, she would never have realised how empty and useless her life had been hitherto, so that when, eventually, she had returned to her father's house, she knew she could not bear to fritter away her time in idleness. Nor, for various reasons, could she bring herself to accept her father's offer of monetary support; and she had resolved to find herself a job.

By sheer coincidence . . . for inevitably she had not seen her friend for several months . . . she learnt of Jenny Spencer's new circumstances . . . that the family had moved away and that Jenny herself was currently working some fifty miles distant in the depths of the Hertfordshire countryside. A letter to Jenny was swiftly answered. Her friend would be delighted to see her again . . . yes, there was a chance of a job, subject to interview. But did Dayle really think she was capable of *this* kind of work . . . arduous, sometimes dirty . . . of living in simple self-catering conditions?

At that time, Jenny had not yet heard the details of Dayle's enforced residence on the island, where she had learnt what hard work meant, where the living conditions had been more primitive than anything Jenny now reckoned to endure. At least Jenny didn't sleep on a camp-bed . . .

When she woke, Dayle could not believe that she had actually slept on the sagging bed, in this ghastly place . . . slept soundly too, despite all the doubts and fears that troubled her mind. Amazingly, the camp bed now felt warm and comfortable and she was reluctant to move. And why should she get up yet? Her expensive wrist watch showed only seven-thirty, and the longer she stayed in bed, the less time she would have to endure in Mac's company.

Things did not look quite so black this morning. Obviously Mac was an unscrupulous man, but he was not the degraded creature she had pictured when she had read the contents of that crumpled envelope. He might not even be the motivating force behind her abduction . . . and if so perhaps he could be persuaded . . . beguiled? She had not altogether lost faith in the powers of her own attraction . . . could she possibly . . .? It would be a dangerous game perhaps, but . . . and it did seem that he had the instincts of a gentleman. His speech was cultured, grammatical, and despite the evident age of his faded clothes, to her discerning eye it was obvious that they were well cut, had once been expensive. Of course they could be someone else's cast-offs. But somehow she did not think so. They fitted him too well for that, moulding to his broad, muscular form and his speech was cultured, with just that faint trace of an accent that he could not quite eradicate.

Dayle had come to the conclusion that he had probably fallen on hard times. But that was no reason to prey on other, richer folk, she thought scornfully. If he was anything of a man he would be out finding himself a proper job, instead of living this drop-out kind of existence. For, from his conversation yesterday, it seemed he made regular use of this island and the cottage he had rescued from decay.

A loud knock on her door disturbed her musings.

'Time to get up,' she heard Mac announce.

Deliberately, she did not answer. Perhaps, if she pretended to be still asleep, he would go away. But the knocking was repeated.

'Come on! We don't keep high society hours here. Chickens have to be fed and the cow milked.'

Then *he* could see to them, she thought mutinously. He'd chosen this sort of existence; let him get on with it.

The door opened and Dayle gave up all pretence that she was asleep, her blue eyes glinting fury at him over the blanket.

'Get out of my room!'

'Not until you get up.'

'I'm not getting up,' she informed him icily; and nor was she, while he was in the room. She was only too aware of the scant protection afforded by the scraps of silk and lace which were all she had on.

She was totally unprepared for his next move. In two strides he had crossed the room and hooking a foot beneath the edge of her bed, tipped it over, rolling her to the floor. Futilely she grabbed at blankets and sheets, but overnight the cocoon had lost much of its efficacy and the folds fell apart, revealing her shapely body, a jumble of arms and legs and the very revealing underwear.

Mac began to laugh, a deep, full-throated sound which filled the small room, grating upon her already exacerbated nerves. He stepped over the scattered remains of her bed and held out a hand, as though to pull her to her feet.

Dayle shrank back against the wall.

'Don't you dare lay your hands on me!' she hissed.

He withdrew his hand, but he did not move away, his strange green eyes fixed intently upon her, as if he could not withdraw them from the distinctly feminine attributes revealed to his gaze.

She tried to reach for the blankets, to pull them about her, to conceal the expanse of creamy flesh which must, she felt, be as flushed with mortification as was her face. But the bedclothes resisted her. Mac was standing on them, and meeting his gaze, she felt something like a current of electricity spark between them, as he continued to stare at her with that awareness in his eyes, a muscle tightening in his cheek, a nerve throbbing at his temple; and the terrible thing was that this magnetic impulse seemed to be mutual, for she felt very strange, very strange indeed, almost as if . . .

'Get out,' she whispered. 'Get out!'

He seemed not to hear her and she saw him swallow before he spoke.

'I hadn't realised just how beautiful you are, Dayle Abercrombie, very beautiful indeed.'

This was just what she had been imagining, only a few moments ago . . . the possibility of finding a chink in his armour . . . but now she was not so certain of the chivalry she had attributed to him. She began to tremble, afraid of the thoughts she knew must be passing through his mind, thoughts that were mirrored in those incredible green eyes. For her part, she had recovered from that one second of lunacy . . . for that was what it had been . . . when she had wondered what it would be like if he *had* helped her up, held her . . . kissed her . . .

As if with an effort, he withdrew his gaze from her face and turned, moving towards the door. He paused there, facing her once more, his expression now unfathomable.

'Get some clothes on.' He snapped out the words. 'And thank your lucky stars I'm a gentleman!'

· Dayle opened her mouth to retort, to express her doubt of that definition, then, realising the foolishness of denying his claim . . . its possible outcome . . . pressed her lips tightly together to hold back the words.

'Good! I see you've learnt one lesson at least,' he said grimly before the door closed soundlessly behind him.

The first thing that came to Dayle's hand was one of the despised plimsolls, and she relieved her feeling by flinging it at the door, imagining that the satisfying thump was made by direct contact with his head.

She dressed, hurrying now, in case he should return to chivvy her. But once fully clothed, she loitered again, reluctant to go down-stairs and face him, still carrying the memory of that sexual awareness she had glimpsed in his eyes . . . and recognised in her own startled response. Beside, once downstairs, the hateful creature would probably find some distasteful chore for her to perform. Hadn't he mentioned chickens . . . and the cow? She shuddered; and then he would probably expect her to cook his breakfast *and* wash up . . . including last night's saucepan. No, now that she felt more secure, protected by the denim jeans and a cotton T-shirt, she would take her time.

She moved towards the window. Her bedroom overlooked the back of the cottage, facing the high ground at the centre of the island, which consisted of peat hags, rough grazing and rocks. High above the island, gulls and other birds circled endlessly, and Dayle felt the first stirrings of interest. If only she had her powerful fieldglasses here.

She could not deny the beauty of her surroundings, or the memory that some such scene must have greeted her father's forebears every morning. Was it possible, she wondered, to experience race memory? Did this scene tug unexpectedly at her heart-strings because once some ancestor had called it home?

'Dayle!' Mac's voice seemed amplified by the narrow stairwell. 'Get down here, if you know what's good for you!'

She felt like shouting back 'Come and make me' but since he was perfectly capable of doing just that, she decided to exercise discretion rather than indulge in bravado. There would be no repetition of that dangerous moment when, for a fleeting instant, she had forgotten that he was her enemy . . . hers and her father's.

CHAPTER FOUR

FOLLOWING the delectable scent of cooking smells, Dayle entered the kitchen, surprised to find it in immaculate order, with no signs of last night's culinary disasters and . . . wonder of wonders . . . a breakfast of bacon and eggs, gently frying.

Mac stood at the stove. He was wearing the same faded jeans and battered sandals, but he had changed his shirt. His strong, blunt profile was towards her, and unseen, she studied the intelligent breadth of forehead, the hard-set chin and firm lips. Something stirred inexplicably within her. He *was* a good-looking man; there was no denying it. If only . . .

'You've time for a dip in the spring before breakfast,' he commented, apparently sensing her presence without turning away from his task. He made deft, flipping motions with a palette knife.

'No, thank you.'

He did turn then, one dark eyebrow . . . incredibly dark when one considered his burnished hair . . . raised in an infuriatingly satirical expression.

'You surely don't intend to go for weeks without washing? This may not be the Ritz, but we have to maintain *some* standards.'

'*I* prefer to bathe in warm water,' Dayle said stiffly.

He chuckled.

'Very well. But *you* will have to carry the water up from the spring and devise some means of heating it. The tin bath is kept on a nail just outside the door.'

A desire to thwart him warred with common sense . . . the knowledge that most certainly she could not neglect personal freshness . . . conflicted too with the doubt of her ability to carry sufficient water; and where *did* one heat it? Obviously not on the small Calor gas stove. The whole thing presented too many complications; and besides, she didn't relish sitting in a tin bath in this cottage, where none of the rooms had locks on their doors. Sighing, she turned away. Knowing Mac, he was quite capable of denying her food until she had done his bidding, and that bacon smelt tantalisingly good.

'You'll find bath towels in the linen cupboard,' he commented to her retreating back view. 'Sorry I can't come and scrub your back!'

She did not deign to answer him.

The spring, Dayle discovered, ran from the direction of the hillside and bubbled briskly along the bottom of the kitchen garden, where, after a nervous look round, she decided it was adequately screened from the cottage windows. She peeled off her clothes and ventured in. The water was shudderingly cold and she indulged in only the briefest immersion. But as she towelled herself dry she was aware of a tingling glow, a sense of well-being, very unlike the lassitudinous sensations she experienced when stepping from a long soak in a piping hot and scented bath. She felt vitally alive and fit, gnawingly hungry, ready for her breakfast.

'That was quick,' Mac commented, as she re-entered the kitchen. 'How many eggs?'

'Two, please,' she said, with a meekness which surprised herself and Mac, evidently, for she was treated to another lift of his eyebrows. But she was so ravenous that she decided she might as well eat before attempting to cross swords further with her captor.

'I believe in division of labour,' he said a few moments later as he set a loaded plate before her, the very sight of it setting her mouth watering. 'When *you* cook, I'll wash up, and vice versa.'

The food tasted heavenly, but she was determined not to praise his cooking and she sought desperately for an alternative topic of conversation.

'There seem to be a lot of birds here,' she ventured, after the first two or three mouthfuls had taken the edge off her hunger and the silence seemed to have lasted an uncomfortably long time.

'Haa is a bird sanctuary.'

'I . . . I don't suppose you have any glasses?'

'You're interested . . . in birds?' His tone was insultingly incredulous.

'I am, actually,' she told him, with a little edge of triumph in her voice, 'very interested.'

She might be useless in the kitchen, or on a boat, but when it came to birds, she was extremely knowledgeable. Her expeditions with the Young Ornithologists had seen to that.

'Good,' he said briskly. 'At least you'll have something to occupy your spare time . . . not that there's much of that.'

Dayle looked at him in patent disbelief. Surely, in a place like this, time must hang very heavily . . . no shops, clubs or theatres to while away the hours; no company other than the wild life and the few domesticated animals to which he had referred.

He answered her unspoken question.

'We have to make the most of the summer daylight. There's the kitchen garden to attend to, peat to be cut . . . and I want to make the cottage entirely weatherproof before next winter.'

'Do you live here all year round, then?' Dayle asked, forgetting in her genuine curiosity that this man was her enemy, that his way of life should be of supreme indifference to her.

'I hope to, some day,' he said rather abruptly. He rose, pushing back his chair. 'Right, you wash up! I'll see to the chickens . . . I've already milked the cow. But don't think you're getting out of it,' he warned. 'You'll be doing it tomorrow.'

Dayle faced him, determined to have this out.

'Just why should I have to do all these things?' she demanded. 'What possible concern is it of yours whether I can or cannot cook, or milk a cow, or . . .'

Mac met her gaze squarely.

'Let's just say,' he drawled, 'that I can't bear parasites, idle creatures who expect other people to anticipate and fulfil their every need.'

Anger warmed Dayle's cheeks. How dared he call her a parasite? *He* was the one who was intending to leech away her father's money!

'But why me?' she persisted heatedly. 'Why pick on *me* to practise your theories?'

He moved towards the door.

'You just happened to be . . . available,' he told her.

'But what has this to do with my father . . . the money . . . you don't seriously expect me to believe that you abducted me, just to . . .'

'You ask too many questions,' he said quellingly. 'I had my reasons . . . and since you're here, why shouldn't I kill two birds with one stone? At least when I decide to let you go, you'll be a complete person, a far more useful member of society.' So saying, he went out, closing the door behind him, leaving Dayle to fume over the washing up.

That remark of his had been the first indication Mac had made
that he *did* intend to release her . . . eventually, Dayle thought, as
she wrapped freshly made sandwiches in cellophane and put
them under the glass dome on the café counter. The park was
now open to the public for the day, and if she knew children, it
wouldn't be long before they were hungry, even if it was only an
hour since they had eaten breakfast. She'd noticed with amusement, when she'd been working in the grounds close to the bus
park, that the first question the children asked their teachers as
they filed up the drive towards the house was 'When can we eat
our lunch?'

Mac had been right about one thing . . . she *was* more useful,
witness her present occupation, but complete? Unaware that she
did so, Dayle shook her head. She was far from complete. Part of
her would always remain back there on Haa Island. She drew off
a cup of tea from the urn and sat down to drink it, before it
assumed the chocolate hue of tea constantly kept hot, and
though she knew it was foolish, allowed herself to go on
thinking . . .

Mac hadn't been long over his chores, returning just as she dried
the last of the dishes.

'Feel like a walk?'

'A *walk*?'

Where was there to walk to? The place hadn't looked very big.
He misunderstood her . . . predictably.

'I'm afraid I can't offer madam a tour of the island in a
chauffeur-driven limousine.'

'I *am* capable of walking,' she snapped. 'I merely wondered
why you asked.'

He shrugged.

'I thought you might care to see the extent of your new home.'

'Don't you mean my prison?'

Nevertheless, Dayle was curious to see the rest of the island.
Knowledge of the territory could be useful, if she ever saw a
chance of escape . . . without the act rebounding upon her father,
of course. She moved towards the doorway.

'But I don't need your company,' she told Mac. 'I'm quite
capable of walking around on my own.' But she did not really
expect that he would let her out of his sight and she was right.

Together they climbed the stony shoulder of the rise she had
seen from her window, and closer to, she could see the gurgling

stream that plunged down its side, the running water tumbling over rocks and stones, pausing at intervals to form tiny pools which, in their turn, overflowed, continuing the cascade and finally forming the natural bathing area she had recently used. They climbed higher still and Dayle could see that this was the central summit of the island, the grass thinner here, the way more stony. The hilltop itself was a flat wasteland, with a panoramic view all around them . . . of the island and, across the bay, the mainland, the clarity of the morning light making it seem so near, and yet for her it was so far away, completely unattainable.

A few sheep grazed the slopes beneath them . . . beasts unlike the sheep to which Dayle was accustomed, for they were horned, some with dark and some with light-coloured fleeces, looking almost goatlike in appearance. They were fleet and sure of foot, indifferent to the presence of the two humans.

'They're Soay sheep,' said Mac in answer to her question, 'a breed that has survived from ancient times.'

'Who looks after them?'

'They look after themselves.'

He seemed different this morning, she thought, a little edgy, as if something had annoyed him. Yesterday he had been talkative, informative, and Dayle had been unable to penetrate his unflagging good nature, despite all her efforts. So it was impossible that she had been responsible for this ill-humour. So what had upset him?

At the far end of the island they came across the traces of earlier habitation, which Mac had told her they would find . . . ancient boundaries, composed of grey, lichened brickwork, some walls shoulder-high . . . tumbledown shells of cottages, the heaps of stone overgrown with grass, nettles and bracken. Here and there were doorways, a fireplace where once peat had glowed warmly, all now in the grip of encroaching plant life. Man might have abandoned this place, but Nature had taken it to herself once more.

The island was a beautiful place. Dayle could admit it to herself . . . though you wouldn't catch her conceding that fact to Mac! It was a strange mixture of the barren and the verdant, smelling of earth and seaweed. Everywhere the seabirds swooped and soared, with plaintive, raucous cries. She stood quietly, absorbing the indefinable atmosphere, experiencing a sense that was almost déjà-vu.

She had never felt so strange, so disturbed and yet so oddly content. It was peaceful here; she had never known such absolute stillness and solitude in her busy social life, and if anyone had asked her, she would have affirmed her horror of isolation and such tangible silence. But here this was not the case. Though the place was deserted, there was no feeling of melancholy to oppress her. Rather, she could imagine the crofters of old working here, making homes, a livelihood for their families, looking after their livestock, repairing, re-thatching the stone-walled cottages, cutting and curing their peats. She felt that she could sense the physical presence of the dispossessed . . . and yet it was a happy presence.

Amongst the tumbled stones, the overgrown peat banks, she could still see visible outlines of once carefully tended gardens. On winter nights her ancestors must have sat around such warmly glowing fireplaces, the men repairing their fishing lines, or fashioning straw baskets, the women knitting or spinning their wool, making gloves and socks. She could imagine the contented conversation, the companionship, the occasional laughter, the warmth, happiness . . . the love of family life.

She had never really had a family, she realised. Angus had done his best to be both father and mother to his only child, but it wasn't the same as being part of a large unit.

'Penny for your thoughts?' Mac asked her after a while.

Dayle started. She had almost forgotten his presence.

'I was wondering what it would be like . . . to live here always.'

He raised one dark, sardonic brow.

'Fallen in love with it already? You? The little socialite?'

'No!' she said abruptly. 'Of course not. I was just wondering about the people who used to live in these houses . . . do you think they were ever lonely?'

Mac shrugged.

'They had their families . . . friends. It would be more lonely to be a stranger in an unfriendly city.'

She looked at him curiously. He sounded almost as if he had experienced such a sensation.

'But what were their lives like?' she persisted. 'Were they happy, contented with their lot?'

'Probably, or they would have sought to change it. Were *you* happy, with the sort of life *you* led?' he countered. 'Would you have changed it, if circumstances hadn't altered it for you?'

'This isn't a permanent change,' she reminded him shortly. 'But yes . . . yes, I was happy, though sometimes . . .'

'Sometimes?' The green eyes were intent upon her unconscious profile.

'Sometimes I couldn't help being curious . . . about other people's lives . . especially the girls I saw in shops, serving behind counters, that sort of thing, and I'd wonder what it would be like to be them.'

'But you wouldn't have changed places?'

'Good lord, no!' She shuddered. 'I should hate to be poor, to have to work to earn money. But I always had a feeling that, in spite of everything, they were freer than I was . . . freer to choose their own friends, boy-friends . . .' she hesitated, remembering her father's machinations . . . 'husbands.'

She turned and looked at him, a puzzled little frown marring the perfection of her brow, as though seeking his opinion.

'Poor little rich girl! Maybe there's hope for you yet,' Mac said lightly.

'What do you mean?' Dayle was on guard immediately. What on earth was she doing, talking like this to Mac, revealing her innermost thoughts, almost as if she had known him for years . . . as if he were a friend of long standing. The trouble was that, unless he was actually issuing orders, his manner was totally relaxed . . . not a bit like that of captor to captive.

'Prickly, aren't you? I was just surprised to find that you do think for yourself, even if physically you're a bit helpless.'

'I may not be a shopgirl,' she countered shortly, 'but I'm quite capable of making up my own mind, making my own decisions . . . choosing my own husband too,' she added thoughtfully, 'when the time comes, even though Daddy . . .'

'You're not engaged, then?' he asked casually, 'never been in love?'

'No, I'm not engaged. In love? No, I don't think I've ever been in love.'

'In that case you haven't,' he stated categorically. 'Believe me, if you had, you'd know it.'

Did that mean he'd been in love with someone? It was very likely . . . after all, he must be in his thirties. Again, Dayle realised just how little she knew about Mac. He didn't talk about himself. He might even be married for all she knew. In which case, she pondered, did his wife . . . or girl-friend . . . know where he was, what he was up to? That he was alone on an island with another girl? Or could this exercise be for the benefit of the woman in his life, a way of raising money to make a fresh start? The idea that he could be using *her* to improve another woman's lot was surprisingly distasteful.

They continued their walk, climbing steadily, as they made their way to the northernmost point of the western coast. Here there were high cliffs, their base jagged with wide inlets. Dayle looked down, impressed, dizzied by the sight, at ledges packed with auks, kittiwakes and gannets. Around them, on the open ground, great skuas rested in the heather.

But far below her were rock slabs and wide ledges, the lower levels washed by the surging seas; while on the dry areas, cormorants nested, the air noisy with their continual coming and going. The upper cliffs were steep and in some places sheer, earthy and clothed with green. On the upper ledges were fulmars, their breeding sites occupied by the chicks, while the adult birds planed stiff-winged up and down the cliff face, then out to sea, as though solely for the joy of flying.

Some time, Dayle vowed, she would escape Mac's vigilance and come here alone to watch the birds, creatures which had always attracted her. She had often envied their soaring freedom; flight must be a glorious sensation, man's nearest approach the soundless acrobatics of a glider plane . . . or the sport of hang-gliding. She had longed to attempt both, but her father, nervous for her safety, had forbidden it, on pain of cancelling her allowance; and wilful though she was, Dayle knew just how far she could go in defiance. On all her bird watching expeditions, she thought, she had never encountered such perfect conditions, free from other human disturbance, been able to come so close to the creatures which fascinated. Alone, it might be possible to get nearer still.

They made their way back towards the cottage, dropping down after a while to the level of the shingly beach. The tide was out, but large and small pebbles still glistened from the recent onslaught of the sea. Rocks, some tilted and sawlike, some square like ruined castle turrets, rose abruptly from the shingled grass of the foreshore, their harsh lines softened by lichens or tussocks of sea pink. The seaweed on the shoreline was still a shimmering, translucent green, amongst which wading birds and ringed plovers scavenged.

'Tern breed here in spring and early summer,' Mac told her,

'and if you come down here at night you'll find eider duck roosting.'

'You seem to know quite a lot about birds,' Dayle ventured.

'I spent my childhood in a place not unlike this . . . a promontory, not an island, but it was possible to get right away from civilisation, to lie on the clifftops and watch the birds and, in those days, to raid their nests. Ever eaten gulls' eggs?'

Appalled, Dayle shook her head, feeling quite sick at the thought.

'Don't turn up your nose,' he advised. 'We may have to fall back on them, if the hens ever stop laying.'

'Never!' she said vehemently. 'You'll never get me to eat one.'

'They're very good . . . much like a hen's egg, only larger, and taste very similar. They just need boiling longer. They never did me any harm, and I ate quite a few when I was a boy.'

Just for a moment, a mischievous grin transformed his face, showing the glint of large strong teeth, and Dayle could imagine the boy he must have been once, tousled of hair, freckled about the face. If one looked closely it was still possible to see the occasional freckle, almost obscured by his healthy tan. It would be so easy, in different circumstances, to like this man, she thought regretfully.

'It sounds as if you like lonely places, that you're not keen on people?' Dayle suggested, reverting to his description of his childhood home.

'I can take them or leave them. Let's say I've only found a few people who are really necessary to me.' Her expression was so obviously questioning that he continued. 'My mother and my sisters, the occasional friend with tastes in common, a colleague I can respect . . .'

'Girl-friends?' she queried.

'A few.'

Dayle felt prepared to believe that there had been more than a few women interested in him. A man with his looks would attract girls like bees to a flower garden. She found herself flushing at the thought. She must stop thinking of Mac as she would any other attractive, normal man of her acquaintance. He was her abductor, an unprincipled stranger . . . and yet she was curious about him, his family, his past. Perhaps, she excused herself, in learning more about him she could discover what had brought him to this pass, to a life of crime. There was little hope, of course, that she could persuade him to abandon his course. But it might be worth a try.

'Tell me about your home,' she invited, as they neared the cottage.

He gave her his hand to help her up the steep ascent from the beach, his fingers strong and warm, so that she withdrew her own as soon as possible, disturbed by the pleasure she found in the contact. His touch ought to be distasteful to her.

Mac dropped down to sit in the heather that fringed the hillside below the cottage.

'It was much like this,' he said reminiscently, looking about him, 'only larger . . . a crofter's cottage. My grandparents started their married life there and my father inherited it.'

'And now?'

'My mother still lives there. My sisters, both older than I are married. One lives in Canada, the other in Australia.'

'Do you live with your mother?'

'No.' His manner became evasive. 'There's only my younger brother at home, but I visit her whenever I can.'

'Is it as primitive as this place?' Dayle asked interestedly.

Mac smiled. It was such a . . . a transfiguring smile, she thought dazedly.

'No. Although it still wouldn't measure up to your standards of comfort. It was one of a number of properties improved at the turn of the century, under the Public Health Acts. A lot of these old croft houses were poorly lit and ventilated . . . very un-healthy. So the thatched roofs were ripped off and replaced by wood covered with felt or slates. My grandfather took the opportunity of having the walls raised and adding two extra rooms upstairs. The earthen floors were covered by wood and the fireplace moved to a gable wall, so that a proper chimney could be installed. Before that the smoke had to escape through a lum, or hole, in the roof.'

'Were you . . . are you . . . very poor?' Dayle felt that she could almost forgive Mac, if his life of crime were prompted by the need to improve his mother's living conditions.

'We weren't destitute, if that's what you mean.' He didn't comment upon his present state of insolvency. 'My father worked the farm and we all had to muck in . . . the girls too. By the time I was thirteen I could shear a sheep as well as the other men.'

'Who looks after the farm now, if you don't live at home?'

His face tautened and his voice became harsh.

'The land was sold off after my father died. He died when I
was fifteen. My mother was determined that I should receive a
good education . . . better myself, as she put it.'

So she hadn't been wrong about Mac. He was not an un-
educated man.

'What sort of education?'

'Public school, then Oxford,' he said briefly. He rose. 'No
more questions. I've talked enough about myself.'

'Just one more,' Dayle begged, as she stood up in unconscious
obedience to his commanding gesture.

'Well?'

'After all the sacrifices your mother must have made, why are
you letting her down like this? You can't tell me she'd approve of
what you're doing now?'

She had expected to hit him on a weak point . . . his evident
affection and respect for his mother . . . perhaps move him to
shame. But his clear green gaze did not falter and unexpectedly a
charmingly crooked smile illuminated his handsome face.

'Perhaps she might not approve the method,' he admitted,
'but I feel sure she'd applaud the outcome.'

Now what was that supposed to mean? Dayle thought crossly.
After all her probing, she was little wiser. Moreover, she felt that,
subtly, she had lost an advantage, by lowering her hostile guard
in order to question him. Now he might be flattering himself that
she would cause him no more trouble. Even worse, he might
have gained the impression that she was beginning to like him!

At this thought, she turned on her heel and made for the
cottage, vowing that she would not repeat her attempts to assess
his character, at least not on such a personal level. What did she
care about his background, his family? All she wanted to know
was how soon she could get away from here. Effortlessly Mac
overtook her, his hand gripping her arm just above the elbow.

'You may as well have a conducted tour of the garden while
we're at it.'

She shook herself free.

'Don't touch me! I don't like it!' She spat the words at him.

'Frigid little thing, aren't you?'

'Only with some people,' she retorted, furious that she could
not feel the revulsion she exhibited. Surely, if he were as despicable, as unprincipled as his behaviour indicated, she should
automatically be repelled by him? Why then did her pulses leap
so strangely at any contact with him? as they had done also at the

expression she had surprised in those narrowed green eyes, earlier that morning.

The garden at the rear of the cottage was completely surrounded by walls. Strangely, neither the walls not the protective shrubs were of any height, yet the area felt curiously sheltered.

'The salt air makes it difficult to grow anything, so we build these 'plantie krubs' ... little stone-walled enclosures ... around our crops. It's surprising the shelter they give. You can be working out here in quite a strong westerly wind and scarcely feel a breath of air.'

The crops seemed to consist mostly of cabbages, potatoes and other root vegetables.

'I had to move bucketsful of stones,' Mac continued. 'It was backbreaking work. I hope to enclose more land this summer and extend the cultivated area. An extra pair of hands will be extremely useful.'

Dayle tightened her lips; she was not going to be provoked into protest. But he would discover, when it came to it, that she had no intention of shifting rocks!

The single cow was grazing in a roughly enclosed area of grass and Dayle could see how the animal might break out from time to time. Shula ... the cow's name ... was not as fearsome a creature as she had expected, being quite unlike the broad-beamed, ponderous beasts she had seen on farms belonging to her father's friends. This animal was fine-boned, with short legs, short, slender horns and a sleek, glossy, black and white coat.

'She's not large,' said Mac, echoing Dayle's thoughts. 'But she's a good milker ... five to eight quarts a day. I'll show you how to milk her this evening.'

'I've no desire to learn how to milk her,' Dayle stated.

'I'm afraid it's a necessary accomplishment. I may have to go away from time to time and apart from the fact that it would be a cruelty to leave the animal unattended, you'll need the milk.'

'You ... you mean you intend to go away and leave me here ... alone?'

Dayle couldn't believe it ... such callousness, such irresponsibility! Suppose she were to be ill, or fall and break a leg? If he expected ransom money for her, shouldn't he protect his investment? But when she voiced some of these thoughts, Mac was calmly unconcerned.

'It may be necessary for me to go over to the next island, yes.

But if you keep to the cottage and its environs, you shouldn't come to any harm.'

'I won't stay here alone . . . I *won't*,' she told him.

He shrugged.

'If it comes to it, you won't have any choice. But let's not cross that bridge until we have to, hmm?'

That didn't suit Dayle at all. She liked to have the future cut and dried, including provision for any emergencies that might arise, liked to have contingency plans worked out for any eventuality. From now on, she determined, she would watch him like a hawk; and if he showed any signs of trying to leave the island, she would attach herself to him like a second skin. *He'd* chosen to abduct her . . . well, he might find it was a different matter, trying to be rid of her!

And now she was separated from Mac for ever. Dayle stared moodily into the dregs of her tea. She was here, hundreds of miles away from him, from Haa Island, and he had not abandoned her. It had been the other way around. *She* had left him . . . running wild . . . as if that were all that was needed to solve her problem, to erase the memory of what she had discovered; and of course it had done nothing of the sort. Her recollections, her hurt, were as fresh as they had been two or three months ago.

'Packet of crisps, miss!'

The piping voice startled Dayle. She stood up and looked over the counter at the diminutive figure in school cap and blazer. Two bright hazel eyes inspected her curiously.

'Last time I was here, you was in the museum.'

'You've been here before then?' said Dayle, as she handed over the crisps and gave change.

'Yeah. Teachers at our school are barmy about this place. *I* reckon it's a good skive for them.'

'Do you like coming here?'

'S'all right . . . in nice weather. But I reckon it's going to rain.'

The sky *had* clouded over and the promise of a warm day had altered subtly to the stolid, sticky menace of a threatening storm. Nervously, Dayle studied the lowering sky. She had conquered most of her inadequacies, but she had never quite overcome her fear of storms. Nowadays she strove to endure them without too much fuss, but as little as a year ago, a storm had been capable of reducing her to a quivering, hysterical mass of fear.

There had been a storm about a week after her enforced arrival on Haa Island. She'd learnt a lot in that week . . . reluctantly at first; then she found the activities passed time which, otherwise, would have dragged interminably; and certain chores had even become enjoyable. Incredibly, one of the most pleasant had been milking Shula. Her first attempts had been grudgingly performed, but after the first two or three times she had found a strange comfort in Shula's enthusiastic welcome, a warm peace, seated with her head against the cow's velvety flanks, as the creamy milk jetted rhythmically into the bucket.

Less pleasant had been the interminable weeding, the clearing of land . . . and carrying stones to build a wall, to enclose the additional garden area Mac planned. Dayle's contribution, despite her earlier resolve of non-co-operation, had been the trundling back and forth with a loaded barrow, while Mac dug out a shallow trench, in which he laid the larger and squarer stones in two parallel rows, filling the space between with rubble.

It had been while they were working on the wall that Mac predicted the coming storm. A westerly wind had risen just after midday and it had been obvious from the first that it bore the promise of rain. But long before this, the wildlife had given warning of bad weather, the sheep edging their way off exposed headlands, down the narrow sheep tracks in single file, while gulls planed in from the sea to spiral into sheltered bays.

It came in sudden gusts at first, out of nowhere, dying away, rising again, then settling down to blow steadily.

'No good trying to do any more work outside, today,' said Mac. 'This is here to stay for a while. I know the signs. We're in for dirty weather.'

They retreated to the cottage, where he proceeded to fasten the storm shutters.

'Is . . . is it going to be that bad?' Dayle enquired nervously.

'Scared?' He rested his hands on her shoulders for a moment.

'No . . . no, of course not.' She shrugged off his touch, even though it had been oddly reassuring. 'I just . . . just wondered, that's all.'

He gave her a disbelieving look, but made no comment.

Despite the shutters, the wind was finding every access available to draughts, beating against the sturdy walls, carrying with it the sound of the rising roar of the sea.'

'Can . . . can the waves reach this high?' Dayle could not hold back the enquiry, even though she didn't want Mac to guess at the extent of her fear.

'Occasionally,' he said, which was not at all comforting to the already anxious girl.

She had always been terrified of storms, even in the comparative safety of her father's solidly built house, but here she felt terribly vulnerable, at the mercy not only of rain and wind, of thunder and lightning, but of the sea too. She could not restrain a shudder at the thought of being engulfed by monstrous seas. Her fertile imagination conjured up all she had heard and read of massive tidal waves, destroying everything in their path, then sucking their victims back into the ocean. She could picture the great plumes of spray now being thrown up on to the beach below the cottage.

'But it's no good sitting around worrying,' Mac said briskly. 'Better to have your hands and mind occupied.'

'Who's worried?' she said, but it was a feeble attempt at bravado and she knew it did not deceive him.

At home, she would have retreated to her bedroom, hidden herself beneath the bedclothes, until the fury of the storm abated. But here there were no heavy curtains to shut out the sky-rending flashes of lightning, to muffle the threatening rumble of the thunder.

Mac moved towards the door.

'Wh—where are you going?' Her voice rose tremulously.

'Just to check on the livestock,' he said calmly. 'Winds of this force could easily blow away every hen we have, and Shula will have to be brought into the byre.'

The byre adjoined the cottage and had once been connected to it by a doorway, Mac had told Dayle, so that access could be obtained from the living quarters. On learning this, she had turned up her nose, but now she found herself wishing that state of affairs still existed. Who was going out there at four o'clock to milk Shula?

'Want to come?'

The question took her by surprise and she hesitated, weighing up the pros and cons. Which was worse . . . to be out there in this awful gale, or to be left alone, imagining Mac being struck by lightning, or blown over the cliff top?

'I'll come with you,' she decided, without stopping to consider why she should be particularly concerned for his fate. Later, when she did stop to question herself, she told herself firmly that it was because her survival depended on his.

She donned waterproof clothing and for the first time admitted Mac's foresight in insisting on its purchase.

Outside, it was even more terrifying than it had sounded. The walls of the cottage must be thicker and more soundproof than she'd thought. She was forced to cling to Mac's arm for support.

Fortunately the chickens, following the example of their wild brethren, the seabirds, had made for cover, and when they led a nervous and lowing Shula into the byre they found the hens already ensconced, damp, dismal bundles of feathers, perched upon the rafters.

'This won't do the crops much good,' Mac said gloomily, inspecting his property.

All Dayle wanted to do was to return to the four sturdy walls of the cottage. She could not understand Mac's tendency to linger, looking out to sea, from whence it was apparent more bad weather was on the way. Huge rollers were coming in, spray being flung explosively up the cliff face.

'There'll be a load of seaweed down there tomorrow . . . that's something, at least.' Mac seemed to find this cause for satisfaction. 'It makes marvellous fertiliser,' he explained. 'In a place like this you have to make the best use of every natural advantage.'

'Can we go back now?' Dayle asked.

He looked down at her, his expression mocking, the coppery hair darkened to the same sleek blackness of his brows by the torrential rain.

'You're definitely not the outdoor type, are you?'

'I've never had to be,' she admitted almost humbly. It was difficult to maintain her normal arrogance in the face of the overpowering elements of Nature; and somehow she didn't think Mac would count tennis and horse-riding . . . both of which she had done in good weather . . . as 'the outdoor life'.

The wind was behind them and as they opened the door of the cottage, their momentum was hard to check. It took their united efforts to close the door, and for additional security, Mac shot the top and bottom bolts.

The storm continued unabated all evening and he insisted that they work on indoor tasks.

'It will keep your mind off the storm; and besides, I believe in using time to its best advantage.'

'On the principle that the devil finds work for idle hands?' Dayle taunted.

Such a moral outlook, she felt, was beyond him. He was just making the most of having captive slave labour!

'Perhaps! Of course,' he added, and there was a strange glint in the green eyes, 'if we were true Shetlanders . . . a married couple for instance . . . there would be other, more relaxing ways of passing the hours indoors.'

Hastily Dayle lowered her gaze. She didn't even dare to think of the implication in his words. Alone here, she was totally at his mercy, if he decided to . . .

'What are we going to do then . . . what jobs?' she muttered.

To her dismay, the chore he produced for her was that of pegging a rag rug, a task which involved cutting up strips of brightly coloured remnants and knotting them through a piece of sacking. This last was hard on fingers unaccustomed to working with rough materials, and at first Dayle made slow progress. Mac, meanwhile, was investigating and cleaning out the black lead range in the living room, which had once done duty in winter, he told her, as both a heating and cooking facility.

'It should be possible to use it again,' he said, as he lay on the floor, his head half extinguished in the surrounding chimney area, his face and hands already considerably blackened.

It sounded, Dayle thought, as though he were serious about taking up permanent residence.

'Would you *really* like to live here always?' she asked, without looking up. She was beginning to find the rugmaking quite absorbing, enjoying the arranging of colours and textures in tasteful patterns, so much so that she was unaware that Mac had ceased his task to study her intent face.

'Yes, I think I would,' he said slowly. 'Of course it would be necessary to return to civilisation occasionally, just to keep an eye on one's business interests.'

This did bring her bright head up, her blue eyes alert with curiosity.

'*You*? . . . have business interests?'

He avoided her gaze, returning his attention to the internal arrangements of the stove.

'I didn't say that,' he returned evasively. 'I meant, of course, that one would need to have other means of support to lead this kind of existence.'

'Why?' Dayle asked bluntly. 'According to you, people used to live very much like this, years ago . . . your ancestors . . . mine, in fact.'

'Yours?' He sat up again.

'Yes, according to my father. His family . . . or one side of it anyway . . . originated from Shetland. I don't know which part.'

'That's very interesting,' he said slowly. 'So you think it would be possible to eke out a living, do you? Without any other financial support?'

'I don't see why not,' she argued. 'What people have done once could surely be done again?'

'Care to try it?' he asked casually, rising to his feet and wiping his hands on an old rag.

'Wh—What do you mean?' She hadn't been thinking of herself but of him.

'Exactly what I say. You're going to be here for quite a while anyway. Time enough to learn self-sufficiency, survival techniques! We could make it a permanent arrangement.'

'I . . . I . . .' she stammered.

Mac sighed, looking down at her.

'As I thought. It's all talk, isn't it? It's all very well to theorise, to suggest that other people do something, but when it comes to actually experiencing it for yourself . . .'

'It isn't all talk,' she said heatedly. 'I could do it, if I had to. I'm not as feeble as you like to make out. But I *don't* have to. I'll be going home some day, when my father . . . I *will*, won't I?' Her blue eyes were suddenly large and pleading.

He sighed again.

'I suppose so.'

'What do you mean? You suppose so?' she cried wildly, jumping up, the rug falling unheeded around her feet. 'You promised! You said . . .'

In her agitation she took a heedless step forward, tripped over the rug and would have fallen heavily, but for his ready arms. She rested against him for a moment, her heart pounding madly; the warmth of him, his arms around her was not an unpleasant sensation; then she recalled who and what he was and struggled wildly to be free.

For a moment Mac restrained her.

'So you don't want to stay here, to try the simple life?'

'No . . . no, of course not. Why should I? How *could* I?' She felt oddly breathless.

He was silent for a moment; then he said something which

stunned her into silence, stilled her struggles into frozen immobility.

'You *could* . . . if you married me.'

CHAPTER FIVE

THE flash and fury of the storm broke over Barnet Country Park and simultaneously, streams of children emerged from farmyard, garden and play area, running for their respective buses . . . teachers in harassed attendance.

Slowly Dayle began to clear the tables of the morning's debris . . . crisp bags, paper cups . . . wiping up the inevitable spills. Often she paused, cloth in hand, to stare dreamily into the middle distance, the thunder and lightning outside a chaotic accompaniment to her equally turbulent thoughts . . . an aid to memory . . .

'M—marry you? *Me?* Marry *you?*'

Mac had still not released her and she'd stared up at him disbelievingly; but he was perfectly straight-faced, no hint of mockery in the brilliant green eyes.

'Is it such an impossible idea?'

'Yes. Yes, of course it is. I'm . . . I'm your prisoner! You don't marry someone who's abducted you!'

He did smile then, a lopsided glint of pure mischief that had a very strange effect upon her pulses . . . or perhaps it was because he was still holding her, her body only a fraction of an inch from his, so that she could still feel the warmth emanating from him, sense the aura of his masculinity.

'You could always make history.'

'No!' Violently she pulled away from him. 'You're talking utter nonsense; and you'd better not get any ideas either, just . . . just because we're alone here together. Why don't you get on with the negotiations with my father, so that I can go home? I suppose you want the money to finish your improvements to this . . . this dump? The money would be more useful to you than I am. You don't need *me* here.'

'Oh, I wouldn't say that,' he drawled. 'There's been quite a marked improvement in you over the last few days. You've actually become quite handy around the place.' He enumerated the points on his fingers. 'Milking, gardening, collecting the eggs

73

... even rug making. We may even have you running up curtains and cushion covers before long.'

'Oh no, you won't,' she interpolated.

'Mind you,' Mac continued, 'you're still a lousy cook, but then the facilities aren't too good. Once I get that thing functioning ...' he indicated the black-lead stove with its oven and pivoting hob for kettles, 'you'll be able to vary our diet a bit ... make bread perhaps?'

'That's all you want, isn't it?' Dayle demanded. 'Someone to work their fingers to the bone, so that you can restore this ... this museum piece! Well, you don't need a wife for that, you need an odd job man ... and if you want to be a hermit and live this sort of life, you just get on with it. You chose the wrong kind of girl!'

'Did I? I wonder?' His lazy smile was challenging and she backed further away from him.

'You keep your distance! My father will pay up to get me back. That's the knowledge that you and your sort trade on ... people's affections ... but he'll hound you to the ends of the earth afterwards, if he finds out you've ... you've ...'

'I've what?' he said softly, 'kissed his daughter?'

'You know I didn't mean ... just ... just kissing.' Dayle couldn't enlarge upon what she *had* meant. 'But you're not even going to do that,' she added warningly, as he showed signs of moving in on her.

'I knew you were frigid.'

Dayle stamped her foot.

'I am *not*? But I don't have to kiss you to prove it. Just because the very thought of kissing you makes me feel sick, it doesn't mean there's anything wrong with me!'

'So the idea of kissing me has that effect on you, does it?'

'Yes,' she said defiantly, 'it does!' Then, before the confrontation could become more dangerous than it already was, before he could demand that he test the truth of her assertion, Dayle turned on her heel and fairly ran from the room, taking the narrow steps to her bedroom two at a time, pursued by the sound of his laughter.

Alone, she began to wish that she had not been so precipitate in her flight, or that the need for it had not arisen; for, up here beneath the roof, she felt nearer to the storm, which still raged unabated, the wind coming off the sea at gale force, great gusts of it. She could hear how it took the tops of the waves, throwing the masses of water against the rocks, could hear it breaking and lling with the sound of breaking shards of pottery.

She undressed and huddled down in the camp bed, trying to ury her face, so that she need not see the glare of lightning hrough the uncurtained windows. Curtains *were* needed, she hought inconsequentially. Perhaps, tomorrow, she would see if he could improvise something.

She heard Mac come upstairs and go into his room. Then the ounds of movement ceased, and with that she felt desperately lone. *He* would probably fall asleep immediately, thick-kinned, insensitive brute, while she lay here wide-eyed and rembling with fear. It was horrible to know that you were the nly person awake, that there was no one to talk to. At home, she ould have rung the bell for her personal maid and demanded a up of tea and other little services, anything, just to keep another uman being in the room.

Dayle was certain that the storm was worse than it had been. robably the cottage would be flattened by a thunderbolt, or truck by lightning. She would be charred into unrecognisable shes and no one would ever know what had happened to her. fter a few years, she would be presumed dead and . . . Tears of elf-pity welled up, as she imagined her father, prematurely aged y grief, having a tablet erected to her memory in their local hurch, perhaps even a stained glass window . . .

She must have slept after all, for the luminous dial of her ratch showed two in the morning, when she woke from uneasy reams to find that the wind had dropped. All she could hear vas the rush of rain, the roar of surf. Then there was a sudden, iolent onslaught of air, which increased until the whole night eemed alive with its clamour. A second or two later the world utside seemed to be engulfed in chaos, flash upon flash, crash fter crash, the wind a screaming crescendo, prevailing over ven the sound of the waves dashing themselves upon the cliffs. he windowpanes rattled violently as though the elements ught to enter, and suddenly Dayle could stand it no longer. Vith a wild cry of despair, she leapt out of bed, flung herself out f the room and into Mac's, without even a preliminary knock. ler eyes still affected by the recent bright glare, she did not otice the shadowy outline of the bed, pulled up almost to the oor, and she fell sprawling across it, startling Mac into instant akefulness.

'What the . . .?' He sat up, hands reaching for her, encounter-g her soft shapelessness.

'Mac! Mac!' she sobbed. 'I can't *bear* it! I can't!' Her tone
voice, the trembling of her body convinced him of her nea
hysteria.

Wordlessly, he disentangled himself from the bedclothes an
her clinging arms, swept her up and carried her downstairs,
place her on the faded settee. It was only as he lit the lamp an
turned to regard her tearstained face that she remembered sh
was clad only in her underwear; the problem of proper sleepwea
had still not been resolved.

As Mac took in her near-nakedness, her struggles to concea
herself with her arms, he swore vigorously and left the room
returning with a blanket, which he flung over her, leaving her
drape it about herself as best she might.

'Do you always sleep like that?' His voice was unnatural
throaty.

'Of course not,' she snapped. 'But I didn't happen to have m
overnight case with me when you snatched me away.'

'Why the hell didn't you get some nightclothes then . . . whe
we were in Lerwick? I can't do *all* your thinking for you!'

'Because I didn't think of it. It wasn't thinking straight. Ho
was I supposed to keep my wits about me . . . abducted from m
own home, shaken to death in that old banger of yours, ha
starved, scared stiff . . .'

'Ah, so you *were* scared.'

'Of course I was . . . wouldn't any girl be? Or were yo
precious sisters such Amazons that they could cope singl
handed with great, brutal men?'

A smile crinkled his face.

'My sisters are diminutive . . . like my mother. But there a
other ways of handling men than by brute force.'

'I know what you mean,' Dayle said furiously. 'But wh
should I be expected to crawl to you . . . plead with you . . .?'

'It wasn't that kind of submission I had in mind.'

'Well, you won't get the other kind from me either,' she sa
recklessly. 'I suppose you're the sort of man who can't be alo
with a girl for a few days without getting ideas. If that's what yo
want, you'd better take a trip to the Mainland, because *I* sha
oblige you.'

'Now that's an idea,' said Mac, as though struck by the sen
of her suggestion. 'And of course you won't mind staying he
alone, will you?'

Her eyes widened with fear. She hadn't really expected him

take up her challenge; she had been driven into using verbal tactics, but her strategy seemed to have misfired.

'Oh, don't worry!' He interpreted her sudden silence correctly, 'when I do go ashore, I'll take you with me.'

'When?' she cried eagerly. 'When will that be? Does that mean you're going to let me go?'

'Not on your life! You haven't been here long enough to complete the cure.'

'Cure? What cure?'

'The cure for your confounded superciliousness, the way you have of treating a man as if he's dirt beneath your feet . . . and your general uselessness.'

'Oh!' Dayle jumped up to rush past him. Better the nightmares of her bedroom than to stay here and endure these insults.

'Sit down!' he commanded. 'I'm going to make you a hot drink and give you some tablets. I guarantee you'll sleep through the crack of doom after that.'

Reluctantly, she subsided. The thought of a hot drink *was* appealing, and she didn't really want to lie awake all night, listening to the clamour of the elements, which still swirled ferociously around the cottage walls.

Dayle eyed Mac over the rim of her cup.

'When . . . when you go over to the mainland, you *did* say I could come . . . can I phone my father?'

'No,' he said uncompromisingly.

'Oh, but . . .'

'We won't be going to the mainland. We'll be going to the next island. There's a small settlement, with a village store, where I usually get my supplies. I don't generally shop in Lerwick.'

'Well, is there a phone there?'

'Yes. But you're not using it.'

'You're . . . you're cruel!' she choked.

'Sometimes,' he said obscurely, 'it's necessary to be cruel to be kind.'

'And you think you're being kind to me, when . . .'

'I'd like to be kind to you, Dayle.' His voice was husky. 'You don't know how kind I'd like to be . . .'

'Don't start all that again,' she begged. 'I . . . I'm not . . .'

'You're not able to cope with it.' He sighed. 'I know. Come on, back to bed with you.'

The tablets he had given her must have been very strong, for when she tried to stand, her legs felt strangely weak and useless.

Seeing this, he lifted her and without any apparent effort carried
her back upstairs.

'Shall I leave our doors open?' he asked, as he set her down
and pulled the scattered bedclothes around her, 'so that you
won't have to hurl yourself into my arms next time you're
afraid.'

'I didn't . . .' she muttered sleepily. 'What a stupid place to
have your bed . . . almost up against the door.'

'I told you one of the ceilings leaked,' he reminded her. 'That's
the only safe place to put a bed in that room.'

Dayle stretched luxuriously and rubbed the back of her hand
across her eyes, in a mannner which he must have found
curiously endearing, for without saying a word, he crouched
down beside the bed and she felt his lips lightly brush across
hers.

Wonderingly, half asleep, she regarded him. It hadn't been an
unpleasant sensation. In fact it had been very pleasant indeed. A
half-smile curled her full lips and Mac drew in a sharp breath.
He kissed her again, and this time it was no light caress, but
firm enveloping pressure and his arms went round her, lifting
her from the bed, to hold her against his chest. With a little sigh
she slid her arms up around his neck, her hands encountering the
thick, coppery hair that waved about his nape.

'Mac?' she murmured, when his lips released hers.

'Hmm?' He was busy running his mouth down the slender
column of her neck, exploring the hollows behind her ears.

'If you weren't such a pig . . . if you hadn't kidnapped me,
think I could . . . could . . .'

'Yes?' he prompted, languor vanished, suddenly alert.

But Dayle was asleep, the tremulous little smile still playing
about her lips.

She'd nearly told him she could fancy him, that night of the
storm, Dayle reflected, as she finished tidying the café to her
satisfaction. She had never experienced a storm since, without
reliving that night. Next morning, she'd put it down to her
traumatic fear of the thunder and lightning, together with her
drug-induced sleepiness . . . for she couldn't *possibly* like a man
who had treated her the way Mac had. Why, she didn't even
know his second name, or anything other than the few details she
had coaxed from him. He could even have a criminal record for
all she knew.

Dayle peered out at the unrelieved grey skies. There were no more parties booked for today and it was unlikely there would be any casual visitors in this kind of weather. She checked to see that the electric tea urns were switched off, locked up the café and hurried across the glistening tarmac still lashed by sweeping rain, to return the key to the office.

'I'm afraid you're right, Dayle,' Tony Ashworth, the Park Manager, said ruefully. 'We shan't have any more customers today. You may as well take the afternoon off. I only wish I could do the same.'

Tony smiled.

'Would you like me to stay and help you with the paperwork?' Dayle offered. She didn't relish the idea of the empty hours stretching ahead.

'I think you might be more of a distraction. Seriously, though . . no, thanks. Fair's fair. It's not your turn for the clerical side this week. I suppose . . .' he hesitated . . . 'I suppose you wouldn't like to come out to dinner with me this evening?'

Regretfully, Dayle shook her silvery fair head. She hated having to appear churlish. Tony, she was aware, had been attracted to her right from the very first day, when he had interviewed her for a post at the Country Park; and she had had to keep him at arms' length ever since. She knew he was puzzled by her apparent stand-offishness, but she had told him nothing about her personal circumstances . . . about Mac. Nobody knew about that, except Jenny.

Jenny had closed up shop too.

'Nobody's going to walk round the garden and buy dripping wet plants,' she observed.

'I hope it clears up tomorrow,' said Dayle as she laid the table for an early tea. 'I'm in the souvenir shop and it's deadly dull in bad weather . . . no trade . . . and I just stand there, twiddling my thumbs and . . .'

'And thinking about the past,' Jenny finished for her. 'Dayle,' she pleaded, 'why don't you get in touch with Mac, tell him where you are? Give him a chance to explain. It might all have been a terrible misunderstanding.'

Dayle shook her head determinedly, her expression grim.

'There was no misunderstanding. He lied to me and that's all there is to it . . . and I'll never forgive him, never!'

'And you'll never stop loving him either,' Jenny said shrewd-

'Maybe not. But there's no need for *him* to know that, so th
he can crow over me.'

Jenny shrugged her shoulders in helpless exasperation.

'I've known you for a long time, Dayle, but I still don
understand you. If it were me, I'd sooner have the whole thin
out . . . explanations on both sides, so that I knew exactly whe
I stood: none of these doubts and speculations. Oh, Dayle, ju
suppose it *was* all a mistake. Just think of what you're missing!

She rarely did anything else, Dayle thought drearily, as sh
dried the pots after their meal. Jenny had a date, so she would b
all alone this evening . . . alone with her memories again. Sh
almost wished she'd accepted Tony Ashworth's invitation. B
that wouldn't have been fair; because she would only have bee
making use of him, raising expectations she could never fulfi
Because there would never be any man in her life but Ma
though it had been a while before she'd admitted it to herself .
let alone to *him*.

She had been icy cold in her manner towards him, the mornin
after the storm, just so that he wouldn't be under any illusion
and for several weeks following that incident she had fought
desperate battle, in an attempt to stifle growing feelings, whic
were just not consistent with her situation; and yet, in tho
weeks, as Mac had revealed more and more of his character
her, she found it increasingly difficult to believe that he was th
criminal that intellect insisted he must be.

For one thing, a man who lived on money obtained l
kidnapping heiresses would scarcely be the sort to work har
and Mac was certainly not indolent. It was a vice she knew h
abhorred. The storm had wrought much havoc on the island an
for several days afterwards he had worked to restore order, har
punishing, physical labour, stripped to the waist, the muscles
his bronzed arms and torso rippling with effort; and he had see
to it that Dayle worked alongside him.

She too was acquiring a tan. There were times when she sti
bitterly resented the damage to her hands and nails, the indign
ty to what she considered to be her position in life; but she wa
beginning to attach less importance to appearance, was begin
ning to discover that working side by side with a man could b
rewarding and sometimes fun. For there were many moments f
humour, though she still found it a little difficult to smile whe
she was on the receiving end of a disaster . . . such as th

occasion, when gathering seaweed for Mac's organic compost heap, she had been taken unawares by a large wave, which drenched her from head to foot, and she had been furious when Mac had laughed uproariously at her bedraggled appearance. There were times, too, when homesickness and concern for her father's safety tortured her; and yet subconsciously, a belief was growing inside her that this man was not the kind to inflict physical injury . . . just so long as his associates were not either . . .

Mac was not only good company; he was a mine of information, and Dayle, who had believed herself to be well educated, found whole new areas of knowledge opening up to her. Then they had their interest in birds in common. The birds were another reason, Mac told her, for his wish to make the island his home.

'One day,' he promised, 'I'll take you to Noss. It's off the east coast of Mainland and far more extensive than Haa.'

One day! she thought. He hadn't even kept his promise to take her to the next island . . . just visible from Haa . . . even though they now had a boat at their disposal. A couple of days after the storm. Simon had turned up with supplies and with a sturdy rowing boat which Mac had, unknown to Dayle, ordered to be delivered to him.

Dayle had looked doubtfully at it. It didn't look a very large craft in which to brave the strong currents which ran between the islands; but Mac was quietly confident.

'It will be perfectly adequate in good weather,' he told her.

From time to time Dayle still raised the question of her release, although as time went by it was becoming more and more difficult to remember that she *was* a prisoner. If she could only be assured of her father's safety, know that his mind had been set at rest about her welfare . . . for although he was still dictatorial from time to time, Mac treated her more like a friend and partner than his captive and sometimes . . . sometimes Dayle had the idea that he would not object to a deepening of that friendship, if she had showed the slightest relaxation in her manner towards him . . . but maybe that was just her imagination.

'Have . . . have you had any contact with my father, since we came here?' she asked one evening, as they sat in what was almost an atmosphere of domestic harmony, she at her rug-making, Mac completing his work on the living room stove.

'No.'

'No? Why not?' It was an indignant squeak. 'You could have asked Simon to post a letter. If you don't contact Daddy, how can he do anything about getting me back? What about the money?'

'What money?'

Exasperated, she glared at his broad back. Was he being deliberately obtuse?

'The money you want before you let me go.'

'I don't want any money,' he said calmly.

'You don't want . . . What *are* you talking about?'

'I've told you what I want. I want to marry you.'

She ignored this ridiculous assertion.

'If you don't want money, what am I doing here? Why bother to kidnap me in the first place?' Then, as he remained silent, '*Mac!* Answer me!'

He sat back on his heels and turned his head.

'I'm sorry, Dayle, but that's a question I'm not prepared to answer just yet . . . not without consultation with . . . with someone else.'

Someone else? Dayle's heart sank. So Mac wasn't acting alone; any progress she might have made, the rapport she'd felt growing between them, was false, since it seemed he was answerable to a higher authority. Her blue eyes narrowed, as she considered this new development. If it wasn't a question of money, then it must be something to do with her father's business interests . . . industrial espionage? Mac didn't want money in exchange for her, because he hoped to obtain something far more valuable from her father . . . for which, in turn, his principal would pay handsomely. She felt sick. To think she had been on the verge of liking this man! But you couldn't have liking without trust. Suddenly she wanted to get away from him, as far away as possible; she was afraid she might burst into tears. Though why she should be so upset, she couldn't imagine. Nothing had changed. She was still being held to ransom; only the form it would take had changed. So why this feeling of depression? she asked herself, as she rolled up her work.

'I'm going to bed,' she informed Mac stiffly.

He acknowledged her statement with an inclination of his head, packing up his tools as he spoke.

'I think I'll follow suit. An early night might be a good idea. I want to catch the tide in the morning.'

'The tide?' She stopped in the doorway.

'Yes . . . oh, didn't I mention it? I'm going over to the next island tomorrow, for one or two things we need.'

No, he hadn't mentioned it and he knew it. Dayle was willing to bet that he'd only just made the plan on the spur of the moment. He probably wanted to make a telephone call . . . to his accomplice. Were they still holding her father? She supposed they must be. If only Mac would let her speak to him again.

'Can . . . can I come with you?'

He stood up, shaking his head.

''Fraid not . . . not this time. You haven't completed your . . . er . . . training.'

Training! What did he think she was? Some sort of domestic pet? No, it was worse than that. She was more like an unpaid slave. She flung her next words at him savagely.

'And just what do you mean by that? What other menial activity have you in mind for me now?'

Mac studied her reflectively, as if debating whether or not he should answer her question.

'Sit down again for a moment,' he invited, doing so himself.

'No! Just answer my question.'

'Answer my question, *please?*' he suggested pleasantly.

She glared at him; but she knew defiance was useless. For someone who exhibited criminal tendencies, she thought scornfully, he was very meticulous about good manners; and if she did not comply, he would not give her the answer she demanded.

'Please!' she said sulkily.

'Very well.' He crossed his legs, his manner very relaxed, in contrast to her own tense indignation.

The movement riveted her eyes upon the strength of his muscular thighs, outlined by the tautness of his denims. Damn it! Why did he have to be so spectacularly attractive, when all she wanted to do was to hate him?

She swallowed, then, determinedly, fixed her eyes at a point somewhere beyond his left ear.

'I don't feel,' he began, 'that you've had enough experience yet . . . of hardship, self-sufficiency . . . of poverty.'

'Poverty?' She picked up the word. 'Why should *I* need to experience that?'

The green eyes were quizzical.

'Don't you know?'

'Of course I don't,' she snapped. 'Would I be asking you if I did?'

'Forgotten your own ambition already?' he drawled, his tone insufferably mocking, 'to marry a poor man?'

Dayle became very still, taken utterly by surprise, then:

'What do *you* know about that?' she whispered.

'Only what I heard . . . from a mutual friend.'

Dayle did sit down then.

'We have a friend in common?' Her tone was disbelieving.

'Oh, several, actually. Even though you once expressed the belief that we didn't move in the same circles.'

'Who?' she demanded. 'Who told you about . . . about what I said?'

'Ah that would be telling! How many people did you tell about your intention?'

Quite a few directly or indirectly, Dayle thought ruefully, remembering that morning at the yacht club, when at least two dozen people must have heard her rebellious words. Any one of them might be known to Mac; could have told him, or passed the story on to a third party. But why should it interest *him?* Unless . . . recent words of his echoed in her brain . . . 'you don't want to stay here? Try the simple life? You could . . . if you married me.'

'So *that's* what you're up to!' She leapt to her feet, thoroughly incensed now, as she felt that the missing pieces of the jigsaw were falling into place. 'That's why you keep on . . . about me marrying you. You think, just because I said I'd marry a poor man, that *you* might qualify. Let me tell you something . . you'd be the very last person I'd consider!'

'Oh no,' he contradicted her, 'because then you'd be breaking the letter of your vow.' And, as she stared at him uncomprehendingly, he continued, emphasising each word, 'because you vowed you'd marry the *first* poor man who asked you . . . I've asked you. There's been no opportunity for anyone else to get their word in.'

By now Dayle's temper was soaring. Fists clenched at her sides, she was literally shaking with anger, and something else . . . fear? But fear of what? She couldn't be held to that rash vow of hers . . . it wasn't legal and binding. Nobody in their right mind would expect her to carry it through. She might lose face with her friends, if they ever heard that she'd passed up the opportunity, she'd claimed to desire. But so what? She'd realised recently that most of those so-called friends of hers were worthless anyway . . . their opinion of no value; and who had taught her that? she asked herself. Desperately she tried to halt the direction of her thoughts, but realisation was in full flood now. It had been Mac . . . Mac, who had taught her how shallow and useless her life had been and . . . necessarily . . . the lifestyle of many of her friends; and what about the gradual change in her attitude towards Mac himself? From thinking of him as an unprincipled villain, she had come to regard him almost as a friend. She dared not consider the further implications . . . the chemical attraction which had sparked between them occasionally . . . for that was all it was; he was all male and she was not unaware of her own attributes.

The new idea was beginning to take hold. So Mac's motives for abducting her had been totally different from those which she had envisaged. Hearing of her declared intention, he had engineered this situation, in order to be the first to ask her to marry him, having first won her confidence . . . though he'd been a little premature. Did he suppose she trusted him already? It was rather a dramatic way . . . a drastic way of going about it. But he would have needed to know if she could stand up to this way of life . . .

Her opinion veered again. No, it wasn't necessary for him to know that; because if he married her, he wouldn't need to live like this. What was she doing, anyway, making excuses for him? He'd be marrying her for her money . . . and *he'd* denied his interest in money . . . liar . . . hypocrite . . .

'Gigolo!' She finished her thoughts aloud on the insult.

'I beg your pardon?' Mac had been watching her for the past few minutes, seeing the conflicting emotions express themselves in her changing expression, but this conclusion had evidently startled him.

'I said "gigolo!" That's what they call men who prey on rich women, isn't it? No wonder you didn't bother to ask my father for any money, since your idea was to marry me . . . counting on getting the lot some day, when my father . . . when he . . .' Her voice broke on a half sob. 'You're despicable! Rotten! You're low-down . . . scum! Well, you needn't waste any more of your time. You can find yourself another heiress. Because if you kept me here for the next fifty years, I *still* wouldn't marry you!'

'That's fortunate,' he said gravely, 'because in fifty years' time, I doubt if I'd fancy you.'

'Oh!' She glared at him. 'You . . . you . . . I hope when you row across to the next island tomorrow that you *drown* yourself!'

She turned and raced up the stairs, before he could see just how miserable disillusionment had made her. Though why she should be more disillusioned, now that she knew his true motives for abducting her, she couldn't imagine.

Predictably, Dayle passed a restless night, and it was later than usual when she woke. At first she couldn't think why she felt so apprehensive; then she remembered. Mac was intent on pressurizing her to marry him. She still found the thought incredible. Before, when she had believed her abduction to be the prelude to a demand for ransom, she had been able to temper her growing liking for him with scornful indignation. But now their duel must, necessarily, take on a different aspect. Now that she knew the truth, would he change his tactics? Come out into the open, trying to sway her by employing his undeniably powerful masculinity? She shivered. She had been unable to hold out against his greater willpower, when he had insisted that she bear her share of the chores; so what chance did she stand of resisting him, if he chose to make a sexual assault upon her senses? She had already discovered that she was not entirely immune to him physically . . . though fortunately she had not betrayed that fact to *him*.

Dayle had momentarily forgotten her sleepy acceptance of his kisses on the night of the storm, her murmured words, not too difficult of interpretation to an experienced man.

It was rather an anticlimax, having steeled herself to go downstairs and face him, to find the cottage empty and silent. Mac was nowhere to be seen. Then she remembered. He was going to the next island today. For the first time in weeks, she would be entirely alone . . . for what length of time? She had no idea how long it would take Mac to row to the next island and back, or how long he would stay there. He might even be away overnight!

She ran out of the cottage. Was she too late? Had he already left? Could she persuade him to take her after all? She didn't want to be here alone, wondering if he was safe. She hadn't meant it, when she'd said she hoped he would drown.

The sky was hazy, with a promise of heat to come, and sound carried clearly on the still air . . . the grinding of the boat on the shingle at the foot of the cliff.

'Mac!' she shouted, scrambling madly down the path. 'Wait for me!'

He was already in the boat and waved a nonchalant hand,

before pulling away, the oars smiting the sea. It gave her a sudden pang to think that he could leave her like this, without a word of farewell. She ran to the water's edge, heedless of the waves lapping her feet, dampening the fabric of her pumps.

'Mac! How long will you be?'

'I don't know.' His voice came back clearly. 'It depends on the weather . . . if it holds.'

'Let me come too.'

'No. Not this time . . . and no wandering round the island on your own. It could be dangerous. Stay put at the cottage . . . there's plenty to keep you busy.'

Dayle had changed in many ways, but nothing could ever touch the inherent, stubborn Abercrombie streak in her nature. Mac had made a distinct tactical error. In one and the same breath he had refused her simple request *and* issued his orders. No one of spirit would accept that sort of treatment, she brooded; and whatever else Dayle might lack, it was not spirit.

'I'm damned if I'll stay cooped up in your rotten cottage all day!' she shouted. Never mind that Mac was too far away to hear her defiance; the very utterance of the words aloud relieved her pent up feelings. 'And when you come back . . . *if* you come back . . . maybe . . . just maybe, I won't *be* here!'

CHAPTER SIX

AND she hadn't been there, Dayle thought, opening up the souvenir shop next morning and taking up her reminiscences where she had left off the night before . . . though she hadn't planned the actual events which had led up to her non-reappearance at the cottage.

But she could not afford to woolgather today. She would need all her wits about her. Even though the visiting schoolchildren were only allowed into the souvenir shop in small parties, they still needed watching. She could sympathise with the young-sters' desire to handle the delightful objects on sale. But if every one of a hundred or so children picked up an item, it swiftly became unmarketable, and sadly, there was always the chance of pilfering. Even the most vigilant teacher-in-charge could not keep her eye on every individual in her group.

Humming under her breath, Dayle refilled the postcard stand and set out a pile of guidebooks. She would be glad when it was her turn to take a party round the house again. Of all her tasks that was the one she most enjoyed, and she took a real pride in having all the necessary information at her fingertips. In fact, wherever she was working . . . in Home Farm, walled garden or the grounds, she was always ready to answer questions put to her by children or adults, for she believed strongly in the aims of the Park . . . to provide an enjoyable day out which was also a worthwhile educational experience for their visitors.

But she enjoyed the shop too. It was amusing to watch the children deliberating over the outlay of their pocket money, to hear the heart-searching that went on over the choice of a present for mother, grandmother, or other relative.

'How about a shopping list with a picture of the Mansion on the front?' she suggested to one small boy, 'or eggs from the hens on our Home Farm?'

The boy looked at her consideringly, his head on one side, as he pondered the important decision, and Dayle's heart lurched as she noticed that his eyes were green, a colour which had the power to move her . . . to move her unbearably. It was not a colour you came across very often, she thought, nor was that particular shade very common. It reminded her . . .

She had often seen just that expression of calculation in Mac's eyes . . . but then she had seen them in many moods . . . mocking, wary, tender . . . *angry*. He had been angry when he returned from his expedition, annoyed to find that she had deliberately disobeyed him, had taken an unnecessary risk . . . but furious at the predicament in which she had landed herself.

For she had kept her threat not to stay tamely in and around the cottage all day. To add to the injury she felt at being abandoned, he had left her a written list of jobs to be done, which included laundry, the digging up of potatoes and the collection of driftwood and seaweed deposited by the last tide. He had at least condescended to feed the chickens and milk the cow.

She would go off . . . for the whole day, Dayle decided. She would take a packed lunch and do something she had long promised herself; she would sit on the cliffs at the northernmost end of the island and watch the birds. She had no fieldglasses, but the birds seemed unperturbed by human presence and she should be able to make fairly close observation of them. The only stipulation she made for herself was that she must be back to milk Shula at four o'clock. It wasn't the cow's fault that her owner was a hardhearted, thoughtless brute.

It was a mild day for autumn and by the time she had made her way over the rough terrain to the northern tip of Haa Island, Dayle was ready to sit and relax and watch the birds soaring above her and out to sea. But after she had eaten her lunch, she found inactivity begin to pall. She would not return to the cottage, however, and the despised chores. Instead, getting up, she wandered along the cliff top in search of some diversion.

A spirit of curiosity prompted her to see if she could get closer to the nesting ground, to have a look at the fulmar chicks, great fluffy balls, twice as large as the parent birds. This would be an achievement to relate to Jenny . . . if she ever saw her friend again.

As far as Dayle could see, from her vantage point, there appeared to be a fairly easy way down to one of the ledges occupied by a nestling, and lowering herself over the grassy edge of the cliff, she found herself with only a short drop to begin her descent. However, once embarked upon the enterprise, she found it was not as simple as it had looked; the route she must

take was precarious in the extreme and required many circuitous
detours. Moreover, the steep way narrowed out considerably in
places and one false step could send her over the edge, with
nothing to break her fall but the cormorants' nests far beneath
her.

Slowly she made her zig-zag way down the cliffside. In places
the going was soft and earthy, offering little foothold; and she
had to take advantage of any conveniently placed rock which
would afford a support. Several times she found herself at a dead
end and had to turn about, seeking an alternative route. Once or
twice she was even tempted to give up and return to the clifftop,
but on looking back, she could not now determine which way she
had come and it seemed easier to go on, though by now she was
feeling not a little afraid and wishing she had not undertaken
such a risky endeavour. What had looked so easy and straightforward from above was well nigh impossible close to. She would
have to exercise extreme caution and common sense, if she were
to survive her rash attempt.

Her progress became slower, as she took a few tentative steps,
crouched on all fours, sat down to manoeuvre her way under
projecting rocks, or slithered a few feet on shifting soil. Many
times she had to lower herself from ledge to ledge, feeling for the
next resting place with her feet.

She was mad to have attempted this, she admitted to herself,
as she paused to catch her breath after one particularly hair-
raising moment, when she seemed to be suspended in bottomless
space; and what if she *did* fall? She took a quick glance at her
wrist watch. It was incredible, but Mac had only been gone four
hours and might not return until evening. If she fell, she could be
lying here, badly injured, for ages before he came in search of her
or, equally well, she could plunge straight into the sea below, as
it boiled around the rocks at the foot of the cliff. Then Mac would
never know what had become of her.

She fought down the rising panic these thoughts engendered.
She was *not* going to fall. She was going to complete her
observation and then find her way back to safety. If she couldn't
go upwards, she would continue on down, until she found a way
around the base of the rocks. She would be back at the cottage
long before Mac returned, ready to give him a nonchalant
account of her day's activities.

A few moments later she was on a level with the first of the
fulmar's nests . . . her objective only a few yards away along the

ledge. Cautiously she approached, fear forgotten now in the thrill of being so close to the chick. The young fulmar, however, did not appreciate its visitor in the same measure and employed a defensive mechanism of which she had never heard. Finding its range with uncanny accuracy, it fired volley after volley of oily vomit from its beak, staining its own front as well as Dayle's light blue jeans with the emission. Moreover, the adult birds were showing signs of agitation, and though Dayle did not think they would actually attack, their swooping flight, close to her head, made it difficult to concentrate on keeping her balance.

She could not make her way forward, since the ledge was blocked by the nest, and on looking behind her, she discovered that the far end narrowed away to nothing. Once again, her only way was down, a route consisting of a steep, earthy slide, terminating in large, jagged rocks. She lay on her back, her legs suspended in space, and wriggled cautiously until her waist reached the edge of her narrow perch. Legs hanging downwards, she felt about until her feet touched soil. From there on it was a matter of edging her way downwards, using her heels as brakes to slow her descent.

Her journey ended on the sea-washed slabs of rock at the foot of the cliffs. It was almost totally rock here, with very little in the way of a beach. She would have a long, hard scramble around the base of the island before she encountered anything in the way of terrain suitable for walking. Also, it seemed to her that the tide was higher than it had been. If she remained at this low level for long, she could find herself trapped . . . not only that, she would be dashed and crushed against the rocks. As she made her way over the intractible surface, it would be necessary to try and gain height. Bitterly, she thought of Mac, on the other island by now, enjoying comparatively civilised conditions . . . meeting and talking to other people, able to make contact with his friends . . . and totally unaware of what she was doing in his absence.

It had been entirely her own fault, of course, Dayle reminded herself, as she cashed up and checked the contents of the till against the till roll. Only she hadn't been prepared to admit it to Mac. She had preferred then to blame him for her uncomfortable state. After all, she wouldn't have been on the island but for him.

The souvenir shop had done well today. With the improvement in the weather, trade had been brisk and she had been kept busy, with only short intermissions in which to indulge in her memories.

It would be fun to do something like this on a smaller scale, she thought . . . to own a property that people considered worth visiting. She would quite enjoy providing refreshments, selling mementoes, knowing that the money was to be reinvested in further improvements. Mac had proposed an undertaking something on those lines. But that had been a lot later . . . several months later, in fact, when she'd actually considered spending the rest of her life with him.

But in the intervening weeks, there had been many other events which she now recalled . . . one of the most vivid being the row they'd had after Mac had returned and finding her missing had come in search of her.

There was absolutely no way of rounding the headland and reaching the safety of the beach on the western side of the island. After several ineffectual attempts, Dayle was forced to accept that she was stuck here, until such time as Mac missed her . . . and that could be a long time. There was no guarantee even that he would search here first . . . and in any event, it might well be too dark by the time he returned and discovered her absence. They were into autumn now and past the time when twilight had extended from sunset to sunrise.

They'd stayed up all night on Midsummer's Eve to see the midnight sunset which the Shetlanders called the 'Simmer Dim' . . . an experience which, despite her recalcitrant behaviour, had reduced Dayle to silent wonder. Mac had chosen a site with an uninterrupted view north over the sea, and as they had watched, the sun had gradually dipped low in the sky, leaving a pale, pearly light, in which the colours of the landscape were still eerily visible . . . orange lichen on rocks and the pink of the thrift. It had been utterly still, even the birds silent in the pre-dawn hush, which had lasted perhaps for an hour. Then there had been a subtle alteration in their surroundings, as the water became faintly luminous once more. Nature had quickened into life again, as birds began their dawn chorus and the gold of the new day spread across the sky, gilding clouds and sea alike.

Yes, there had been almost endless daylight for about four weeks, but that was nearly three months ago and she was aware that today's milder weather had been the year's last benison. Soon the northern winter would be upon them, with heavy rains and gales. Already the nights were sharp and cold, and she might well be out here tonight, with only the protection afforded by her jeans and thin sweater, amply warm enough that morning. Once more she berated her own foolhardiness.

She had often thought since what a good thing it was that she'd discovered the cave.

She came upon it accidentally in one last frenzied attempt at traversing the rock face. Caves . . . or the idea of them, for this was her first experience of one . . . had always held a fascination for Dayle; and now this one evoked recollections of stories devoured in childhood . . . of smugglers, hidden treasure, or . . . delving deeper into the past . . . the places where prehistoric man had made his home, dragging his chosen bride there by her hair. This cave was cold and dark and it smelt strongly of seaweed, but it was protection of a sort.

The cave was deeply incised into the cliff face, black, mysterious, almost spooky and uncannily silent, for it was so deep that no sound could be heard either of wind or sea. It seemed, much to Dayle's relief, that the waves did not reach this refuge, since the floor beneath her feet felt loose and dry.

She shivered. The air was chill, but at least she was safe from drowning. With the knowledge that no other course of action was open to her, she settled down to wait, and gradually fell into an uneasy slumber.

When she woke, she was chilled to the bone and the luminous dial of her watch showed six o'clock. Six o'clock! That meant she had been here all night. For it had been almost eight when she had discovered the cave. If Mac had returned last night he must have been aware for hours of her absence . . . had perhaps been searching for her? Or had he just shrugged his broad shoulders and gone to bed. Somehow she didn't think he was that callous, even though he might assert that she deserved the piteous condition in which she found herself.

Her cave now seemed a doubtful refuge. While she was hidden away here, Mac could not possibly discover her, and cut off from all sound, she would be unaware of his presence on the cliff top above. Hastily she made her way out into the early morning light.

It had rained overnight, was still raining slightly, a thin, unpleasant mizzle. In the distance, the sea and sky were a drab grey, while beneath her was turmoil . . . the ocean boiling and heaving, while long ranges of waves, almost obscured by their own spray, rushed in succession towards the rock face, the shock of their impact echoing among the crevices.

Suppose . . . suppose the sea had been like this last night when Mac returned? Suppose his boat . . . a frail craft in her eyes . . . had been overturned? He might have been drowned and she . . . she would be immured here for ever. How she wished she hadn't made that stupid remark about him drowning! She would be haunted all her life by the thought that she might have ill-wished him.

For more than an hour she sat huddled hopelessly on her rain and windswept perch, unwilling to return to the cave in case there were signs of rescue, yet terribly, mortally afraid that there would be none. Then, above the sound of the dashing waves, she heard something. Somewhere far, far above her head, a few pebbles had been disturbed, falling past her with a clatter.

She looked up. All she could see was Mac's face. He must be lying flat on the cliff edge to peer down at her. But oh, what a blessed sight! She felt her eyes fill with tears of relief, but whether for his safety or her own imminent rescue she could not be sure.

At first his words were blown away by the rising wind, but at last she caught their meaning.

'Have you found the cave?'

She could only nod. Useless to pit her own voice against the tumult of sound.

'Go back inside,' he articulated, 'and keep going . . . as far as you can.'

She was mystified, but she obeyed.

On the seaward side, the roof of the cave was about six foot high, enough to accommodate her, though a tall man like Mac would be forced to stoop; but farther in the roof became lower, as the floor climbed, and finally she was obliged to proceed on all fours. But despite fatigue and a feeling of malaise, her spirits began to soar. There must be another way out of here, an exit that Mac knew of.

The silence was still oppressive, the passage a tight fit, and just as she was beginning to feel decidedly claustrophobic and as though she could go no further, she saw a glimmer of light ahead, filtering into another, smaller cavern, its exit blocked by fallen rocks. But she could see the sky, could hear Mac's voice, and there was just sufficient space for her to scramble painfully through. She could understand why Mac had been unable to come to her; his broad frame would never have passed through the opening, or negotiated the tunnel like passageway through which she had crawled. Then she was out in the rain, buffeted by the boisterous wind . . . but best of all, Mac's arms were round her and she felt unutterably safe as he held her in an iron grip, his face against her hair, and she heard his heart beating its strong tattoo.

The feeling of security did not last for long. Almost roughly, he pushed her upright and she saw that his face was a rigid mask of anger, the green eyes almost black with the intensity of his fury.

'You pigheaded, foolhardy, suicidal little idiot!' he stormed. 'What on earth possessed you to pull a crazy trick like that?'

As he spoke, he was marching her over the rough, tussocky heather of the headland, apparently not caring that she stumbled every few steps, as reaction to her narrow escape set in.

'How dare you go off like that . . . especially after I specifically told you . . . thoughtless . . . irresponsible . . .'

His deep, angry tones were just a muffled accompaniment to her agony, as she let him half drag, half carry her along . . . frozen, almost insensible, and yet admitting miserably to herself that she deserved his censure.

It seemed as if they would never reach the cottage and she could not remember the point at which he must have lifted her in his arms to carry her . . . only aware some time later of a cessation of the elements, of being wrapped in a blanket and lying before a roaring fire. A fire? She turned her head. She was in the living room of the cottage and the stove was working, the crackling roar of driftwood and peat warming the room . . . warming her.

Then a cup of steaming hot liquid was being held to her lips, a hand supporting her head, and the lecturing voice continued.

'Going off and leaving the place unattended! I come back to find none of the chores done, the chickens waiting to be fed, the cow distressed because she badly needed milking . . .'

'Is that all that concerned you?' Dayle snapped, but it was a very feeble snap. She felt terribly ill. 'What about me? I'm well aware that I come low down on your list of priorities, but . . .'

'Yes, you do!'

'You . . . you callous, unfeeling brute!'

But he hadn't meant it, Dayle recalled, as she drove down to the local bank with Tony Ashworth, to lodge the days' takings in the night safety deposit box.

Mac had been worried out of his mind when he'd found her missing; but it had been a long time before she'd discovered just how much he cared for her safety . . . a very long time; because not only had she felt ill, she had *been* ill for quite some while.

Fortunately, her illness had only taken the form of a heavy feverish cold, otherwise the outcome of her adventure might have proved disastrous indeed, for the bad weather which had blown up had closed in the island for several weeks, making it impossible for anyone to visit, or indeed to leave. Goodness knows what would have happened if she'd needed a doctor.

Dayle had never known what it was to feel really ill. The usual childish ailments had afflicted her only lightly and she had always received the best of care; and to do him justice, Mac had looked after her as well as any trained nurse. When he had realised just how rotten she felt, his harangue had ceased. He had brought her bed downstairs, setting it up in the living room close to the fire, and there it had stayed for nearly two weeks.

Dayle had little recollection of the first of those weeks, only a confused memory of blinding headaches, sore throats, coughs and sneezes; of someone lifting her head to give her drinks, of hands that bathed her perspiration-drenched body in order to reduce her fever. It was not until afterwards that she realised that it had been Mac and only Mac who had performed these intimate tasks for her; that on his shopping trip to the neighbouring island, he had brought back, amongst other things, nightdresses for her to wear and that he had needed to change these for her, during her delirium.

By the end of the second week she was able to sit up and take note of her surroundings, but she was still as weak as a kitten, thought not too weak to notice and marvel at Mac's efficiency, his seeming tirelessness. Besides looking after her night and day, he had still coped with the daily chores and had contrived to make the living room a more comfortable place. His purchases had included readymade curtains, which now hung at the window, and colourful throw-over rugs disguised the faded condition of the settee.

With the stove now in operation, hot meals were more varied and appealing, and one afternoon, as she half sat, half reclined in the snug warmth of her bed, he demonstrated another of his talents . . . breadmaking.

'I bought the ingredients, intending to teach you to make it,' he told Dayle ruefully, as he set out flour, butter, salt and baking powder on the scrubbed wooden table, which he had carried through from the kitchen.

It was the first reference he had made to the day of his trip and not another word of reproach had passed his lips about her reckless escapade. When she thought of all that he had done for her since then . . . and the realisation of some of the tasks he must have performed brought the hot colour to her cheeks . . . Dayle felt bitterly ashamed of herself and with an absurd desire to gain his good opinion, to prove to him that she was not the thoughtless idiot he believed her to be.

'It's quite a simple recipe,' Mac continued 'and very handy when it's impossible to get fresh bread.'

She watched carefully as he measured out eight tablespoons-ful of plain flour, a teaspoonful of baking powder, and added butter and salt, mixing well. She was determined to learn, so that next time he was away from the cottage for any length of time she could surprise him.

'It's best to mix it with your hands, until you have a good, greasy dough,' said Mac, suiting action to the words, 'but you need cool hands, otherwise the butter melts and makes a mess.'

Strange, Dayle thought, to watch him performing a woman's task, and yet it didn't make him any the less manly, any more than it had made her less feminine to assist *him* at *his chores* . . . for she had long since recognised that fact that there was nothing demeaning in physical labour, that it could actually be reward-ing.

Nobody could ever fault Mac for lack of masculinity, whatever he did, with those raw good looks of his. He could be tough and ruthless; he was supremely self-confident, logical and efficient, yet he was not insensitive. Despite their relative positions, he had never been unkind to her. Oh, he had lashed her with his tongue a few times, especially in the early days, when she had resisted his attempts to teach her various skills, but he had never ill-treated her . . . and when he had been angry, it had always been justified, as on the occasion of her rescue. But he had never yet praised her. Absurdly, she had the longing to do something really well, something which would merit praise from him.

She watched his face, so intent upon his task, the well-shaped mouth drawn into a firm line of concentration; and her gaze strayed to the robust chestnut colour of his hair, waving crisply about his head. From there it was a natural progression to his shoulders . . . shoulders wide and strong enough to take the weight of responsibility, that made a woman feel she would be happy to rely upon him . . . and his hands, that now were involved in bringing the dough to just the right plasticity . . . they could be both strong and tender, and she found herself wondering how they would feel in a caress, in the intimate exploration of a woman's body.

With a start she recalled her wandering thoughts. She must still be a little light headed from her illness, to permit such ideas to cross her mind. She had better concentrate on the bread making.

Having arrived at the proper mix, Mac added water, and Dayle watched with some concern the resulting gooey mess. Surely that wasn't right? He looked up and observed her worried frown. He gave an amused laugh.

'Don't despair! This is where you keep mixing, no matter what. Sooner or later all this ooze disappears and you get a nice dough.'

Sure enough, that was the eventual outcome of his labours and he proceeded to break up the dough, rolling it into small balls. These balls of dough he placed in a large earthenware pot, which he stood over the glowing range, turning them from time to time, until after thirty minutes or so he showed her the rolls, which gave off an aroma as delicious as anything she had smelt issuing from a bakery. He offered her one.

'They're supposed to be eaten the same day,' he told her. 'That's the only snag. Bread made like this soon goes stale.'

As she ate the appetising result of his culinary efforts, Dayle pondered again on the enigma of this man. He was a strange mixture . . . of prejudices, arrogance, capability, but also of extraordinary kindness and gentleness. If he could be like this with someone who had constantly defied and annoyed him, caused him so much inconvenience, what would he be like with someone he loved? There she went again, she told herself crossly, but somehow it was impossible to halt her train of thought.

How ironic that she should find herself in the position where she did not want her captor to think badly of *her*. She wondered if, in other circumstances, they could have been friends. Suppose . . . suppose, because of her recent illness, she could play on his sympathies, could persuade him to return her to her father? Wouldn't that prove that he was not altogether bad? a fact she already suspected; and once back in her familiar surroundings, it might be possible for her to do something for him . . . or rather, persuade her father to help him. Surely Angus could find Mac a position in one of the many business enterprises in which he had a controlling interest? In time Mac might even rise to a seat on the board . . . then she need have no objection to marrying one of her father's co-directors . . . She suddenly realised where her thoughts had led her. She was actually considering *marrying Mac*! And to her horror, she also realised that she had been staring intently at him for several minutes and that he was aware of this and of her heightened colour, the fact that her eyes had widened wonderingly.

'Dayle?' His deep, quiet voice was questioning.

'I'm . . . I'm sorry, did you say something? I was miles away . . . th—thinking. . .'

To her alarm, he rose and came towards her.

'Very interesting thoughts, to judge from your expression. Care to share them?'

'Oh . . . oh . . . no. No, *you*, wouldn't find them a bit . . .'

'Sure about that?' He stood over the bed, looking down at her.

'Quite sure,' she said, more firmly than she felt, for her heart was performing the oddest gymnastics.

'Hmm!' He sounded disbelieving, but to her relief did not press her further.

She decided it would be prudent to introduce a safer topic of conversation.

'I . . . I've never thanked you for . . . for rescuing me . . . for looking after me,' she said hesitantly. He said nothing, apparently waiting and she continued. 'But I *do* thank you, very much. I . . . I could have died of exposure, or . . .'

'Yes, you could.' Mac's voice when he did speak was slightly husky. 'Don't ever give me a fright like that again.'

'*You* . . . you were . . .?'

'Of course I was,' he said explosively. 'How do you think I would have felt, having to break the news to your father that . . .' He stopped short.

Dayle looked at him incredulously. What would *he* have cared about her father's feelings? But he seemed to anticipate the question that hovered on her lips and skilfully he avoided the enquiry.

'Tomorrow,' he said, 'I think we'd better have you out of that bed. Time you got your sea legs back.'

'Sea legs?' She regarded him doubtfully. Did he mean they were going on a boat trip? Could . . . could he be going to take her over to the mainland? Would the plea she had planned prove unnecessary? Perhaps he had been concerned enough by her recent illness to want to return her to her father? After all, if she had died while she was in his hands, she supposed he could have been accused of manslaughter.

To her astonishment, a thought which once would have filled her with relief, with excited anticipation now affected her with a strange sensation that was almost . . . dread? Oh, she wanted to go home, to see her father . . . of course she did . . . but not to stay. Once she had assured him of her safety, seen for herself that *he* was safe, she . . . Oh no, it wasn't possible, but that was how she felt . . . She wanted to come back . . . here . . . to the island . . . *to be with Mac!* She couldn't bear the thought that she might never see him again. What on earth was the matter with her? Could she still be slightly feverish?

'Yes,' he said, before she could analyse these thoughts through to any conclusion. 'I want you on your feet and well enough to be left for a short while.'

'*Left?* You're going to . . . to leave me again?' This was not at all what she had expected and her voice was tremulous, accusing. How could he do it, after what had happened last time?

He crouched down, bringing his face disturbingly close to her and took her hand.

'Don't worry. I think you've learnt your lesson and I won't be gone so long this time. But I do need to make another trip before winter closes us in. Once that happens it will be three or four months before I can use the boat again.'

'You . . . you mean we have to stay here, all through the winter?'

A moment ago she had been reluctant to leave Haa Island. Now her emotions were veering in the opposite direction. It wasn't so much that she wanted to return to civilisation . . . not as desperately as she had once wanted it . . . though that would be all right with her if Mac were going too. But she did want to straighten out this matter of abduction. She wanted Mac to clear himself, both in her eyes and in her father's.

'Of course,' Mac was saying calmly, 'you've only seen the island in summer . . . at its best. How can you judge it on that alone?'

'Judge it . . . why should I want to judge it?' she said with an attempt at indifference, but she knew the answer before it came.

'You have to know the best and the worst, before you marry me.'

There it was again . . . that suggestion that she might marry him, and he was confusing her. If he really wanted to marry her . . . if, as he had implied, that was his true reason for kidnapping her, why hadn't he just got to know her in the normal way, and then proposed to her? Because, her other self replied, *you* wouldn't have had anything to do with him . . . not in those days. Despite all that talk about marrying a poor man, you were a snob. You'd have turned up your nose at him; and her father wouldn't have been in favour of such a match either, she reflected. If she ever got back home, she supposed he would recommence his efforts at matchmaking again. She wondered with a touch of curiosity if the Callum person was still hanging about, waiting for her to make a reappearance. Or had he got tired of waiting and found himself another heiress's father to suck up to?

Suppose . . . there was no harm in supposing, so she allowed herself to toy with the idea. Suppose she *did* agree to marry Mac . . . and the thought was oddly exciting . . . there would have to be certain conditions of course. She would want to be absolutely certain that he *had* arranged for her father's release. But there was something else she needed to know. What exactly did Mac want . . . expect . . . of her?

'If . . . if I *did* marry you, I . . . I suppose it would just be a marriage of convenience, wouldn't it? I mean, just so that you could get your hands on some money to . . . to carry out these ideas of yours?'

She waited breathlessly, not really sure what she was waiting for, yet knowing it was important.

Mac stared at her for so long that she thought he was never going to answer. Not that she needed to hear his words of confirmation. He had been so cool, so matter-of-fact about this proposition all along that she knew it was prompted by nothing more than the mercenary desire to possess her father's fortune some day. If there had been any other reason . . . if he had entertained any spark of actual feeling for her, she would have known. At last he replied, his tone curt.

'Naturally! What else did you expect?'

CHAPTER SEVEN

WHAT she had expected . . . hoped, rather . . . Dayle thought ruefully, as she relaxed in a hot scented bath, preparatory to going out for an evening with Jenny, was that Mac would declare himself to be in love with her . . . a love he had miraculously discovered during their weeks alone on the island. She wouldn't have minded him marrying her for her money . . . well, not so much . . . if he'd loved her as well; but he'd made no pretence of it . . . at least, not then. The pretence had come later, she thought bitterly, and she'd been fool enough to believe in it . . . because she'd *wanted* to believe it.

'Ready, Dayle?' Jenny was hammering on the bathroom door.

'Almost. Give me another minute or two.'

Ten minutes later she ran downstairs, to find Jenny waiting impatiently.

'Sorry!' she said contritely. 'I forgot the time.'

'Daydreaming again, I suppose. Dayle, how much longer are you going to go on living in the past? You keep saying you want to sever all ties with Mac, forget about him, and yet I know you never stop brooding about him. The trouble is you're on your own too much. Why don't you go out with Tony Ashworth occasionally? You know you've only got to crook your little finger for him to come running.'

'I know. But it wouldn't be fair,' Dayle said bluntly, 'when I don't feel anything for him. I'd only be making use of him.'

'But you might come to like him. What's wrong with him?'

For an instant, a smile lit Dayle's normally serious face.

'You sound just like my father, in the old days. But it's no good you matchmaking, Jenny. There's nothing at all wrong with Tony. I even like him . . . like him too much to play such a rotten trick on him, encourage him, when I'm not free.'

'You could get a divorce.'

Yes, she could get a divorce, Dayle thought drearily . . . and she supposed it would have to come to that some day, if she thought there was any way of achieving it, without her having to face Mac. Because she *had* married Mac in the end . . . even though, for a while, it seemed as if *he* had forgotten the idea . . . or changed his mind.

Once he was sure Dayle was fit to be left, Mac had made his trip to the next island, resisting all her pleas to be allowed to accompany him this time.

'I'll take you in the spring. If you decide to marry me, we'll need to . . .'

'In the spring?' Dayle could not prevent the astonished query.

'At the earliest,' he confirmed, then, ruefully, 'You're not ready to be my wife yet, are you?'

And what the hell did he mean by that? Dayle had plenty of time to brood upon his statement, during the four or five hours he was gone. Hadn't she done enough to prove that she was hardier than she looked? Hadn't she successfully performed every task he'd set her? She could even make bread now . . . his way . . . and she hadn't baulked when he'd killed off one of the older hens and shown her how to prepare it for the table. What more did he expect of her before he condescended? Hey, wait a minute, she told herself. Surely the condescension was on her side, not Mac's? What was she getting so indignant about? She couldn't be in *that* much of a rush to marry him . . . could she?

Dayle decided it was time she stopped these random musings and considered the position seriously, logically . . . endeavoured to interpret her exact feelings for Mac. Firstly, she wasn't afraid of him. Strangely, she never had been. She respected him for his self-sufficiency, his fairness . . . he was never unjust; and she was *almost* certain that he was not an habitual criminal. But did she *love* him . . . with *all* that that implied? Mental, spiritual and physical commitment?

She could not ignore the evidence of the throb of her pulses, on the occasions when he had touched her; even his nearness awoke strange urges in her, so she could not deny the effect of his masculinity on her senses, but that was not enough.

Then she remembered that agonising hour on the cliff face, when she had dwelt on the possibility that Mac's boat might have capsized, that he might have drowned . . . and instantly she felt again that agonised wrenching of both mind and body, the awful premonition of bereavement.

Awed by this revelation, she rose to her feet and wandered

restlessly about the ground floor of the cottage. Suddenly she
was in no doubt whatsoever . . . probably, instinctively, she had
known it all the time, but she had needed to come to terms with
the startling idea . . . to spell it out for herself. She *did* love Mac,
and . . . her hands went to cheeks suddenly flushed . . . she did
want to marry him, with every fibre of her being . . . she *wanted*
him. But . . . and this applied a damper to the sudden fires of
sensuality that threatened to possess her, so that she longed
ardently for his return . . . he didn't feel that way about her. He
had been only too ready to agree that any union between them
would be one of convenience.

It was as well that she had this period for reflection. Somehow
she couldn't think clearly when Mac was around. If he hadn't
gone off and left her today, if he hadn't made that statement that
she was not ready for marriage . . . made his own prosaic
intentions so clear . . . she might have been stampeded into
revealing her feelings: and she knew now that that was something she must never do.

If she agreed to marry Mac . . . and she was not sure now that
she should . . . it would mean a whole lifetime of keeping her
emotions in check, never letting him see how much she loved
him; and suppose, later on, he met someone else, someone he
could care for? It would mean hiding her jealousy then . . .
perhaps even being asked to release him from their agreement.
Was she prepared to take those risks? Perhaps it was a good
thing Mac did not seem to be in a hurry, that he was prepared to
wait until spring. But of course that only underlined his lack of
emotional involvement.

Though she was sure now of her love for him . . . it explained
so many reactions in herself that she had not understood at the
time . . . she needed longer to consider the wisdom of following
her instincts, of taking such an irrevocable step. If Mac had been
in love with her, he would not have been able to wait to . . . Well,
anyway, he would have insisted on an immediate decision.

She was almost uneasy when she heard the sounds of his
return, the door opening, his footsteps in the tiny hall, and she
swallowed nervously before she turned away from the stove to
greet him.

'H—hallo. Your meal is almost ready. Did . . . did you have a
good trip?'

He nodded, coming closer to investigate the contents of the
saucepan, and with her new knowledge of herself, Dayle had

difficulty in behaving naturally, forcing herself not to flinch away as his arm brushed hers. Such unnatural behaviour would instantly betray her self conscious reaction to him, and Mac was not stupid . . . far from it. It wouldn't take him long to put two and two together, to realise that she was far from indifferent to him; and in the circumstances that would be mortifying.

'I telephoned your father,' he said casually, as they sat over their meal.

Dayle dropped her fork and stunned by this intelligence, could only stare at him.

'Well, don't you want to know how he is?' Mac asked irritably. 'That was the first question he asked me . . . about *your* welfare.'

'I . . . I . . . of course. How is he? Where is he? Is he still . . .?'

'Your father is at home,' Mac said brusquely. 'He's in good health and . . .'

'Oh, I get the picture,' she interrupted him scornfully, 'and will remain so, as long as I continue to behave myself.' There was nothing like a reminder of Mac's treatment of her father to act as a restorative to common sense.

He shrugged.

'They're your words.'

She had waited then, waited for him to add that her good behaviour included agreeing to marry him . . . that was the logical progression, wasn't it? But he hadn't mentioned it, either then or at any time during the next four months . . . the months of winter.

Those four months had seemed the longest of her life, Dayle thought, as she sat beside Jenny in the little red Mini they had bought between them. They were on their way to a dance in the nearest town. Usually Dayle refused to accompany her friend to such functions. She did not want to dance, to be held in another man's arms. But tonight Jenny had pleaded that she had no escort, that she did not relish going alone, and since Jenny didn't have too much fun on her limited income, Dayle had not liked to refuse.

She had spent those four months constantly on edge, aware that her attraction to Mac was growing, so that she did not know which was the most unbearable, to be close to him in his indifference, or to be parted from him.

Every evening, in the warmly intimate atmosphere of their sitting room, she had been supremely conscious of his presence, afraid to brush accidentally against him, or to meet his gaze too squarely, in case she betrayed the intensity of her feelings; and always she had been waiting for him to bring up the subject of marriage . . . afraid that he would, disappointed when he didn't.

Once she had been well enough to resume her chores, she had been involved in a flurry of activity . . . of preparation for the winter months ahead. Throughout the summer, Mac had gathered in a store of peat . . . the soft, brown substances, remains of moss, heather and other plants, compressed and compacted . . . and built it into a stout, weatherproof stack. But there was still driftwood to be collected and stored in a corner of the byre. Twice a day they went down to the beach, taking rope with them to tie up large finds, filling sacks with smaller pieces. There were potatoes and other root vegetables to be dug up and stored.

It was a monotonous routine, but it had to be observed, and despite her almost constant mental preoccupation with her unrequited feelings for Mac, Dayle was aware that life must go on as usual. In a place like this, your heart might be breaking, she thought wryly, but your back ached too . . . you still had to eat and sleep, feed live stock . . . Not that her heart was actually broken, of course, but it was decidedly bruised . . . by the knowledge that her love for Mac was a useless, wasted emotion.

Autumn had suddenly changed to winter . . . so suddenly that it seemed to Dayle that only one day she had been watching gannets climb high in the blue sky, wheeling against the wind on barely moving wings, to plunge down into the sea, or, from the kitchen window, seeing goldcrests perched on thistleheads . . . and the next day the view outside was hidden by unceasing, pitiless rain, the sky seeming to hover over the cottage roof.

It was difficult now to determine where night began and ended, when the days too seemed to be spent in almost perpetual twilight. All day long the sun made no more than a low arc in the sky. Now Dayle saw the reason for their large stores of lamp oil and candles.

'There'll be nothing but rain and gales until spring,' Mac told her. 'We shall have to exercise strict economy, consider the use of every bit of peat, every drop of oil or the candles that we use . . . if our supplies are to hold out.'

First thing in the morning and last thing at night, her bedroom was uninvitingly cold, and she thought how different it would be if they were married, dreamt wistfully of a warm body against

hers, providing both heat and security . . . and something else
which she only dared to dream about in the privacy of her own
room, for fear that her expression should betray her.

Mac's boat had to be dragged up the cliff path and tied and
weighted down with large stones, for, as he explained, quite
heavy vessels could be lifted and tossed away in a high wind.

The winter seemed to go on interminably, chores performed to
a regular background of dismal sounds . . . the howling wind,
sudden swirls of fiercely blown rain, the vexed disturbance of the
sea. The windows clattered continually in their frames, and
Dayle was thankful that Mac had taken time during the lingering evenings of summer to make the roof weatherproof.

Going out to the byre was a major undertaking; one had to
dress as carefully as if for a ten-mile hike, in waterproofs and
wellington boots, for the ground was sodden with the perpetual
rain. Going to the spring was unpleasant too, the wind lashing
water from carefully carried pails.

Yet there were peaceful moments too, evenings when the rain
ceased briefly and the wind dropped. They took advantage of
such rare occasions to relax, to go out for a breath of air, to stand
on the cliffs watching the moon rise out of the sea and listening to
the little sounds which broke the stillness . . . the startlingly
human sound of a sheep's cough . . . the little unidentified
rustlings in the grass. Dayle never ceased to marvel that any
creature could survive these conditions.

At times like these she felt closer to Mac, her perceptions
heightened, and once, when he threw a casual arm about her
shoulders, she felt herself tingle with pleasure . . . a sensation
followed rapidly by the sharp pang of desire which she must
disguise.

How had *he* endured those long weeks, without revealing anything of his body's cravings? For he *had* desired her . . . though it
had not been until after their marriage that he had admitted the
tight rein he had been forced to place upon himself . . . desired,
not loved.

Looking back, Dayle saw that there had been just one occasion when that control had almost slipped . . . one tiny clue to the
fact that he was not physically indifferent to her, but at the time
she had not recognised it for what it was.

It had been one evening, when Mac had retired early. He felt,
he said, as though he had a cold coming and planned to dose

himself up and have a good night's sleep.

Dayle was reluctant to go upstairs; her bedroom would be cold after the almost luxurious warmth of the living room; they kept the fire in all night so that there was warmth to come down to next day. The first one up each morning stirred the fire, cleared the ashes and added fresh peats to the glowing embers.

She decided that Mac's withdrawal was a good opportunity for her to have a bath. Usually they arranged it so that the non-bather remained in the kitchen until given the all clear. But tonight she had the whole of the ground floor to herself.

They had carried up several pailsful of water that afternoon and there would be enough to fill the tin bath and yet leave sufficient for breakfast time. The water heated up surprisingly swiftly, by using several large saucepans standing closely together on the top of the range.

Dayle undressed and filled the bath. It was heavenly to be able to sit here and soak, with no fear of an impatient voice asking if she had finished. If she had an instant's nostalgia for a large, full-size bath, full of scented crystals, she banished it. That was an unattainable luxury. This was here and now and she would make the most of it.

Drowsy with the warmth of the water and the radiant heat of the fire, she did not hear the creak of the stairs, nor the opening door, but Mac's startled exclamation did rouse her and she turned to see him in the doorway, his dressing gown pulled about him, his bare legs indicating that he wore nothing beneath it . . . in spite of the fact that he felt the onset of a cold, she thought, in the instant before her eyes travelled upwards to meet his.

His eyes were devouring her, glittering emeralds in the lamplight, while a nerve in his temple twitched uncontrollably. He took an impulsive step towards her, then stopped. She could not speak, could only stare at him, as though invisible bonds held them eye to eye. He parted his lips as though he were about to say something, but only a strange croaking sound issued from his mouth before he wheeled round, slamming the door behind him.

Dayle sat there, completely immobile, hearing him go into the kitchen, heard his returning footsteps pause outside the door, then go slowly up the stairs. It was several moments before she regained her wits and reached for the towel, drying herself in a frenzied haste now to have her nightclothes on and her bedroom door fast shut between her and Mac.

That was another thing which had puzzled her at the time.

After his second trip for supplies, he had produced a bolt and fastened it to the inside of her bedroom door. She had never used it until that night, when some strange instinct prompted her to do so; and she had never been quite sure afterwards whether she was glad or sorry that she had. For, after about half an hour, when she was almost on the verge of sleep, she had heard him try her door and heard what sounded like a muffled curse as it resisted him.

Yes, that had been the only time Mac had nearly betrayed himself . . . and she could not help wondering what would have happened if her door had not been locked.

The dance floor was already crowded, when Dayle and Jenny checked in their coats, and as usual there seemed to be a large preponderance of women over men; not that this worried Dayle. She didn't care if nobody asked her to dance, but she knew it mattered to Jenny. Apart from the fact that her friend loved to dance, she was a romantic soul, hoping every week that she would meet the man of her dreams. So Dayle was pleased rather than otherwise, when she saw Tony Ashworth amongst the men lining the edge of the floor. At least *he* would partner Jenny.

She was dismayed, therefore, when he headed in their direction, but instead of approaching Jenny, invited *her* to dance. Dayle's hesitation was only fractional. Despite her reluctance, she knew it would be bad manners to refuse, especially as she had no good reason for doing so. She smiled apologetically at Jenny as she rose and allowed Tony to take her in his arms.

'I've never seen *you* here before, Dayle.' His tone expressed pleasure that she was there tonight.

'No . . . I don't usually go dancing, but . . .'

'Why, Dayle?' he asked curiously. 'You're a good dancer, you're young . . . and *very* attractive.' His hold tightened a little, 'and yet ever since you came here, you've lived in that cottage like a recluse. You're not *shy* are you?'

'No,' she said quietly. 'I'm not shy, Tony. I just prefer a quiet life.'

'But don't you want to meet people . . . have boyfriends . . . get married?' He sounded puzzled.

Dayle was deliberating over whether or not she should tell him the truth, when the music ended and in the noisy hubbub of conversation that ensued, the opportunity was lost. Tony returned her to her seat, but did not seem to be in a hurry to leave;

and finally it was Jenny who asked if he would like to join them.
He accepted with alacrity.

For the rest of the evening, he was meticulous in dividing his
attentions between them, but it was obvious to both girls that it
was Dayle who held his interest . . . a fact that was particularly
noticeable whilst they were on the floor, when his embrace was
far more intimate than during his dances with Jenny. Predictably, during the last waltz, he asked if he might see Dayle home;
but she was adamant.

'I came with Jenny. I can't leave her to drive home alone.'

But she was aware that he took his dismissal reluctantly and
he referred rather pettishly to her behaviour next morning, when
she went to the office to collect her float for the till. There were
several people coming and going on similar errands and Dayle
did not want to be drawn into a discussion which might prove
acrimonious.

'I'm sorry, Tony,' she murmured, 'but I can't stop to talk
now. I . . .'

'O.K.' His voice was equally restrained, 'but we *have* to talk
some time. Come out with me tonight and . . .'

'No. No . . . I can't. I . . .'

'*Dayle!* For God's sake! What *is* it with *you?*' He did raise his
voice this time and she was aware of curious glances, as she
hurried away.

She was on the main reception desk today, issuing tickets
which covered admission to house, farm and garden and she was
glad that it was a job requiring all her concentration . . .
especially when the rates for large parties had to be calculated.
Even so, at the back of her mind all the time was the hope that
Tony was not going to prove an embarrassment. She did not
really want to tell anyone else about her life before she came to
the Country Park, but if he grew too persistent, she would be
forced to tell him she was married. Consequently, when she was
relieved for her coffee break, all the thoughts she had repressed
whilst on duty, came at once to the fore.

The dance last night had reminded her unbearably of another
dance . . . that which had been held to celebrate their wedding
. . . an old Shetland custom, Mac had told her.

It had been early March before he brought up the subject of
marriage again, by which time Dayle felt she had experienced all
the rigours of weather the island had to offer. For, in the New
Year, there had been frost and snow; and Dayle woke one

morning to a white silent world, which seemed to have awed even wind and sea into immobility. A few flakes were still falling and the snow lay everywhere, planing into smooth contours the island's harsh irregularities. In places the drifts were extremely thick, beginning to be soft on top, and it took their combined efforts to clear a way to the byre, where they found a hard-packed mass blocking the door. They had to dig their way in before Shula could be milked.

Inside, Dayle was surprised to see a fine layer of snow covering everything, except Shula herself and the floor immediately beneath her, where the warmth of the beast's body had melted the drifting flakes. The overnight gale which had brought the snow had driven it through almost imperceptible crevices in walls and roof.

Their chores done, they had taken a walk, just for the sheer pleasure of it, to admire the immensity of the scene, which had a beauty of its own, unsurpassed even by the almost forgotten attributes of summer. The sea was a smooth, glassy swell, reflecting back the shapes of the snow-laden clouds, its former fury reduced to a faint hissing and sighing, as it rose and fell upon the whitened, rocky shore and a weak sun cast a strange light over hill, rock and promontory.

There were several consecutive days of calm, when seagulls alighted near the cottage, scavenging for food, accompanied by their smaller brethren, starlings and sparrows, which had some-how survived the winter.

February was an uncertain month, fine one day, yet another day bringing fresh falls of snow and cruel frosts, the cold bone-biting. But then, as the year moved into March, there were signs that the long winter was almost over, as a warmer air stream blew across the island.

'We'll soon be able to use the boat,' Mac said one morning, as he stared out over the sea.

'We?' she ventured.

'Yes. We'll be going over to the other island for a few weeks.' He paused, then added, with a challenging ring to his voice, 'We have to establish a three-week residence period, before we can be married in the church there.'

It had been so long since he'd mentioned this subject that his words came as a distinct shock and Dayle found herself totally unable to reply.

'I take it you've no objection, since you've nothing to say?' His tone was satirical and it angered her, because of his assumption of her complacency . . . that she had no say in the matter.

'That's where you're wrong,' she retorted. 'You take a lot for granted, don't you? I've never said that I'll marry you.'

'Oh, but I think you will.'

For the first time in weeks he was looking at her as if she were a woman and not just the faceless companion of his endeavours on the island; and it unnerved her, even though she knew it was only the revelation of his male urges . . . that any woman would have looked good to him after these long months of an unnatural existence.

'I've given you no reason to think that.'

'Perhaps not,' he admitted, 'but I do know that you'd go a long way to ensure your father's safety.'

She tensed. Oh no, he wasn't starting that again!

'I thought you said my father was home again. You told me . . . If *you* lied . . .'

'Calm down! I didn't lie. Your father is at home . . . always has been. You can telephone him when we go over, find out for yourself that I'm telling the truth.'

So her father wasn't a prisoner . . . unless it was in his own home. Mac must be very sure of himself . . . he must have some hold over Angus Abercrombie. Otherwise her father would have been moving heaven and earth to discover her whereabouts. She turned and began to walk back towards the cottage.

'And what do you think my father's going to say when I tell him you want to marry me?' She threw the words back over her shoulder.

Mac's grin was infuriating, as he drew alongside.

'I don't think he'll object too much.'

'You mean he *daren't*,' she cried furiously. 'What sort of life do you think we'd have, based on the knowledge that you forced me into marriage?'

'I forced you to come here,' he returned, 'and it hasn't been too bad an existence.'

'For whom? You may be used to this kind of life, but I wasn't . . . and anyway, I didn't mean our way of life, I meant the way we . . . we feel about each other.'

Mac held open the door for her to precede him and followed her into the living room before he answered.

'How *do* we feel about each other?' He sounded mildly interested.

Dayle concentrated on pulling off anorak, woolly gloves and cap; and when she did not answer him, he moved closer, throwing his own outdoor wear on to the settee. He put his hands on her upper arms, turning her so that she had to face him.

'I asked you a question. I said how do we . . .?'

'I heard!' she snapped.

'But you're not certain of the answer?' His voice was lightly teasing, that irritatingly independent eyebrow mocking her.

'I'm quite certain of *my* feelings at least.' She tried to shrug his hands away, but he retained his grip of her, angering her into an enlargement of her statement. 'I despise you.'

'I see.' His reply was noncommittal, but she sensed a tension in him. 'And how do you suppose I feel about you?'

This was more difficult and she swallowed convulsively, unsure of her ground.

'Come along,' he persisted. 'I credited you with more imagination than that.'

Damn him! Why didn't he let go of her, give her a chance to steady herself? It was the first time in weeks that he'd come near her . . . touched her, and this renewal of his attention was unnerving, awakening all the tensions and sensations she had believed to be finally crushed. But she must answer him. The sooner she did so, the sooner she would be freed . . . an urgent necessity, before the tremulousness she felt revealed itself in an actual shaking of her limbs.

'I would imagine that you feel nothing for me,' she forced herself to say. 'It's my money you covet, isn't it?'

Her words had the desired effect, for he flung her away from him with such force that she felt her legs strike against the settee and she sank down on to it, relieved of the necessity of standing.

'So you've learnt nothing in these past months,' he said, 'of companionship, friendship . . . mutual respect . . .'

That wasn't true, she thought. She *had* learnt to value Mac's companionship, and she did respect him . . . up to a point, the point where he became an adventurer, after her fortune. Friendship? She shook her head slightly at the word. She didn't understand herself. In spite of everything, she wanted more from Mac than friendship.

He misunderstood the slight negative movement of her head.

'So we have nothing to base a marriage on?'

'Even . . . even if we did have those things,' she said slowly, 'is that going to satisfy you . . . us . . . for ever? Whenever I've

thought about marriage, I expected more than just . . .' Her
voice trailed away at the expression in his eyes.

'*You* were the one who stipulated a marriage of convenience,'
he reminded her, lowering his great length to sit beside her.

She edged away.

'Yes, I know, and I . . .'

'Of course, if you've changed your mind . . . I wouldn't like
you to get the idea that I'm totally impervious to your charms,'
he told her; and somehow the space between them was reduced
. . . to nothing . . . his powerful figure unnerving in its closeness.

'I . . . I . . . wasn't . . .'

'And I think I should demonstrate that fact at least once . . .'

'Oh, no . . . no . . .'

But it was too late for protest, as his arms confined her and his
mouth covered hers ruthlessly, passionately. Even through the
thickness of her sweater, Dayle could feel the hard bone and
muscle of him, crushing her breasts, the uneven rise and fall of
his ribcage. He pressed her down against the cushions of the
settee, the imprisoning weight of his body arousing an aching
longing within her. While his lips held her captive, his hands
were seeking out the ribbed welt of her sweater, moving up
beneath it to explore silky flesh that curved and pulsated at his
touch. She could not help or hide her response to him; just the
warmth of him against her was intoxicating, and each touch of
his hands sent quivers through her . . . down, down, until she
was tinglingly, vibrantly alive with sensations that cried out to
be appeased. But just as she felt she could hold her feelings in
check no longer, that she *must* cry out her love and need of him,
Mac drew a deep breath and pushed her away, rising to his feet
as he did so.

She stared up at him, bereft, bemused, her mouth trembling,
and saw that his own normal composure was severely shaken.
She had to fight an urge stronger than any she had ever known,
so that she did not leap up and throw herself into his arms, beg
him to carry his lovemaking to a satisfactory conclusion; for she
felt hollow, unfulfilled, every nerve awakened to erotic vulner-
ability.

'Mac?' She whispered his name questioningly, wondering
why he was staring at her, his expression angry rather than
tender.

Why should he be angry with her? She had not repulsed him.
Perhaps she should have done . . . perhaps he now despised her

or the easy victory he had won . . . but his assault upon her had
been so unexpected, so swift the storm he had roused within her
that there had been no time to ponder upon the rights and
wrongs of resistance.

'Does *that* reassure you?' he asked at last, his voice coming a
little raggedly.

'R—reassure me?'

'About the benefits conferred by marriage.'

She continued to meet his gaze, but her blue eyes were bleak.
So that was what he thought it was all about . . . just a blind
gratification of the senses . . . and that was what he thought she
wanted. Were all men like this, relating emotions only with sex?
Had men no romance in their souls? Hadn't he heard of *love*, its
mental expression rather than the physical? Dayle knew she
could never be satisfied with the mere expression of sensual
pleasure, to be an object of his passing lust. It would be a
profanation of all her girlish dreams. Better the marriage of
convenience he had suggested, based purely on his need for her
money . . . as far as she was concerned they need not even live
together once the ceremony had been performed. But how to tell
him that, how to make it sound convincing, when her throat was
still thickened with the desire he had aroused?

Mac made it easy for her.

'Well, what's it to be? Business . . . or pleasure?'

She found her voice, managing to imbue her words with a note
of distaste.

'Business, thank you. If that's what you call pleasure!'

CHAPTER EIGHT

SHE was uncomfortably certain that Tony would not be content to accept her rejection of his friendship, her refusal to discuss it, and she was reluctant to re-enter his office at the close of business for the day. She had hoped that there would be others present, so that she could deposit her takings and make her escape, but an annoying discrepancy between recorded figures and cash had taken her some time to rationalise and Tony was only waiting for her monies before closing his books.

'Don't go, Dayle,' he said, as he entered her takings into a large ledger. 'I want to talk to you.'

She couldn't very well refuse. Technically, Tony was her superior; he had employed her and he could fire her; and she did not want to lose this job. Apart from the fact that she enjoyed her work, Jenny was here, and she felt that her friend was her only link with her former life, the only one to whom she could speak of personal matters . . . a therapy she needed from time to time. Of course she would not always have Jenny; her friend was bound to get married some time, but until then . . .

She shifted from foot to foot as she waited. Somehow she must placate Tony, and it seemed there was only one way to avoid giving offence; she must tell him the truth . . . or just a sufficient amount. So, when he closed his account book and pushed it away from him with an air of finality, she drew a deep breath and took the plunge.

'Tony, I . . . I know what you want to talk about, and I'm sorry if you thought me rude and . . . and unsociable last night. But there's something you ought to know, then perhaps you'll understand why I . . .'

'I can make a good guess.' He stood up and came round the desk towards her. 'It's pretty obvious that you've been hurt at some time. There's a look in your eyes occasionally . . . But you'll have to put it behind you eventually, Dayle. Not all men are rotters.'

'Mac wasn't a rotter. He . . .'

116

She stopped. Wasn't he? Wasn't that the very label she'd pinned on him, when she'd left him?

'Well, whatever he was, he must have given you a rough time; and to do that, he couldn't have been in love with you. Nobody who loved you could ever hurt you, Dayle.' Tony's voice was suddenly husky.

No, Dayle agreed mentally. Mac hadn't loved her. Oh, he'd pretended to, when he'd seen that nothing else would get him what he wanted. But it was her father's money he'd been in love with.

'Why not try to forget him, hmm? Give someone else a chance to make you happy again? I . . . I'd like to try, to be the one who . . .'

She recoiled.

'Tony, please! It's no good. You . . .'

'I always thought you liked me, Dayle?' His fresh, open countenance bore a hurt expression, and Dayle rallied her wits. She must get this over, as cleanly and as painlessly as possible, before more misunderstandings arose.

'I *do* like you, Tony, which is why I'm going to tell you the truth. I'm not free. I'm married . . . separated from my husband.'

There was silence, while he stared at her disbelievingly. Then his gaze shifted to her left hand.

'You don't wear a ring,' he said accusingly, 'and there's no mark where it . . .'

'I only wore my ring for a few hours,' she told him quietly.

'You realised you'd made a mistake?' Tony said eagerly. 'But you could get a divorce, you . . .'

Dayle shook her head. Oh, she'd made a mistake, she thought wearily, but not about her feelings for Mac. Her mistake had been in believing that he shared those feelings . . . worst of all . . . she shivered with the humiliation that always overtook her, when she remembered that she had let him see just how much she loved him.

Despite her scornful repudiation of Mac's lovemaking, her assertion that she would prefer their marriage to be kept on a business footing, he had not been deterred from his plans. Why should he have been, with all that he had to gain? Oh, he had shown his displeasure that she should find his kisses distasteful . . . the knowledge must have dented his male ego a little . . . but she supposed that having gone this far, having abducted her, trained her to his ways, held the threat of her father's safety over her head, he was unlikely to admit defeat and tamely let her go; and so, a couple of days later, they had gone over to the next island.

'Who'll look after the animals?' she asked him, when he confirmed that they were leaving. This alone was evidence of how much she had changed. She would never have realised the need for such arrangements a few months ago.

'There's a fellow I know, a keen ornithologist, who's willing to spend a few weeks here and keep an eye on things.'

Dayle's eyes narrowed. Mac hadn't been off Haa Island since the autumn. He must have made these plans then. Oh, he was infuriating, so cocksure, so certain of her compliance.

'And suppose I don't agree to all this?' The words were an extension of her thoughts. 'Suppose I refuse to marry you? You can't force me up the aisle. We're not living in the bad old days . . . no minister of religion will marry an unwilling bride.'

'But you're going to appear willing, aren't you? Or do I have to remind you about your father?'

She was silent, biting her full lower lip. Mac had the one unanswerable argument. Selfish she might have been, accepting as her right all that her father had given her, but she *did* love Angus, and these last few months had taught her a lot . . . altered her values. Besides, did she really want to refuse? Wasn't there a sneaking hope within her that once they were married, Mac might come to appreciate her for herself and not just for the money she could bring him? After all, they had co-existed fairly amicably up to now, even if her participation had been under duress at the start. She sighed. She would just have to wait and see; but pride compelled her to make reluctant admission of his ascendancy over her.

'All right! So you have a hold over me . . . a pretty unfair one; because you know no decent girl would do anything to endanger a member of her own family. You can marry money, Mac, but it can't make you a gentleman!'

She had the satisfaction of seeing him flush, but whether with anger or mortification she couldn't be sure.

There was very little conversation between them, other than that of necessity, as they made preparations for their journey; and Dayle made no attempt to break the silence as he rowed, but sat idly in the stern, watching their progress; and it did not occur

o her until afterwards that she had experienced absolutely no
eelings of nausea.

Steering his way with oars alone, Mac threaded a route
hrough a maze of rocks, some clear of the water, others awash or
ubmerged, and she realised just how much a prisoner she had
peen. She would never have dared to attempt the crossing alone;
or the complexity of the tides around the island, the problems of
etting a course and then landing would have made it impossible
or her, even if she had been able to handle a boat.

Once they were clear of Haa, the breeze freshened and steep
ittle waves slapped against their bows, but still she felt no
liscomfort.

It was a long hard pull to the next island and occasionally Mac
ad to rest on his oars. Dayle could not help admiring his
letermination. She wondered if he always achieved what he set
ut to do and if so, why he had not made more of a success of his
ife. With his grit and tenacity, he could have been at the top
f some profession or other. She just could not equate his un-
crupulous behaviour with the other character traits he dis-
played.

The island was in sight and Dayle could just discern the
utlines of buildings . . . houses, smaller crofts on the hillside
nd a church. Was that the church where? . . . she swallowed
nervously.

'Landing at Slu-voe with a full boat can be a tricky business,'
Mac observed. It was the first time Dayle had heard the name of
heir neighbouring island. 'A lot depends on timing . . . the tide
. . If you arrive too early or too late, there isn't enough water to
nake it safely.'

Dayle saw what he meant, as they neared the landing place,
he approach narrowed by rocks and large stones. She had the
choice of jumping into the icy water and wading, or being
carried, but she was not permitted to make that decision for
herself.

Mac waded ashore and made the boat fast, and then, while
he was still dithering, swept her up into his arms and made a
second journey, holding her clear of the tumbling surf. It was the
irst time he had touched her since he had made love to her; yet,
lespite their waterproof clothing, the unromantic, prosaic manner in which he carried her, she was instantly aware of him, his
ace close to hers, so that she could feel the warm breath of his
xertions upon her cheek, smell the indefinable, pleasant mascu-

line odour of him. All too soon, it seemed to her, she was unceremoniously dumped and he began to unload the boat . . . swiftly, for it was a tricky business since every so often a swell carried the vessel to the furthest extremes of its painter.

With a curt jerk of his head, indicating that she should carry her share of their luggage, Mac led the way up the track towards the small island settlement. As they drew closer, she could see that it was even smaller than she'd thought . . . the cluster of houses, one general store and, standing at a little distance, the church, its graveyard a meadow by the sea.

But they did not stop at the village itself; instead, Mac strode on up the hillside towards one of the crofts.

'Hannah and Fergus Blain are old friends of mine. They'll put us up until the wedding,' he said.

'They . . . they know about me, then?' she enquired nervously. He nodded.

Just what did they know? Dayle wondered. Surely, if these were respectable people, Mac hadn't told them how she came to be here, that theirs was to be no ordinary marriage?

He certainly seemed at home, she thought, as, with only a cursory knock, he entered the building. The layout was very similar to the one they had left on Haa, except that it was all on one level, with four ground floor rooms instead of two up and two down.'

'Hannah? Fergus? It's me . . . Mac!'

A voice from the door to their right answered his greeting and bade him enter.

Dayle caught her breath as she followed him, for, apart from the fact that there was more comfort here, they might have been back in their own croft. *Their own croft?* Yes, she realised, she had come to think of its as theirs. But there was no time for introspection, for already Mac was introducing her to the heavily built, rosy-cheeked woman, who sat in a comfortable armchair to the side of the stove.

'Hannah, this is Dayle,' He hesitated briefly, then added: 'My fiancée.'

'Please, don't get up,' Dayle begged, as the elderly woman laid aside her knitting, which looked very complicated to her inexperienced eye.

Her hand was taken in a firm, warm grasp.

'No trouble, lass. You'll be wanting a bite to eat, no doubt. Mac, take your lassie through to the bedroom and unpack your bits, while I call Fergus. He's away out to the byre these two, three minutes.'

The room to which Mac showed her was as neat and as comfortable as the living room. No camp bed, Dayle was pleased to see. But was *that* the bed? Wooden doors, about a foot off the floor, their surface ornamented with cut-out shapes of hearts and diamonds, stood open to disclose an area about six and a half feet long and four feet wide, made up with plump pillows and quilts.

'We'll just dump the bags for now. If I know Hannah that meal will be on the table by the time you've run a comb through your hair.'

Not that that was an easy task these days, Dayle thought ruefully. The wind and salty spray had whipped her hair, almost shoulder length now, into multifarious tangles.

'Here, let me.' Mac had been watching her ineffectual struggles and now he took the comb from her, his strong hands, despite their size, deft and efficient.

The feel of him close to her, his hands firm yet gentle in her hair was unbearably seductive and she longed to lean back, to feel the hard, muscular length of him supporting her. But she fought down the impulse and took her comb from him with a brief word of thanks.

Fergus, Hannah's husband, proved to be a short man, pensive, slow-moving, bony-faced, his hair a token close-cropped fuzz around his head, so that not only the flesh of his face but that of his scalp too was brown and weatherbeaten. He was a man of few words, but Dayle felt that his keen blue eyes were summing her up.

'You'll be away down to the kirk this afternoon, then, to see the Minister?' Hannah suggested as they ate.

Mac nodded.

'And then you'll be over to the mainland, for a dress and such like?'

'No.'

'No?' Hannah looked shocked. 'But you'll not be expecting the lassie to be wed in yon jeans and sweater?'

Mac looked uncomfortable, but he was adamant.

'We won't be going over. We're staying here until after the wedding.'

Hannah said no more, but her gaze upon Dayle was reflective and the girl felt herself colouring. Whatever must the old couple think of her . . . a bride who had made no preparation for her wedding? They must think it a hasty, ill-planned affair. Perhaps they even thought . . . her colour deepened . . . that she *had* to get married. It was as well for the sake of her composure that Fergus swiftly dispelled that idea.

'Talk sense, woman,' he said. 'Where would the lass have kept fine dresses, living on that wee island these months? No need that I can see to go gallivanting off to the mainland.' Head on one side, he looked at his wife with a grin and Dayle could see traces of the good-looking, wheedling suitor he must once have been. 'Happen you could contrive something, Hannah?'

'Aye, mebbe,' she said drily. Then, to Mac: 'Away with you now, before the Minister settles himself down to his afternoon nap.'

Although Dayle had deliberately held very little conversation with Mac since they left the island, she could not forbear to question him about Hannah and her husband . . . such likeable people, she thought.

'Have you known them long?' she asked.

'Since I was a lad. Hannah is an old friend of my mother's. I used to come here for a week or two every summer, and I've kept up my visits ever since.'

'How . . . how much do they know . . . about us . . . me?'

'Enough!'

Which told her precisely nothing, Dayle thought crossly, as they walked up the path to the manse, adjacent to the tiny church.

There was nothing to distinguish the Minister's house from those of his flock, and *he* didn't look a bit like a parson in his old workaday trousers and shaggy Shetland pullover. He settled them down in twin, comfortable, but baggy armchairs in his study and took his pen, and for the first time Dayle learnt the full name of her husband-to-be.

'Dayle Abercrombie?' The minister rolled her name on his tongue. 'A Scots name?' He raised shaggy brows.

'Like mine—but some of her ancestors were Shetlanders too,' Mac put in.

Dayle would have wondered why he seemed so anxious to stress that fact if she had not read of the history of mistrust between Shetlanders and the Scots; that, centuries ago, the Shetlands, together with Orkney and Fair Isle, had belonged to Norway, who had traded them to James the First of Scotland as part of a marriage dowry. But the islanders had never considered themselves to be Scots.

'And Alastair MacAlastair,' the minister continued, his pen moving slowly, painstakingly across the page.

Dayle stifled a giggle. What a mouthful! Her amusement did not go unnoticed.

'Now you know why my friends call me Mac,' he observed.

'So, lassie,' the old man had set down his pen and was looking at her, 'your ancestors were Shetlanders?'

'On my grandmother's side,' she confirmed.

'And what would their name have been, d'you know?'

'My grandmother's maiden name was Magnusson.'

'Ah, the old Scandinavian heritage.' He looked pleased. 'I'll show you something later that may interest you. But now . . . first things first . . . you want to marry young Mac here, hey.'

There was an awful silence. Dayle hadn't expected the question, though she suspected it was only routine . . . part of the old man's standard procedure; and she couldn't think how to answer him. It would be awful to tell a lie to a minister of religion. Then relief flooded her. She wouldn't be telling a lie; because, whatever impression she had striven to give Mac, however foolish of her it might be, she *did* want to marry him. She opened her mouth to speak, but the Minister forestalled her.

'Of course you do, lassie, or you'd not be here. It must seem a foolish question, but we have to do these things properly.'

He bumbled on through the arrangements . . . the date, the time, the number of guests expected. He did not seem surprised that it would be a quiet affair. Of course he could not be expected to know that, had she been getting married in London, the daughter of Angus Abercrombie would have merited St. George's, Hanover Square and a congregation of hundreds.

'And will your father be giving you away?' He broke in on her thoughts.

'I . . .' She looked helplessly at Mac.

'No,' he said smoothly. 'Unfortunately, Mr Abercrombie can't get away just now. But my fiancée *would* like to telephone her father. I was wondering . . .?'

'Of course, of course!' The Minister indicated the instrument on his desk. 'You're very welcome. The telephone in the village eats up the coins before you've scarcely said a word, and besides, there's no privacy with all the coming and going and Hamish listening to every word that's said.'

There wasn't any privacy here either, Dayle thought resentfully as Mac dialled the number for her. He obviously didn't intend her to speak to her father out of his hearing. The old Minister did suggest that he left the room, but Mac politely detained him.

'I'm sure Dayle has nothing to say that we can't hear,' he said, and for an instant, to Dayle's jaundiced eye, his normally attractive smile resembled the crocodile's evil leer at its victim.

Her father's voice sounded very far away and a pang of homesickness smote her, so that she could hardly speak.

'Dayle? Are you . . . are you still with . . . er . . . Mac? That is his name, I believe.'

'Yes, Daddy.' She didn't know how to go on. How did you tell your father that you were going to marry a man who had held him hostage for your good behaviour?

'Is everything all right, child? You sound . . .'

'Yes, yes, I'm O.K. But what about you, Daddy? You're . . . you're not having any . . . any difficulties?' That was as close as she dared come to asking him if he were under restraint of any kind.

In his turn, Angus Abercrombie hesitated and when he spoke again Dayle sensed that he was choosing his words with care. Was someone listening at the other end?

'You're still . . . er . . . co-operating, I take it?'

'Yes, Daddy, but I . . .'

'You and this . . . Mac . . . still getting on well?'

'I suppose you could put it like that. Daddy . . .' she took the plunge, 'You know you said . . .' She shot a swift glance at the Minister, in conversation with Mac, and lowered her voice. 'You said "do *anything*"?'

'What's that, Dayle? Speak up , love, I can't hear.'

She repeated herself.

'Yes, I remember saying that.'

'Mac has asked me to marry him.' She held her breath and waited for the roar of outrage that she felt must come. But her father's reply was mild.

'And have you agreed to do so?' He sounded wary.

She supposed she had; she hadn't much choice really. But she must make one last try at gauging Angus's reactions.

'Is . . . is it all right with you, Daddy?'

Dimly, in the background, she heard the old Minister mutter something about such filial respect being rare, and saw again the mocking glint in Mac's smile.

'You're willing to do this thing? If so, it's all right by me, my dear.' Her father's voice was flat, almost expressionless. If only she could speak with him face to face! But it seemed she did have to go through with this, or surely he would have found some way of telling her so, even if he were not alone.

'Yes, Daddy,' she said wearily. 'Yes, I'm . . . I'm willing.' She knew she must end this conversation quickly, or she might burst into tears. It was so long since she had seen her father, her home, her friends. Would she be allowed to visit Angus, once she was married to Mac? 'I . . . I have to go, Daddy. G—goodbye. T—take care.'

Careful. Her voice had almost cracked on the last words. The Minister would think it odd, if she broke down.

'Goodbye, Dayle. You take care too. Bless you.'

He couldn't have said 'bless you *both*', she thought, as she replaced the receiver. It had been the poor line which had distorted his last words. She turned to face Mac, hastily blinking back the tears as she did so.

He had crossed the room to her side and unexpectedly his arm went round her shoulders; and for a moment she could have sworn that he had sensed her distress, that there was sympathy in the brilliant green eyes. But of course it was all a show of affection for the Minister's benefit, she reminded herself.

'So that's settled, then.' The Minister rubbed his hands together with satisfaction. 'And now, my dear,' to Dayle, 'that little surprise I promised you.'

She would rather have left the Manse now and gone for a brisk walk on her own, in an endeavour to fight down the misery that had engulfed her ever since she had heard her father's voice. But the old man was urging them into the passageway and out through a side door into the churchyard.

'I won't show you the church just now. You'll have plenty of time on Sunday and over the next three weeks. But there is something I want you to look at . . . just down here.'

He led the way across the graveyard, an isolated corner where the village tapered out towards the sea. It was shaggy with marram grass, and the lurching grave stones were moss-grown. Near the ancient boundary wall, patterned with ochre and orange lichen, was a group of stones older than the rest, flat slabs sunk into the turf, which was beginning to close over them; their inscriptions were encrusted and difficult to read, but the Minister indicated them with conscious pride.

'There you are! I know every stone in the churchyard. I recognised the name immediately. There are your Magnussons, my dear . . . maybe the very ancestors you spoke of.'

Dayle gave him one incredulous look, before dropping to her haunches to inspect the stones. He was right. The dozen or so slabs bore dates stretching back to the eighteenth century. These could well be her grandmother's people, her grandmother's home . . . before she had gone away to Edinburgh and married a Scotsman. Had her family disapproved of this linking with the traditional enemy? She fell into a mood of brooding reminiscence. Here, as on Haa Island, she could sense the past, was aware of her roots, even though the details were unknown to her. What would these ancestors think of her own marriage? Would they have disapproved of its manner, or would they be glad that a descendant, if only on the distaff side, was coming home to be married in the land of her forebears, whether by fair means or foul?

She turned to Mac, her blue eyes shining, not with tears now, but with excitement.

'I must come back and copy out these inscriptions for my father. He always meant to trace his ancestors, but . . .' She turned to the Minister. 'Is there any way I can check whether these were my grandmother's family? Would there be any record here of her?'

He nodded vigorously.

'Surely, surely, child. If she was born here, her name would be registered at her christening.'

'Her first name was Kirstane,' Dayle said excitedly. 'Could we look now, please?'

He shook his head regretfully.

'I shall have to delve deep into the old registers. They're stored in a steel-lined chest . . . the damp, you know. But I will look out the appropriate year for you, as soon as may be, and you shall have a copy . . . as my wedding gift to you, hey?'

'Are there . . . are there any Magnussons living here now?'

Dayle had a sudden crazy notion that, if there were, she would invite them all to her wedding. At least she would have relatives there then, however distant. But the old man was shaking his head again.

'Alas, no all gone. I suspect your grandmother may have been the last of her line. But we shall see, we shall see.

And with that, for the moment, Dayle had to be content.

She and Mac had gone back to the churchyard a week later and at her dictation, he had written out the history of her grandmother's family . . . for Kirstane's name *was* in the register, her parents' only child. Dayle had intended to give the information to her father, but she still had it, tucked away at the back of a drawer, because it was her only memento of Slu-Voe, the place where, for a few brief weeks, she had been happy, had believed that she had found permanent happiness. It was her only tangible memory of Mac too, and the sight of his handwriting, strong and decisive, was one she only permitted herself occasionally, for it was too evocative of the man himself. The only other memory of him was something she dared not dwell upon, for it induced in her a very real, physical anguish.

'You could divorce him!' Tony's voice, the repetition of his statement, brought her back to the present. 'After all, if your marriage was never consummated . . .'

'Oh, but it was,' Dayle said softly and the old hunger swept her . . . hunger that would never again be appeased.

'You poor kid!' Tony was all compassion now, his arm around her shoulders, but it was evident that this emotion had only increased his own desire for her. 'Good job you didn't get pregnant . . . bad enough having to support yourself.'

Was it a good thing? she wondered dully. If, in the first few dreadful weeks after she'd run away from Mac, she had discovered she was carrying his child, wouldn't it have been an excuse to swallow her pride and go back to him, make the best of what she had, ignoring all the lies and deceit. She had often tried to imagine Mac's child, herself carrying it . . . giving birth to a son or a daughter with Mac's green eyes and burnished hair. She never doubted for a moment that any child of his would inherit his characteristics . . . the very dominance of him precluded any other possibility; and mightn't the fact that she had been bearing his child have changed everything? Mightn't his assumed affection have developed into the real thing?

'How on earth did a girl like you get involved with a rotter like that?'

Dayle gave a short, bitter laugh. It was such a fantastic story.

Looking back, she could scarcely credit the details herself; such a
tangle of deviousness and deception that it had taken her some
time to unravel the whole of it.

'It's a long story, Tony.'

'I've got plenty of time,' he said eagerly. 'Come up to my flat
for coffee and . . .'

'No.' She shook her head. She had hoped that the knowledge
that she was married would deter Tony from his pursuit of her,
but it didn't seem to have had that effect. If anything, it
appeared to have whetted his appetite still further. Hadn't
someone told her that some men preferred experienced women?
She sought for a legitimate excuse to hurry away.

'I . . . I want to get our evening meal over early, so I can go
through my notes on the history of the house. I always like to do
that, when it's my turn to do the tour, just in cast I forget
anything.'

'You know it backwards,' he said, but he released her, albeit
reluctantly, and with a sigh of relief Dayle left the office and
hurried back to the cottage.

'You look a bit fraught.' Jenny eyed her friend consideringly
as they sat down to eat. 'Tony?' she said perceptively.

'Yes. I decided to tell him about Mac. Just that I was married.
I thought it might . . .'

'Put him off?' Jenny shook her head. 'Not Tony. He's really
got a thing about you. He . . .' she hesitated, 'he'd make a good
husband, Dayle. I've often thought so.' She sounded a little
wistful and Dayle looked sharply at her. Did Jenny like Tony
that much? Had *she* been blind?

'As far as I'm concerned,' she said bluntly, 'he's all yours.
After Mac, no one could . . .'

After Mac no one could satisfy the hungry urges of her body.

She had been aware for a long time of her physical response to
Mac and in those three weeks before the wedding, it seemed he
had suddenly decided to foster that feeling, had deliberately
played upon her susceptibility to him; and he hadn't wasted
much time. His campaign had begun that very first night they'd
spent at Hannah and Fergus's croft.

They'd strolled back, Dayle full of her discovery in the
churchyard, and Mac had let her chatter on . . . perhaps, she
reflected afterwards, so that it wouldn't occur to her to ask a
certain question . . . a question that hadn't occurred to her until

much later that evening, as they sat, all four of them, in
Hannah's cosy living room; and before she had had time to
formulate the sudden problem which had sprung to mind,
Hannah's words answered it for her.

The elderly woman looked up at the clock that ticked comfortably on the overmantel.

'I don't know about you folks, but I'm for my bed. Fergus has
to be up early to tend to the stock.' She smiled at Dayle. 'I expect
you'll be knowing all about that?' Then, to Mac: 'I'm sorry
we've such limited facilities for guests ... just the one spare
room, but happen you'll not object to bundling?'

With that she moved towards the door, and Fergus, the habit
of years apparent in his obediently prompt movement, followed
her.

'You'll put the lamps out, Mac?' said Hannah, and then the
door closed behind husband and wife.

Dayle was taut with a nameless fear, a wild surmise, her
stomach muscles contracting with a sharp sensation she did not
wholly recognise.

'What ... what did she mean, only one bedroom ... and
what's ...?'

'You'll see.' Mac rose and extinguished the lamps. In the
resulting darkness, he took Dayle's hand to guide her around the
furniture. The contact of his palm against hers, the sudden
doubts in her mind, combined to make her shiver.

'Cold?' He pulled her against his side, as they traversed the
short distance to the bedroom. 'You'll soon be warm.' His tone
was meaningful.

The lamps in the room were already lit ... Hannah, no doubt
... and Dayle turned to Mac, expecting, hoping that he would
bid her goodnight and go, but instead he was closing the door
behind him.

'Wh—what are you doing?'

'I should have thought that was obvious. Or do you prefer the
bedroom door open at night?' He assumed a concerned frown.
'It's less private like that.'

She faced him squarely, her blue eyes challenging, daring him
to give her the answer she dreaded to hear.

'Where are *you* sleeping?'

He looked immoderately surprised ... the hypocrite! she
thought.

'Why, here, of course.'

'Oh no, you're not!'

'Give me one good reason why I shouldn't.'

Dayle floundered. She knew it wasn't right, but how to express her conviction in coherent words . . .

'I . . . Hannah couldn't have meant . . .'

'Oh, but she did.' And then, at her startled expression, 'My dear girl, what do you imagine they think we've been doing for the last six or seven months?'

'You mean you . . .?'

'They think I've finally decided to make an honest woman of you.'

Dayle's cheeks flamed with anger . . . and embarrassment. Well he still wasn't sleeping in this room with her. There was only one bed for one thing and . . . Oh! He didn't intend . . . he couldn't . . . He most definitely was *not* going to anticipate the wedding ceremony, if that was what he thought. In any case, she'd made it quite clear before they left Haa Island that there wasn't going to be anything . . . anything like that, even when they *were* married.

'I'm not sleeping with you,' she said flatly.

Mac's gaze encompassed both her and the box bed.

'Oh, I think there's room for both of us.'

'I didn't mean that,' she snapped. Oh, horror of horrors, he was actually beginning to undress, or at least he was removing his shoes and socks and now the thick sweater, revealing the hair-roughened flesh of the broad chest that she had seen only once before. Dayle watched him in hypnotised fascination, but to her relief he went no further.

'You do the same and get in.' He jerked his head towards the bed.

'No! I. . .'

'Or do I have to undress you myself?'

'Don't you dare!'

This couldn't be happening, she thought wildly. In all the months she had been on Haa Island, she had never seen this side of Mac. Never by word or deed had he ever given any sign, shown any inclination to . . . He surely wouldn't force her to . . .?

'Don't look so scared,' He was actually smiling! 'You heard what Hannah said about "bundling". I'm not suggesting anything more daring than that.'

'Bundling? I don't understand. What does it . . .?'

'Bundling is an old custom. Our northern ancestors were not

such prudish folk and in large families, living in small houses, it was often difficult for courting couples to have time alone together. So they devised bundling . . . the lovers were permitted to spend the night together in the girl's bed, lying fully dressed in each other's arms.'

'I bet it didn't stop there,' Dayle said sceptically, then blushed again, as she realised the implication of her words.

Mac seemed amused.

'Perhaps not. It must have been hard, if they were really in love. But we don't have that problem, do we? So it shouldn't present any difficulties. Now,' he added pleasantly, 'let's get into bed, shall we?'

She contemplated defiance, but she knew it would be useless. Mac would just sweep her up in those strong arms of his and deposit her in the cupboard-like structure, and worse still, he might carry out his threat to undress her. With trembling fingers she removed her shoes and the thick woollen socks, then hesitated over her sweater.

'Come on,' he said impatiently, 'you can't sleep in that. You won't feel the benefit of it in the daytime if you do.'

Slowly she removed it, unaware that the reluctant deliberation was more provocative than any swift gesture on her part, then folded her arms across her breast, in an effort to reinforce the scant protection of a fragile, lacy bra. She looked again at the bed. Once in there, she would be trapped by Mac's large frame.

'You . . . you get in first,' she told him.

'So that you can slip out the moment I'm asleep? Not likely! In with you.'

And then he did the thing she had feared, lifting her easily, one hand beneath her knees, the other warm on the bare flesh of her waist, and walked with her to the embrasure. He turned back the quilt and set her down. The available space for them seemed horribly narrow. There was no possibility that their bodies would not touch. Then he had doused the lamps and she lay rigidly, as she felt him slide in beside her, his thigh hard and intimate against hers.

There was a breathless silence and Dayle was sure he must be able to hear the erratic thumping of her heart; while, try to still them as she might, she was sure her limbs were trembling convulsively.

'Which side do you normally sleep on?' he asked.

'I . . . I don't know.' And her brain was so bemused by her

senses, that, for the life of her, she couldn't remember.

'Well, we can't lie flat on our backs all night,' he said reasonably, 'there just isn't room. So either you lie on your left side and I'll snuggle up to your back, or we'll settle for the other way round.'

Dayle tried to concentrate on the problem, and as she did so, the obvious dangers of being held against him made her opt swiftly for the alternative.

'You turn *your* back,' she said decisively, and thought she heard him chuckle, knew that he would have had no difficulty in following her reasoning.

For comfort, it was necessary for Dayle to draw up her knees and fit herself into the curve of Mac's body . . . like two spoons, she thought a trifle hysterically. She felt horribly self conscious .ʾ. . she had never shared a bed before, with anyone . . . and she was very aware of him, of his warmth, of the male scent of him.

'Relax!' he told her.

It was impossible to relax, with her face only a hairsbreadth from the smooth, silky skin of his back, so that a move on the part of either of them might bring her face against his flesh and at the thought, she imagined her lips feathering the line of his backbone. It was a dangerous thought, for it set in train a host of other imaginings. Suppose, in the night, he turned towards her. Suppose he was tempted to . . . Suppose, half asleep, she were unable to hide her reaction, unable to resist whatever he . . .

She remained in a state of tension for a long time, then, finally lulled into a sense of security by his deep, regular breathing, she too began to drift on the edge of sleep.

CHAPTER NINE

'BARNET Hall was the home of the Earls of Barnet, until the last Earl died in 1979. The Museums Department of the County Council run it now as a public amenity.'

Dayle recited a few facts about the history of the house, before starting her first guided tour of the day. Generally, a tour of the entire building took about an hour, depending on the mobility of her hearers and, quite often, upon their age and nationality. She had known a group of bored schoolchildren cover the course in half an hour with no questions asked, whereas a small group of absorbed adults could easily run over their allotted time.

'The oldest part of the hall dates back to 1540 and was added to by subsequent generations . . .'

This party was totally comprised of adults, some of them quite elderly, and with her quick ear Dayle had picked out at least one American accent. She would be called upon to rack her brain for every little detail, and she was glad she had insisted upon doing her homework the previous evening.

'Below stairs, we have the kitchens, very much modernised, of course, since the family lived here until 1975; and next to the kitchen, the former servants' quarters have been given over to an exhibition of agricultural implements and tools, many of which were used on the Home Farm, which you will be visiting later.'

Dutifully the party followed her upstairs and down, and Dayle began to notice one little woman in particular dogging her heels, her alert, inquisitive eyes on Dayle's face as she spoke, rather than upon the exhibits. It was disconcerting, especially as Dayle began to feel that the woman's face was somehow familiar. Had she met her before somewhere? Was she supposed to know her? But surely none of the local people would come on a guided tour. Someone from the past, then? She had always had a dread of someone discovering her whereabouts. Jenny, of course, was sworn to secrecy, even in her communications with her own family.

'In the dining room, note the imposing fireplace, made from

wood grown on the estate and carved by local craftsmen.'

She must keep her full attention on what she was saying. She had almost fluffed the answer to a question then. Determinedly, she ignored the small woman. She was probably just a type and her imagination was playing tricks. Mentally, she dwelt in the past so much that if she had known this woman before, she must surely have remembered.

'The library contains many fine examples of sixteenth-century furniture and a large Chippendale mirror, unique of its kind, which reflects the whole length of the room . . .' She talked steadily on and was soon immersed once more in the history which fascinated her.

'The Wedgwood bedroom has a sliding panel by the fireplace, which leads to a concealed passageway, used in the past, it is believed, for discreet assignations, during large house parties . . .'

What had gone on in that magnificent fourposter bed? Had its many occupants over the years achieved the same happiness, the same fulfilment that she and Mac had contrived to find in a sanctuary barely a quarter of this bed's size?

Dayle had no idea how long her hard-won sleep had lasted, before the dream began . . . she had imagined it to be a dream at first . . . when the throbbing ache in the pit of her stomach started making her shift restlessly, until finally her eyes fluttered open, to find that this was no dream, that at some time Mac had turned to face her, so close that their lips were only a breath apart and his hand was caressing the fullness of one breast, and it was this insidious seduction that had stirred her body into wakeful awareness. Impossible to pretend that she was still asleep, for already, instinctively she had curved against him, and he needed no further invitation to capture her in a hard, sensuous embrace.

His nearness electrified her; the skilful pressures of his muscular body were driving her insane with desire. She strained against him, seeking a more intimate contact, and his hand left her breast to run down over the curve of her hips.

Heart drumming against heart, they lay, mouths locked in a seemingly endless kiss. The passion Mac moved in her was a live, painful thing, and she knew an obsessive desire to have that pain assuaged. He too seemed to be engulfed in this hot sweet tide; the sensuality in him, which until now she had only imagined, freed from restraint. She tried in every way her body seemed instinctively to know, to convey to him her longing to be possessed, and an access of warm rapture flooded her as he began to whisper words of love.

He *loved* her! She could scarcely believe it. Sooner than she had anticipated, her dreams were coming true. He might have set out to gain her for more mercenary motives, but miraculously, something deeper, more precious had intervened, and if he had not forced their present sleeping arrangements upon her, she might not have known it for another three weeks, until after they were married . . . for it was only their proximity, she felt sure, their proximity and the enveloping intimacy of darkness which had freed his tongue.

She drew a great breath of ecstasy, as she dreamed of the coming three weeks, the bliss there would be in talking of their love, seeing the day of its consummation draw gradually closer. Her stomach knotted at the thought. How were those weeks ever to be endured; for it never occurred to her for a moment that they would not wait. To Dayle, making love in the fullest possible sense was something you did after marriage; but lying here in Mac's arms, she realised just how difficult such restraint could be . . . and if they were to sleep together like this every night, what unbearable torture it would inflict upon both of them; and she knew Mac shared the leaping, throbbing ache that racked her . . . she could feel his body's betrayal of his need.

'Dayle?' He whispered her name, but it was a question, a plea, and she knew what he demanded of her and her senses clamoured to grant that request. But a tiny corner of her brain urged her to postpone that ultimate intimacy until its proper time.

'No, Mac . . . please!' Desperately she fought the insidious ecstasy, the fulfilment of which was only a touch, a whispered assent away. She pushed aside his hands that sought privileges she was not yet ready to bestow.

'Why, Dayle? You love me . . . you must do. Your body can't lie, even though your lips might deny it. This won't be just a business arrangement, will it?'

'No, no, of course not . . . and . . . and I *do* love you, Mac.' It was sweet to say it at last, to savour the fact aloud on her lips and the fervour in the murmured words left no possibility of doubt. 'But oh, darling, can you understand? I want us to wait, until . . . until . . .'

'Three weeks!' It was a groan of sound. 'Dayle, does it matter to you so much? When we're to be married anyway?'

'Yes,' she whispered faintly. 'Yes, it does. Mac, please, help me. It would be so easy to give in to you now, but I should regret it, I know I should.'

And now, Dayle thought, her body throbbing unbearably with the memory of that night, she sometimes regretted that she had not submitted. For then she would at least have known three weeks of fulfilment, instead of the one night, whose memories must last her for the remainder of her days.

She found she was staring at the embroidered hangings of the fourposter, all other thought and action suspended, encapsulated in that one moment of time, while the members of her party either stared at her transfixed face in bewilderment, or, more tactfully, roamed about the apartment, inspecting its fittings for themselves. Perhaps they thought she was about to have some kind of fit.

'I'm sorry!' She tried to laugh off the moment, to banish the exquisite torture which had seized her innermost being. 'I fell into a brown study, didn't I? The past always has that effect on me.'

There was relieved laughter, as they accepted her words at face value, believing that she referred to the distant, historic past and not a mere six months ago . . . her own past.

She finished the rest of the tour, rigidly banning her mind from further wandering, and was gratified by the enthusiastic thanks she received, as they returned to the entrance hall. Only the small, elderly woman lingered after the rest of the group had dispersed. She came straight to the point.

'I do know you, don't I? You are Dayle Abercrombie? Angus's daughter?'

Dayle flinched. She had convinced herself that the woman was a stranger and this confrontation, following upon her almost unbearable attack of physical nostalgia was almost too much for her. There was no point in denying it, but still she hesitated.

'I'm sorry. Should I know you?'

'Perhaps not. I only came to your house once, about two years ago . . . to a dinner party. My son, Reggie . . .'

'Oh, of course!'

Now Dayle remembered. Reggie Parnell had been one of the hopefuls, one of the first young men presented for her consideration, after her father had decided it was incumbent upon him to find her a husband, made in the mould he considered suitable for his only daughter's spouse.

'I heard that you'd moved away, but the last time I saw your father, he was curiously reticent on the subject.'

Yes, he would be, Dayle thought, particularly since . . . but the woman was still talking.

'I must tell him I've seen you and how well you're . . .'

'No!' Dayle exclaimed, then, more quietly: 'Sorry! I didn't mean to sound rude, but I'd rather you didn't mention it.' She thought rapidly. 'My . . . my father and I had a . . . a difference of opinion and he doesn't know where I am. I . . .'

The little woman tut-tutted.

'Such a shame, my dear. Don't you think you should make it up? Such a pity when children drift away from their parents.'

'I'm afraid that's not possible,' Dayle told her. 'Please, I must ask you not to mention that you've seen me.'

'Very well,' the woman said stiffly, 'but I do think . . .' She walked away, still shaking her head, and Dayle wondered uneasily if she would keep her promise. It would be disastrous as far as she was concerned, if Angus discovered her whereabouts; for there was a very real danger that, through him, Mac would trace her.

To Dayle's suprise, Mac had respected her request that their love should not be consummated until they were married; though there were moments during the days that followed when they were both tested to the limits of their endurance to curb the urgency that filled their veins whenever they were alone together.

There had been no more bundling. That would have put too much of a strain upon both of them; and yet they both shrank from Hannah and Fergus knowing of problems which concerned them alone. So instead Mac had used a sleeping bag on the bedroom floor, rolling it up and concealing it each morning. But even so, the fact that they were in the same room was a stringent test of their resolution, and Mac's goodnight kisses were sometimes prolonged and threatening to get out of hand. The box bed, which had once seemed far too small to Dayle, was now large and achingly empty to its one occupant. But somehow the three weeks passed, and though the nights seemed long, spent in an agony of wakeful, physical yearning, the days were easier to endure.

After Haa Island, Slu-Voe seemed large, with more scope for exploration and with people to meet. The islanders as a whole seemed delighted to meet Mac's future wife . . . the more so upon hearing of her ancestry . . . and despite the fact that he was a Scot obviously held him in so much affection and respect that the last of Dayle's doubts of his character began, imperceptibly, to fade; for surely these kind, honest folks could not be deceived in him.

The islanders worked hard at various crafts, the results of which were sent by the weekly mailboat to the mainland for sale. There was handloom weaving on a small scale, basket weaving and even a small bakery, which supplied the islanders' own needs.

Hannah was an industry in her own right, for she was one of the few women on the island who retained the old skill of Shetland knitting. One week she would be turning out a gaily patterned fishermen's jersey, the next a fine, delicate lacy shawl with rows of as many as four hundred and eighty stitches, of intricate design, the needles flashing in the lamplight, as her fingers flew and the garment or shawl literally grew before the eyes. Even when she was working with half a dozen colours, Dayle never saw her wools in a tangle.

'There was a time,' Hannah told Dayle, 'when I was just a slip of a girl, when only the needles of our women kept us from starvation. The fishing failed, d'you see, and we sat and knitted the old patterns and sent them to the mainland in exchange for food.'

Most of the food nowadays seemed to be home-produced, the fishermen's efforts supplementing the farmers' contributions of vegetables, flesh and fowl.

Mac showed Dayle how to fish from the rocks, a handy method for stormy weather conditions, when to put out in a boat would be a foolhardy undertaking. A bamboo pole was used, the ten-foot line ending in three hooks, each dressed with a wisp of feather. This was a skill at which she became surprisingly adept. The whole rod had to be plunged into the deep water, reaching as near to the bottom as possible, drawing the rod through the water in a scything action. More often than not this exercise swiftly had three fish dancing on the hooks, which she than had to learn to gut.

Besides the various cottage industries, there was the village shop, which was more than just a convenient provider of necessities. During the course of the day most of the population of Slu-Voe would pass through its doors, to stand and exchange news in its atmosphere, redolent of the smells of paraffin, blended with bacon, apples, cheese and coffee . . . so that shopping became more of a social occasion.

And there was the dress to alter.

Hannah had not forgotten or discounted Fergus's suggestion, and one evening, shortly after Dayle's arrival at the croft, Hannah beckoned to her, indicating that she should follow her into the main bedroom. There, laid out on the large, old-fashioned bed, was a full-length creamy dress that had once been white, fashioned in the exquisite lacy Shetland design which Hannah's fingers still produced so fluently.

'This was the dress I wore for my own wedding,' she told Dayle. 'I made it myself. I was a mite plumper than you, but with a stitch here and there I think we may contrive.'

'Oh, but I couldn't!' Dayle protested. '*Your* wedding dress . . . and you've kept it all these years! I'd be terrified of something happening to it.'

Hannah laughed, a fat, jolly chuckle.

'Bless you, child, I'll never wear it again. What use would I have for such a dress at my time of life, even if I could squeeze myself into it . . . which I can't; and don't talk to me of family heirlooms either. Fergus and I never had chick nor child, so there's no one to pass it on to. Mac's the nearest I've ever had to a son and I'd like fine for his bride to wear this.'

Dayle could only accept, gracefully and thankfully. For she did want to look nice for her wedding day, and Mac had not yielded an iota about a shopping trip to the mainland.

'A poor man's wife has to learn to contrive,' he told Dayle.

She didn't know what he expected, she thought indignantly; true, there were bolts of material on the shelves of the all-purpose store, but she had no skill with a needle, or the faintest idea how to use a pattern. She supposed, after they were married, she could learn. But would there be any need? They would have her money then, for as things were, she supposed her father could not do other than make a generous marriage settlement.

And so several hours were happily spent in fitting the dress and adjusting it to Dayle's measurements. She was a lot taller than Hannah and the dress that had been full-length on the older woman hung to mid-calf on Dayle, but the effect was still charming.

For some time, Dayle had sensed that Hannah was intensely curious about her relationship with Mac, yet was too good-mannered to pry; but while they were working on the dress, it was inevitable that their conversation should centre on the topic uppermost in their thoughts.

'Not long now, then?' said Hannah one afternoon, as they fitted the dress and she made slight, deft alterations to waist and bodice. 'Nervous?'

'Yes . . . yes, I suppose I am,' Dayle admitted.

She wondered, not for the first time, just how much this kind, motherly woman knew of her circumstances, but dared not ask, in case she inadvertently let slip some intelligence Mac had not confided to his friends.

'You'll be all right with Mac,' Hannah observed, her tone comforting in intent. 'He's a good lad. He's been a good son to his mother and almost like a son to me.'

Hannah couldn't know what Mac had been up to these last few months, Dayle decided. She was so obviously honest and straightforward herself, she could never approve of abduction and enforced marriage. Dayle felt a little sad to think how disillusioned Mac's friends would be if they ever discovered the whole truth, which was another reason for discretion on her part; she must not let slip anything that would hurt them. And yet, if she had not been in love with Mac, she knew that she must surely have begged Hannah's help in escaping such a liaison. Which was why Mac had not brought her to Slu-Voe before, she thought darkly. He was too intelligent not to realise the effect upon her of having a female confidante. No, he'd waited until he was sure of her complete enslavement to him. He must have been certain of her, even before she had admitted her love, and though she was almost completely happy, the thought of his arrogant confidence still rankled a little. She could have been completely happy if it were not for the unprincipled way he had contrived their present situation.

Hannah was eyeing her consideringly; evidently there was still something the older woman wished to say, and for a blunt, forthright woman, her words were chosen with surprisingly hesitant care.

'Mac is a good man. Don't let anyone or anything convince you otherwise, lass. There may have been times when you've wondered . . . still will be occasions, perhaps.'

'Hannah, are you trying to tell me something?'

The older woman shook her head, then, the denial apparently conflicting with her natural honesty, nodded.

'Aye, mebbe I am . . . in my own way. Trying to, without betraying a confidence. It's difficult, but just remember this . . . things are not always what they seem, and if you love a man, you have to trust him.'

That was the trouble. Did she entirely trust Mac? How could she, when this whole affair had its beginnings clouded by doubts of his intentions . . . his motives. But she did love him, heaven help her, even so. Surely your heart couldn't lead you astray? She sighed. If only Hannah would be more explicit; but whatever Mac had told her, it was certain that she put loyalty to him first. Had Mac told her the whole truth? She shifted restlessly.

'Hold still, lass, or I'll be pinning this to your skin! Just be patient. I'm certain Mac will tell you all you want to know, in his own good time. Now, it's of no use you looking at me with those great blue eyes of yours, because I've said all I'm going to say. But just you remember it, if ever you're uncertain or things look black. Off with you now . . . and look forward to your wedding day!'

Dayle had hoped for a fine day for her wedding . . . the old superstition 'happy the bride the sun shines on' imbued with a new significance, now that it applied to her, and she was distressed to wake early to the unmistakable sound of wild weather, a wind that beat around the little croft, rumbling in the chimney, while sheets of rain drove slantingly across the island.

'Oh, Mac!' she wailed. 'It's raining!'

He rolled out of his sleeping bag and crossed the room, to peer through the curtains at the gloomy prospect outside.

'You're right!' was his laconic comment.

'But Mac, it will ruin everything! I did so want everything to be perfect for my wedding day.'

He came towards her then, leaning over to plant a kiss upon the tip of her short, straight nose.

'Everything *will* be perfect.' But his tone carried an extra depth of meaning that had nothing to do with the ceremony, the dress or the weather and Dayle felt herself blushing, glad that the predawn darkness still filled the room.

'Oh well,' she said, with an attempt at lightness, 'perhaps by the time we get up, it will have cleared a little. We may as well get a few more hours' sleep.'

'As an insurance against getting very little tonight?' Mac enquired teasingly, his words serving to deepen her confusion.

She had expected that, having surveyed the weather, he would return to his sleeping bag, but he seemed disposed to linger, seated on the edge of the box bed, leaning over her. There was an electric awareness in the atmosphere and she could read his mind as clearly as if he had spoken his thoughts aloud.

'Mac,' she began falteringly, but the sound was cut off at source as his lips pressed against her throat and burnt a trail downwards to where her breasts rose and fell to the sudden agitated intakes of breath, the warmth of his mouth, the knowledge of his desire an insidious bewitchment of her senses.

His hand followed where his lips had led, a disruptively sensual caress, as he cupped each breast in turn, his mouth possessing itself of the rosy tips in a manner which sent ecstatic shudders through her, so that her body craved to yield to him. He was inciting feelings in her, whetting appetites whose existence she had never suspected and especially not within herself.

She was totally unprepared for the leaping passion that seemed to fire the whole of her being, and it was a temptation to utterly abandon herself to this infinite pleasure, to allow it to mount until they both reached a point where there would be no turning back.

But that must not happen . . . only a few hours more and it would be their undeniable right to satisfy these urges, as deeply and fully, as often as they desired. She trembled at the thought and the sensuous shudder seemed to increase his fervour.

'Dayle . . . after all, we are to be married today. Does it matter so much, if we . . .?'

'Yes! It does . . . it does to *me* . . . please!'

Of course if he'd really loved her, it would have mattered to him too, Dayle thought, as she waited for her next party of tourists. If Mac had loved her with even half the total commitment she had begun to believe in, then the postponement of their consummation of love would have seemed as right, as sacred to him as it did to her. But he had flung away from her with no lingering words of affection, no reassurance that he understood, had gone out . . . as she learnt afterwards . . . into the elemental conflict that was as violent as his own, as he fought back the physical need that had threatened to swamp them both.

The next tour of the house was without incident and Dayle took her lunch break, glad to find that Jenny's free time had coincided with hers. She was anxious to discuss that morning's development, to share her anxiety that Reggie Parnell's mother might betray her whereabouts.

Jenny, however, was philosophical, practical.

'You can't expect to vanish for ever, you know, Dayle,' she said reasonably. 'Not unless you leave the country. Sooner or later you're going to have to face up to your life. O.K., so you needed a breathing space . . . needed to get away from Mac and from your father. When you first came here, I agree that you were in no fit state to think rationally about the way you'd been cheated. But you *have* had time now, and if you're going to make anything of the rest of your life, you'll have to come to a decision soon.'

'What decision?' Dayle said drearily. 'All I want to do is to forget.'

'But you won't, will you? Do you think I don't know how you spend all your waking hours . . . the hours when you're not working . . .? and I'm not sure sometimes that your personal life doesn't intrude even when you are working.'

Dayle flushed guiltily, recalling how badly her concentration had slipped only that morning.

'You'll have to make up your mind,' Jenny persisted. 'Whether you're going to forgive and forget the dirty trick that was played on you, whether you're going to do what . . . if you're honest . . . you really want to do . . . go back to Mac.'

'I wouldn't go back to him,' Dayle interrupted indignantly. 'Not now that I know the truth . . .'

'What *is* the truth?' Jenny asked sceptically. 'Are you sure you know?'

'I know what really matters,' Dayle asserted, 'and that's that Mac never really loved me. Oh, O.K., so we had a physical thing going for us . . . and I daresay we could have built some kind of life around that . . . some women could, I daresay, but not me. I want more than that.'

'Yes,' Jenny agreed, her voice unusually sharp. 'You want perfection. You want it all . . .'

'If by all, you mean I wanted my husband to have respect for me as a person, to love me, even when we're not actually performing the physical act of love, then yes, I *do* want it all . . .

and I won't settle for less, even if it means remaining single all my life.'

'But you're not single,' Jenny pointed out, 'and it's scarcely fair to keep the man tied to you if you don't want him. So you're going to have to come out of your funk-hole some time . . . to divorce him.'

Dayle had to admit the truth of her friend's words, but somehow she still shrank from taking that ultimate, terribly final step. Once she divorced Mac that was it . . . he was no longer hers in any way, and she wasn't sure she had the courage to face that knowledge. It was ridiculous of her, inconsistent . . . she knew that. Perhaps, as Jenny said, it was unfair too. But she denied her friend's insistence that she had had ample time to come to a decision. She hadn't.

When she had first come to the Country Park, she had resolutely banished all thoughts of her life with Mac, and of the day of their wedding in particular and of the dreadful days that followed. It was only recently that she had allowed memory full rein, and there had been a kind of therapy in it. But so far she had not allowed herself to relive the actual wedding, the night of ecstatic realisation . . . or the anti-climactic, destructive aftermath, and until she could face these incidents squarely, realistically, she felt she was not ready to take that decision Jenny insisted was demanded of her.

It had still been raining when Dayle decided to get up. The thought that this was her wedding day was causing the strangest flutterings in her stomach, making sleep or even relaxation impossible. She was still a little nervous of facing Mac, after the way he had stormed out, apparently incensed by her insistence on further postponement of their lovemaking; but he appeared perfectly calm and normal at the breakfast table, though his bright coppery head was still darkened by the rain into which he had plunged.

After breakfast, she went out alone on to the hillside, staring out to sea from whence the weather came, and after a while it seemed to her that the run of the waves had changed, that the raindrops were pattering against the croft instead of racing past in angry slanting fingers. Low down on the horizon there appeared a suggestion of light . . . murky, reluctant, but light nevertheless. Distant islands began to take misty shape, until at last there was a large area of bright sky veiled by the rain. Then, seemingly at a great distance, the sun came out, bringing the dead, grey sea to life with a thousand sparkling colours and every blade of grass beneath her feet bore a diamond drop of rain.

She had expected that her wedding, held in the late afternoon, would be a small, quiet affair, with no relations there on either side . . . with perhaps only Hannah, and Fergus of course, who was to give her away, in the congregation; but she had reckoned without the friendly interest of the Shetlanders, their affection for Mac. The entire population of Slu-Voe, except for the aged and infirm, was there in force, crowding the tiny church to overflowing.

Dayle had regretted the lack of flowers, due to the season, with which to decorate the altar, but every housewife on Slu-Voe, it seemed, had a hoarded treasure of artificial spring flowers, which, overnight, had been skilfully arranged, so that in the church, lit only by flickering candles, they seemed the genuine article; and from somewhere a bouquet had been provided for her . . . a spray of white heather.

'For luck!' Hannah told her.

Dayle paused, her hand tightening on Fergus's arm as she looked around the church, exclaiming with delight.

'It's beautiful,' she whispered. 'Oh, people *are* kind!' And she felt the prickling warmth of unshed, happy tears behind her eyelids.

'Aye, it's fine enough,' Fergus agreed, 'but you should see it at Harvest Festival . . . sheaves of corn, marigolds all over the pulpit, pyramids of turnips, cabbages and potatoes on the steps . . . loaves of bread, great churns of milk . . . aye, and fish too. There's a grand sight if you like!'

How like a man, to find beauty in the prosaic needs of life; but the little chuckle Dayle gave dried her tears and she lifted her head to glide up the aisle at Fergus's side, proudly confident in Hannah's exquisitely dainty dress, her gaze fixed on a pair of broad shoulders, the back of a head whose hair gleamed with copper lights in the candlelight, to meet green eyes that looked into hers, worth more than any emeralds, whose colour they faithfully represented.

The service was a simple one, yet still strangely moving, the old Minister's words uncomplicated, yet coming straight from the heart; and Dayle knew, when he wished them joy, that he meant exactly what he said. When had Mac found an opportunity to buy the ring? she wondered, as he slipped it on to the third

finger of her left hand . . . there were no jewellers' shops on
Slu-Voe.

They signed the register and Dayle peered curiously at her
new husband's signature . . . 'A. C. MacAlastair.'

'What does the middle initial stand for?' she asked.

His grin was teasing.

'You found the Alastair a bit overwhelming. I don't think
you're quite ready for the second shock.'

And, all unsuspecting, she laughed with him.

Among the secrets kept from Dayle, not least was the party
planned to follow the wedding; but first there was another
custom to be observed. Followed by the entire congregation, the
bride and groom formed a procession, led by a fiddler, which
wended its way to every house on the island where old or infirm
people had been unable to attend the ceremony, so that they
might have a part in the rejoicing.

The tiny village hall, whose presence Dayle had not even
suspected, tucked away as it was behind the church, had
been gaily decorated and a buffet of surprising variety loaded the
tressle tables. After everyone had eaten and drunk their fill there
were lively speeches and toasts, followed by energetic dances.

The dancing was prefaced by the strains of the Bridal March,
then, without pausing, the fiddler quickened his tempo to the
whirling pace of a reel. Dayle found herself drawn into eightsome
reels, Lancers, barn dances, Shetland reels, all with Mac as her
partner, his eyes never leaving hers all the while, dark with the
promise of what was to be, once the merrymaking was over and
they were alone.

The Gay Gordons followed, then a schottische, polka,
Dashing White Sergeant, Strip the Willow, until she was dizzy,
but even the concentration needed to follow the steps could not
drive out the singing knowledge from her heart that soon, very
soon, she and Mac would be really one . . . 'one flesh', the words
of the marriage service had emphasised, and she yearned for that
unity.

It was the early hours of the morning before Mac whirled her
to the side of the floor.

'This will go on until dawn,' he murmured. 'You don't want to
stay until then, do you?'

Suddenly shy, she still contrived to meet his eyes, her own
clear, honest and full of her love for him.

'No,' she whispered. 'No . . . I don't want to stay.'

Unobtrusively, he led her out of the hall and across the
arkend fields . . . to the croft.

There was no objection from Dayle tonight to the close
onfines offered by the box bed . . . no need to retain garments, to
aaintain the semi-respectable tradition of bundling. With
ngers that trembled, they undressed each other, pausing as
ands and lips made delightful discoveries, new ways in which
ach might pleasure the other, until at last, in lamplight, they
ood for an instant as though to savour more fully the delights to
ome. Then Mac lifted her in his arms, his lips on hers, her
reasts brushing against the soft mat of his chest.

Once in the box bed, he turned to close the carved doors
ehind them, enclosing them in an enchanted world of intimacy,
s though nothing existed beyond the confines of this six-foot by
ur-foot world . . . as indeed, for them, it did not.

He handled her gently, but with knowledge and expertise,
irring her body with unerring sureness, and she responded
tuitively to his needs, his hard, muscular body sensuous to her
xploring hands. There was a delicious moment, their naked
odies entwined, before he urged the hardness of his thighs
gainst hers and she knew at last the exaltation of both giving
nd receiving.

hey had known the kind of rapture Dayle had dreamt of, but
ever imagined could so exactly match her dream, and then they
ad slept, close in each other's arms, awakening at dawn,
verwhelmed once more by passion and its inevitable conclu-
on.

Dayle shook as though with an ague, as she allowed herself to
member in agonising detail every kiss, every word, every
ovement of their bodies, moving in climax, the perfect dove-
iling of two becoming one; and it was only with a tremendous
fort that she forced herself to leave the cottage and return to her
ities up at the Mansion, instead of running up to the sanctuary
her room, to cry her heart out for all that she had lost.

CHAPTER TEN

JENNY seemed determined to press Dayle for a decision, now that the subject had been raised between them.

'Have you thought any more about what we discussed at lunch time?' she asked that evening.

Dayle nodded.

'And . . .?'

'I don't know, Jenny . . . I really don't. In one way I'd like to get it all straightened out, but . . . but suppose Mac doesn't want to see *me* again?'

'You couldn't blame him if he didn't,' Jenny said drily. 'It's not exactly a friendly thing to do . . . to walk out on a man, the day after his wedding, without a word of explanation . . . not even a farewell note. For all he knew, someone else might have abducted you.'

'It's scarcely the sort of thing that happens to a girl twice in her lifetime,' Dayle observed with a wry twist of humour.

'You could have misunderstood,' Jenny said, not for the first time.

'There was no misunderstanding what I heard,' Dayle maintained stubbornly, 'no way he could excuse his behaviour . . .'

Mac's intention, he told Dayle next morning, when there was time to speak rationally of other things, was to spend the rest of their honeymoon on the Mainland.

'There's so much there I want to show you. I want you to meet my mother . . . and my brother. I wish you could meet my sisters, but maybe we'll visit them too, some day, when . . .' He stopped abruptly and Dayle knew that he must have been about to say 'when we can afford it', and that could only come about when her money was in his hands. It embittered the first day of her married life just for a moment, then she brushed the thought aside; it wasn't as if she had only just learnt of his monetary needs; she had gone into marriage with her eyes wide open in that respect at least.

148

Shaking off the languidity of their first blissful night together, Mac told Dayle they must be up betimes, because Simon was coming over to take them to the mainland in his fishing boat, and from then on the day rushed by at a rapid pace.

There was time only for heartfelt thanks to Hannah and Fergus, and fervent promises to visit them again very soon, before they were on their way, and Dayle stood looking back at the island where she had known such fulfilment.

'We'll spend a couple of days in Lerwick, getting to know each other better, Mac said meaningfully, bringing the colour into her cheeks that such words could still provoke. 'And I'd like to take you over to Noss . . . the bird sanctuary.' He hesitated. 'I've been thinking of opening Haa to the public . . . in the summer months, that is. What do you think of the idea?'

'What would it involve?' Dayle queried cautiously.

'Someone on duty to see that the visitors had a bona fide interest in birds . . . that they were not disturbing them . . . keep an eye on the litter problem.'

'Would you charge?'

'Not for admission to the island, but I *was* wondering, how about providing refreshments souvenirs . . . that kind of thing?'

'Sounds all right to me,' Dayle agreed, but she was puzzled nevertheless. With her money to look forward to, why was Mac worried about such a small financial return? The season could only be a very short one at best and the interest in birdwatching a limited one.

'Right! We'll look into it, then,' said Mac. 'When we've nothing better to do!' He brushed her lips with his own and under Simon's interested eyes . . . knowing he could not have failed to hear Mac's loaded remark, she blushed again; and with a little skip of her heart, found she was thinking yearningly of the night to come. Making love to Mac was still too new an experience to be able to contemplate with equanimity.

'And then we'll go south to Scotland,' Mac continued, 'to visit my mother.'

'Does she know about me?' Dayle asked wonderingly.

'Not yet . . . but what a pleasant surprise she'll have!'

Mac's mother was destined to forgo that surprise, but it was not until later in the day that this fact became apparent.

On the mainland, a car awaited their use and they drove over the route to Lerwick, a route which Dayle had traversed in the opposite direction with such very different feelings. Now, she could look at the grey houses of Lerwick with a less jaundiced eye. She was a changed person from the girl who had passed this way six months previously; she had experienced something so remote, so different from her old existence . . . a way of life surrounded by sea, totally cut off from the intrusions of civilisation. She had sampled the fears and the exhilaration . . . not only of loneliness, but of love, of desire, and now she had known the joy that surpassed all others, that transcended fear.

Yet in a way she *was* afraid . . . afraid of having left that splendid isolation, in case a change of scenery should, in some way, mar this new perfection she had found. If only one could hold time still, she brooded, encapsulated in one's most splendid hour.

It was difficult to shake off this mood of foreboding, and yet she knew she must. Time could not be halted and, she reminded herself, there were moments to come, equally precious, equally worthy of memory. If only she had known . . .

The hotel Mac had chosen was a modest one . . . a commercial hotel, his choice showing a restraint she could only approve even if her soul did cry out for the romance of a bridal suite in some exotic far away place. Anyway, she chided herself, this was only the continuation of their honeymoon, and last night had been spent in as unusual a setting as the most romantic heart could devise, its events more than satisfactory.

They unpacked their few belongings and Mac suggested that they lunch at the hotel, then go out to renew their acquaintance with Lerwick.

'After all, you *did* see it in somewhat different circumstances,' he teased.

She smiled in rueful agreement.

'I'll go down and order lunch, then . . . and you can join me when you've powdered your nose.'

Oh, the small things that dictated fate. If he had only waited for her! Those few moments would have made so much difference and yet it would only have postponed the evil moment . . . eventual discovery had been inevitable.

Suitably freshened up, Dayle began the descent of the narrow stairway that led to the reception desk and foyer, where doors led off to office, residents' lounge and dining room. Halfway down she heard the sound of male voices, loud, their volume probably increased by the liquid lunch their owners had just imbibed.

'Well, if it isn't old MacAlastair! Where have you been all
ese months? Properly dropped out of sight, didn't you? Not
ke you rich boys to miss all the goings on. One of your firms
ade a big killing in the City, I hear.'

And the other voice, infinitely more damaging.

'Callum MacAlastair, as I live and breathe; old Abercrom-
e's latest blue-eyed boy!'

Dayle stood, riveted to the spot, her presence mercifully
ncealed by the bend in the stairs. At first her brain utterly
fused to translate the facts her ears had just related. But at last
 sense of outrage began to outweigh shock. There could be
solutely no misunderstanding what she had just heard; the
vo loud voices had laid it absolutely on the line . . . everything
 e needed to know about Mac . . . the mystery of his middle
me, the means by which he had learnt of her declared
tention to marry a poor man. He was no more poor than her
ther . . . Her father? Oh no! He couldn't! Had her father known
 e true identity of her abductor right from the start? Oh, the
 miliation, the devastating realisation that Mac . . . she sup-
sed she should call him Callum now . . . someone her father
d trusted, had even proposed as a husband for her, had cold
oodedly kidnapped her, won her trust while betraying her
ther's . . . toyed with her affections. What kind of man would
 such a thing? Deliberately make a girl fall in love with him,
cause she was a rich man's daughter? Greedy, grasping,
aricious . . . wasn't his own fortune enough for him? When she
ought how she had bared her very soul to him, let him see how
uch she loved him! Dayle cringed, as she remembered her very
actical demonstrations of that love . . . and he had callously
ken all that she had offered. How had he expected such a
lationship to prosper? The man wasn't an idiot, so he couldn't
riously have imagined that his deceit would never be dis-
vered.

How had he planned to cope with *that* revelation? Or had he
pected her to be so completely ensnared by the chains of
ysical dependency by then that she would not protest over-
uch? If so he had mistaken his victim. Love him she might, but
e was no clinging, dependent vine! Ironically enough, he
mself had seen to that, with his tough course of training in
lf-sufficiency. Dayle fought back the threatening tears. This
as another lesson learned . . . that it was a hard world men like
ac inhabited, not the harshness of life on a primitive island . . .

that was just a toy to him, she thought scornfully . . . no, like he
father, he was from the hard jungle of the business world, nc
hesitating to employ its ruthless measures. Well, she could b
hard too, from this moment on.

She wasn't sure how long she stood there; how long it took fc
all these thoughts to career through her mind; but it suddenl
occurred to her that Mac would shortly become impatient, tha
he was quite likely to come in search of her. Well, he wouldn'
find her. She had no formulated plan of action, no idea where sh
would go as yet, or what she should do. Like a wounded anima
her only instinct was to run, to hide, to lick her wounds i
private. To think was to act. Blessing the fact that Mac had give
her some money for shopping, that she carried her handbag, sh
ran through the foyer as though pursued, thankful that th
dining room doors were closed, and out into the street.

Fortunately, before she had gone very far, she came across
taxi rank and leaping into the leading car gave the first instruc
tion that came into her head:

'The airport . . . and hurry!'

All the way she was constantly glancing over her shoulder
fearful of pursuit. Had Mac discovered that she was missing
Did he suspect yet that she had run away, or would he suppos
that she had not been able to resist the idea of shopping, that sh
had slipped out on some vital errand? It was a pity, she though
that she had not had time to leave a misleading note.

After a while he would certainly begin to worry. Well, let hir
worry, she thought savagely. No anxiety he might endure woul
be sufficient to pay for all the anguish he had caused her . .
When she thought of the months of her life he had wasted!

She alternated her fearful glances behind with anxious look
ahead, watching for the first signs that they were approachin
the airport. Suppose there were no regular flights to Aberdee
. . . or suppose today's flights were finished? How little she kne
of such things. Her father's secretary had always been respons
ible for booking their air tickets. Dayle had no idea even c
prices. Perhaps she would find she hadn't enough money. Th
thought of having to wait ignominiously at the airport until Ma
found her was unbearable. As she had feared, it took most of he
slender horde of money to pay for her ticket. She would have jus
enough, if she was miserly in her spending, to buy food for two o
three days; for, of necessity, she would have to hitch-hike th
length of Britain.

It seemed an eternity until her flight was announced and she was safely in her seat, the aircraft taxiing down the runway.

Dayle closed her eyes; she did not want to take a last look at Shetland. As when she had left Slu-Voe that morning, her emotions would be too mixed for comfort.

'Oh, Mac . . . Mac!' she yearned. 'Why did it have to be this way? Why couldn't we have met and fallen in love normally? Why did you have to lie and cheat? How could you pretend to be in love with me? You didn't even need the money!'

'I think that puzzled me more than anything,' Dayle told Jenny. 'It still does. Why did he agree to do it, if he didn't need money?'

'Didn't you ask your father? After all, he was in on it, wasn't he?'

'No, I didn't ask him. After he'd told me his part in the affair, I couldn't bear to speak to him. All I could think about was packing a few clothes and drawing enough money out of my bank account to live on, while I looked around for a job. Once Daddy had admitted everything, I just wanted to get away. I didn't care if I never saw either of them . . . Daddy or Mac . . . again.'

'And do you still feel that way?'

Dayle hesitated.

'I don't know. I've calmed down a bit, I suppose, and there are times when I miss Daddy . . . we were quite good pals most of the time. I suppose that's why it hurt so much . . . that he could play such a dirty trick on me; and I keep remembering how worried I was, when Mac first kidnapped me, thinking that he might have harmed Daddy. I can't forgive Daddy for what he did . . . or forget it . . . but he's still my father. I'm glad he's safe . . . and you can't stop loving someone just like that, can you?'

'Any more than you can stop loving Mac!' Jenny observed. 'Just as a matter of interest, which of them do you blame most?'

Dayle looked at her friend, a puzzled frown making furrows between her blue eyes.

'That's the strange thing. I know now it was all Daddy's idea in the first place, that I ought to be angrier with him, but . . . but I'm not. I'm furious with Daddy, but I *hate* Mac for agreeing to his scheme.'

Jenny nodded shrewdly.

'As I thought! You're still in love all right.'

'How do you work that out?'

'Oh, come on, Dayle, be your age! If you didn't like the man
you wouldn't really care what he'd done. You'd just be content
to despise him and reckon yourself well out of it . . . get a divorce
But you *hate* him . . . that's a pretty violent swing of emotion
isn't it? Don't you have to hate him, to stop yourself loving him?'

Jenny's insight was uncannily accurate; she had put into
words a puzzle that Dayle had been ruminating over for several
days.

'You're right, of course,' she said slowly. 'I suppose I've
known it all along, but I didn't want to admit it to myself. I tried
to tell myself it was all a hangover from the . . . the physical
thing, you know . . .'

She meant the way her body still cried out for Mac's, but she
trusted to Jenny's common sense to formulate the words she
hesitated to speak, even to such a close friend.

Jenny was nodding sympathetically.

'I won't deny you've had it pretty rough, old thing . . . first the
fright of the kidnap, then the "will he, won't he?", then thinking
you've got it made . . . only to find your idol's feet were a pretty
outsize fit in clay boots . . . and to top it all, that ghastly journey
home, wearing just what you stood up in. You were lucky to
make it intact!'

She had been lucky, in that respect. Dayle still shuddered when
she remembered that seemingly endless trek from Aberdeen to
the outskirts of London, wearing only jeans and sweater. She
had walked a lot, but she had also been fortunate in obtaining
several lifts . . . some of them from very decent people; but there
had been a couple of lorry drivers whose ulterior motives for
being helpful had been less honourable and she could have found
herself in a very nasty situation, if they had been real villains
instead of blustering, bluffing brutes.

By the time she had staggered into Angus's house she had
been tired, hungry, filthy and in no fit state to enter into battle
with her father, as she had originally intended. So it was a relief
that her arrival coincided with office hours and she had most of
the day in which to clean herself up, rest and prepare her
indictment; though even then she had not realised the full extent
of her father's perfidy, still casting Mac in the role of the
principal villain.

She was in her own suite, which seemed vast after months in
the tiny rooms of the croft, when she heard the discreet purr of

the Rolls-Royce, followed by the thud of the garage door and then her father's unmistakable tones in the front hall. She came out on to the upper landing, in time to hear the housekeeper apprising Angus of his daughter's return.

'Miss Dayle is back, sir.'

'Dayle? Here?' There was no mistaking his surprise. 'Alone?'

There was no relief in his voice. Well, there wouldn't be, would there? It was not as if she'd been abducted by a complete stranger. Whatever hold Mac had over him, at least her father had known her kidnapper's identity.

Dayle had had plenty of time to work things out during her long trek and during her wait for her father's return. For some reason . . . financial probably, such as a projected merger . . . Mac, or Callum as she must remember to call him now, had asked to meet her, with a view to proposing marriage. Her father must have told him of her outspoken reluctance to make his acquaintance, warned him of her likely rebellion, her threat to marry out of hand the first poor man who offered, and Mac . . . no, *Callum*! . . . had hatched his plot accordingly.

She walked slowly down the stairs to face her father, her legs trembling slightly, but her chin held high. Before the evening was out, she would have the full truth out of Angus; then she would know what steps to take.

'Dayle! Lass! It's good to see you!' Angus advanced, arms outstretched, but Dayle merely presented a cool cheek for his kiss. 'What are you doing here? I thought you were on your honeymoon?'

She was aware of the housekeeper's discreet interest, the maids coming and going on errands.

'Shall we go into the study?' she asked stiffly.

She preceded Angus and waited until he had shut the door before she turned to look at him.

'Well, Daddy?' Then, as he raised interrogative shaggy eyebrows. 'Oh, come on, Daddy don't pretend you haven't got a lot of explaining to do.'

He sat down behind the large mahogany desk, toying with a letter opener.

'What do you want to know?' he said cautiously.

'Everything,' she said firmly. 'You must realise by now that I've discovered who Mac really is . . . Alastair *Callum* MacAlastair.' She said the name with angry distaste. 'What sort of hold has he got over you, that you dared not report him to the police, that you meekly agreed to him marrying your daughter?'

'Hold? Over me? What are you talking about?'

'Daddy! Will you stop pussyfooting about? Can't you see, I
have to know the truth . . . all of it?'

'You and Callum did get married?' Angus asked, endeavouring to get a glimpse of her left hand.

'Oh yes,' she said bitterly, holding it out for his inspection.
'We got married all right, but if you're wondering where the ring
is, I removed it . . . the minute the plane for Aberdeen took off.'

'And how do you feel about Callum? Come on?' as her face set
mulishly. 'If you want the truth from me, then you can do no
less.'

'All right!' she burst out. 'If you must know, I fell in love with
him . . . but you needn't gloat, because I couldn't go on loving a
cheat and a liar. I . . . I despise him . . . I *hate* him!'

'You must feel the same way about me, then,' Angus said
sadly, and suddenly he looked very old, his wide shoulders
sagging, his leonine head sunk between them.

'You? Why should I hate and despise you?' Dayle's voice
faltered, as a dreadful premonition seized her.

'Because I arranged the whole thing! No . . .' he lifted a hand,
as her lips parted in a prelude to indignant speech, 'hear me out.
You really put the wind up me, Dayle, when you threatened to
marry just anyone, so long as he was poor . . . and not *my* choice
of a husband for you.'

'I had a right to choose my own husband,' Dayle asserted
angrily, 'but I probably wouldn't have carried out my threat.
What chance did I ever get to meet that sort of man anyway?'

'I couldn't take the chance,' Angus said wearily. 'You've
always been wilful. I see that now; and I knew Callum was the
right sort of man, the sort to master you . . .'

'*Master* me!' It was an outraged cry.

'Yes.' Angus's voice became stronger as he expressed his
conviction. 'I suddenly realised that I'd spoilt you, my girl. I'd
brought you up to a certain way of life . . . with expectations, but
no knowledge of how to handle the money that would be yours
. . . a prey for any unprincipled scoundrel; and then there was
always the chance that you wouldn't always be rich. Nothing is
certain in this life. Investments can fail. It happened to poor old
Spencer. It could happen to me; and I couldn't see you coping
with sudden poverty.

'Spencer? You mean Jenny Spencer's father?'

Angus nodded.

'It seems he made a whole series of unwise investments. If he'd only consulted me first, I'd have told him, but . . .' He shrugged. 'About a month after you 'disappeared' I heard he'd gone bust. It was too late to help him. They've left the area, gone up north somewhere . . . him and his wife . . . to the Midlands, I think. He's got a brother there who's promised to put something his way.'

'And Jenny?' Dayle asked, her own problems temporarily shelved.

'Got herself a job somewhere, I'm told. I don't know where. Doubtless one of your yacht club pals will be able to tell you.'

'Poor Jenny,' Dayle said slowly. 'How awful for her!'

'Yes, well, that could have been you my girl . . . and how would *you* have managed, hey?'

Dayle could not deny that she would have been absolutely useless, once upon a time . . . before Mac . . .

'So you set me up?' she accused.

'I did what I thought would be best for you,' said Angus, a note of pleading in his voice. 'Mac and I had been good friends for some time, despite the difference in our ages.'

'You mean, he didn't have any hold over you?'

'Lord no! he . . .'

'But what about those letters . . . the threats . . .?'

Angus's expression was a mixture of embarrassment, shame and . . . contrarily . . . pride in his own ingenuity.

'That was my idea, so you wouldn't smell a rat . . . later, when you *were* kidnapped. I knew if I made a big enough show of being worried and then carelessly left one of the letters lying about, you wouldn't be able to resist . . .'

'Of all the dirty, double-crossing, low-down tricks!' Dayle jumped to her feet. 'And to think that I actually worried about you . . . imagined you being held prisoner somewhere, being threatened . . . imagined you . . .' her voice broke slightly, 'being worried about *me*, when all the time you and that loathsome man . . Oh, how you must both have laughed!'

'No, no, it wasn't like that. After you'd gone . . . when you rang me and I had to pretend . . . well, I felt an utter heel, but . . .'

'And Mac . . . I mean Callum . . . when I think of how he . . . No decent man, or a man with any pride, would have agreed to abduct a girl he'd never met, couldn't care two hoots about . . .

and agree to marry her, sight unseen. Unless of course you paid him? I suppose it *was* quite an incentive, being eventual heir to the Abercrombie millions.'

'Good lord!' Angus said incredulously. 'You mean to say he hasn't told you? You've got it wrong . . . that part of it. Callum didn't . . .'

But Dayle was no longer listening.

'It's no good, Daddy. I don't want to hear any more about the whole despicable business; and most of all, I don't want to discuss *him.*'

'At least let me explain his part in it. He . . .'

'No, no, *no!*' she cried vehemently.

She was already filled with disgust and humiliation to think how she had been bought and sold. Like . . . like a *prize cow*, she told herself. She already knew enough of Mac's appalling part in this conspiracy. Her heart was already broken. To know more, to have to bear the weight of further hideous knowledge, would kill her.

'Wait, Dayle. You have to hear me out,' said Angus, as she hurried towards the study door, her face averted to hide the tears that streamed down her cheeks.

But she did not pause until she reached her own room, where she slammed and locked the door behind her and despite Angus's earnest entreaties, refused to emerge.

That night, when the household was in darkness, Dayle crept from the house, taking only the barest essentials with her . . . a few of her most sensible clothes and her bank book. She didn't want to be beholden to her father for anything, ever again. She had to get away, before Mac traced her to her father's house . . . she had to be alone somewhere, to think things out.

The next day she drew out some money, enough to see her over the next few days, then mailed the book to her father. That money was rightfully his; she hadn't earned it; and in future she didn't want anything that she hadn't gained by her own endeavours. Using a callbox, she telephoned all her friends, until she obtained news of Jenny's whereabouts.

She took cheap lodgings in a town several miles from her home, while she waited for a reply to her letter to Jenny, in which she briefly outlined her dilemma. Jenny had obtained an interview for her with Tony Ashworth and from there her new life had begun.

And I've always been grateful to you for getting me this job, Jenny.'

'But it was only a stopgap, Dayle, surely,' her friend insisted. 'O.K., so you're enjoying it for the present, but do you really want to go on working here until you're as old and bent and grey as Miss Wilson?'

Dayle had to smile at this reference to the head gardener.

'I suppose not.'

'Then make up your mind what you're going to do. I don't like to think of you all alone here, brooding, while I'm away.'

'You're going away?' Dayle was surprised. She thought her friend had used up all her holiday allowance.

'Yes. It's Mum and Dad's twenty-fifth wedding anniversary the week after next. They want me to go up for a few days. They're having a family party, to celebrate that . . . and the fact that things are looking up a bit for them. They'll never be fabulously wealthy, of course, but they'll be comfortably off . . . and I suppose after hitting rock bottom that *is* worth celebrating.'

'I'm very pleased for them,' Dayle said sincerely. She had always got on extremely well with her friend's parents.

'So just you get yourself sorted out before I go. Then I shan't ruin my holiday worrying about you,' Jenny ordered.

CHAPTER ELEVEN

DESPITE Jenny's strictures, Dayle was no nearer to a decision about her future one Thursday morning a couple of weeks later as she helped her friend to load her suitcases, her parents' anniversary present and various other packages into the Mini. Jenny was to have the use of the car they shared for her long weekend in the Midlands.

'Don't forget to have the tyre pressures checked at the first garage you come to,' Dayle reminded her. She sighed, remembering her own smart little Mini, still, presumably, garaged at her father's house. 'I wish we could afford a better car. I'll be surprised if this gets through its M.O.T. next month.'

'We'll worry about that when it happens!' Jenny, looking forward to her reunion with her parents, was too elated to worry over such details. 'Now, don't you forget! While I'm away, instead of daydreaming, do some serious thinking.'

Smiling her acknowledgement, Dayle waved Jenny away, then wandered back into the cottage, suddenly quiet and empty after all the activity of departure. The next few days would be very dull without her friend's exuberant presence and the matter-of-fact way she had of dispelling Dayle's blues. Sunday would be the worst day, when there were no chores to be done . . . unless one was on duty at the Home Farm, when, of course, the livestock still needed attention.

She cleared away the breakfast things; she had insisted that Jenny make an early start on her journey, refusing to allow her to wash up. Then, locking the cottage door, she made her way to the office to report for duty. She found Tony Ashworth impatiently awaiting her.

'Could you take over for the morning?' he asked. 'The Head of the Museums Department wants to see me . . . just a routine matter, I think, but he prefers a face-to-face report to a written one. Think you can cope?'

Upon Dayle's assurance that she was perfectly well able to manage for the few hours required, he continued:

'There's nothing important outstanding, so it should be very quiet for you . . . just a matter of taking telephone bookings for parties.'

'Stop fussing, Tony!' Dayle laughed. 'Anyone would think I'd never minded the office before.'

'Right! I'm off! Oh, before I go, there's a letter for you on the desk. Looks as if it's been astray somewhere. The postmark is nearly two weeks old. I'd have brought it down to you, but I was pushed for time.'

Tony rushed away and Dayle settled down behind his desk. Incuriously, she reached for the letter; she rarely had any correspondence of importance. Then she stiffened. It was from her father. The envelope was a fat one and when she slit it open, the reason for the thickness became apparent. There was an enclosure the handwriting on this envelope also unmistakable . . . bold, black and upright . . . Mac's.

Angus had covered sheet after sheet, and delaying the moment when she must make a decision about Mac's letter, Dayle began to read her father's large, sprawling writing. Angus was not normally a man who wrote personal letters. He usually preferred to dictate his correspondence to his secretary. It must have been quite an effort for him to write a letter of this length.

'Dear Dayle, I ran into Minnie Parnell yesterday. You'll remember her son Reggie, no doubt.'

Damn, damn, damn. So Mrs Parnell had not kept her own counsel after all. She hadn't been able to resist telling Angus that she'd seen his daughter . . . and where. Meddling busybody! Dayle read on.

'I was very grateful to her for giving me news of your whereabouts. It obviously didn't occur to you that I might be worried about you, and in particular about your marriage.'

Dayle snorted. It was more likely that Angus was worried about his financial dealings with Callum MacAlastair. Her disappearance had probably caused a considerable rift in *that* lute.

'You should have given me a chance to explain more fully . . . about Callum's part in my plans for you. Frankly, I don't think you've been fair to the lad.'

Fair! *She* hadn't been fair? Did Angus think it was fair to take Mac's part against her?

'He's been in touch with me, of course . . .'

Yes, he would have been. Mac wasn't one to let grass grow under his feet. What did he want . . . his wife back, or a divorce?

'. . . worried out of his mind about you, until I told him I'd seen you, that so far as I knew you were all right . . . just blazing mad with the pair of us, and gone off to sulk somewhere.'

Had Mac been worried about *her*, or about the threat to his carefully contrived marriage of convenience . . . the probable loss of a second fortune? And how dared Angus accuse her sulking? She had good cause to be aggrieved, but he made her sound like a petulant schoolgirl, instead of a mature woman who had been wronged.

'Of course you may not bother to read this. The mood you were in when you came home, I wouldn't be surprised if you tore it up. But in case you have decided to read on, I think you should know the whole truth.'

Did she want to know the truth? She was in two minds whether or not she should do what her father had feared and tear up his letter. Had she the courage to read on? In the end simple curiosity won the day.

'O.K., so I'm sorry about the fright you had, the anonymous letters and so on . . . and all the unnecessary work I put you to for the dinner party. Of course you've guessed that I cancelled the party to leave Callum a clear field. I stayed at the office that evening, until I thought you'd be well clear . . . I'd given the household staff the day off.'

Yes, she had wondered how Mac had achieved his abduction uninterrupted, never suspecting then that he'd had 'inside' co-operation.

'I knew you'd be safe with Callum and he promised me to give you a taste of the kind of life you'd never experienced.'

It seemed he'd promised to marry her too. How *could* he? Now that she knew Callum MacAlastair, she just couldn't see him as a man who would agree to a marriage of convenience. He was too . . . too *male*, the kind that would want to seek out his own mate.

'. . . to knock the rough corners off you.'

Wasn't that supposed to have been the task of the expensive Swiss finishing school? Dayle wondered wryly.

'I thought a few weeks of hardship might bring you to your senses . . . rid you of your crazy ideas. After all, it's as easy to fall in love with a rich man as with a poor one.'

How very true! and she *had* . . . hook, line and sinker, to use one of Mac's fishing terms; and he'd been after a big catch, when he'd cast his bait in her direction.

Her father's letter had been written over two days apparently, for the next section bore a different date, the writing even more hurried.

'Callum called here a few days ago. He has to go abroad on business for the firm, and he was hoping I might have some news of you, before he went.'

Dayle's breath caught in her throat, as she read on hastily, to see if Angus had revealed her whereabouts.

'I hadn't seen Minnie Parnell at that date, of course, so I wasn't much help. I told him to write to you and if I heard anything, I'd forward his letter. He's probably stated his case better than I could. But I think you owe it to him to meet him and talk things out. He is your husband and he deserves a bit of consideration, after all he's done for you . . . so read his letter.'

If Angus hadn't finished on that note, Dayle might have opened the enclosure bearing Mac's writing; but she felt that she was being pressurised. Her father had interfered in her life once, to disastrous effect; he was not going to tell her what she should do or should not do . . . and as for that bit about 'all that her husband had done for her' . . . Her face was cynical as she stared at Mac's unopened letter. Her initial reaction was to destroy it unread, but somehow she could not bring herself to actually tear it up, and throw it away. In what she told herself was a cowardly fashion, she thrust it into the deepest recesses of her handbag, once more postponing a decision.

But what about her father's letter? Should she answer it . . . or telephone him, beg him to keep her whereabouts secret? But would he do that? The whole tone of his letter indicated that he was on Mac's side. Of course he would be; men always stuck together; and in any case, defending Mac was probably Angus's way of justifying his own behaviour. Dayle decided it was pointless to appeal to her father. Besides, with his letter being so much out of date, he had probably passed on the vital information by now. How long had she got, she wondered, before Mac followed it up? Not long enough, she decided, for her to be able to move on before he came in search of her . . . for somehow she had no doubt that he would. She was bound by the terms of her contract with the County Council to give a month's notice and she couldn't see Mac giving her that much grace.

So, if she wasn't going to run away, what was she going to do? If Mac turned up at the Country Park, she could refuse to allow him over her threshold, refuse to speak to him; or she could face him and make it quite clear that she wanted nothing more to do with him . . . that she wanted a divorce. But would she be able to go through with it, be able to convince him? Dayle knew that she was still so susceptible to her burning memories of Mac that it would require consummate acting to hide her reactions, to maintain an indifferent front . . . particularly if he set himself out to be persuasive.

Suppose . . . she swallowed, and simultaneously her insides twisted convulsively . . . suppose he tried to touch her, kiss her even? She would be lost before battle was even commenced.

There was one other way she could protect herself, of course. She could pretend that there was someone else in her life now. She was sure, if she appealed to Tony, he would stay close at hand, act the part of the devoted boy-friend with convincing realism; but was it fair to ask this of him, when she knew that Tony himself was already more than half in love with her?

She wished Tony had not been so accurate in his prediction of a quiet morning in the office; a few telephone calls would have proved a welcome distraction from her thoughts, and the hours dragged interminably. Several times she retrieved Mac's letter from her handbag and turned it over in her hands, wondering what it contained. Were they words of condemnation or of love . . . an indictment of her behaviour, or a plea for her to return to him? She couldn't imagine Mac pleading.

She was relieved when Tony breezed in, his manner more relaxed now that his meeting with his superior was over.

'Well, there's a turn-up for the book,' he announced, as Dayle relinquished his desk to him. 'The County kept *that* a pretty close secret. Still, I'm glad we didn't know about it before today. It's saved us all a lot of worry.'

'Kept what a secret? What kind of worry?' Dayle asked curiously, glad to shelve her own problems.

'It seems we could all have been out of a job. But, as things have turned out, we might be better off in the long run.'

'Tony, do come to the point,' she begged.

But he was looking at her, his head slightly on one side, a mischievous grin on his pleasant features.

'No! No, I think I'll keep you in suspense a bit longer.'

'Tony!' she wailed. 'You mean thing! Rousing my curiosity like this!'

'I'll make a bargain with you,' he said. 'Come out to dinner with me this evening and I'll tell you the whole story . . . before the rest of the staff get to know.'

'Oh, but . . . I don't think . . .'

'No dinner, no story!' he threatened. 'And I warn you, you'll be sorry . . . because it's quite a tale.'

Dayle deliberated. It *would* be lonely at the cottage this evening, with Jenny away for the first time since Dayle had come to work at the Park. Then, too, she was a little nervous about being on her own just at present. Her father's letter had made her very apprehensive. Suppose Mac were to turn up, out of the blue, while she was all alone? Alone in the cottage, she knew she would be completely at his mercy; she knew Mac too well to suppose that he would let her escape before she had heard what he had to say. He would restrain her by force if necessary, and that meant physical contact . . . she shuddered . . .

'All right, Tony, and . . . thank you.'

It was only fair to Tony that she should make the best of her appearance that evening, Dayle decided. But it was rather pleasant, too, to have an excuse for dressing up again; she went out so rarely that the two good dresses she had allowed herself had scarcely been worn.

She chose the strappy, cocktail-length dress in a peacock blue that set off the silvery fairness of her hair and deepened the blue of her eyes. She had always had a good figure, but a healthy outdoor life had given a new bloom to her complexion, and she was rewarded for her efforts by the undisguised admiration in Tony's eyes.

'I've waited a long time for this,' he observed, as he steered her towards his car, one hand at her elbow, 'but by golly, it was worth waiting for!'

She paused, looking at him anxiously.

'Don't get the wrong idea, Tony. This is only a . . . a friendly outing, to discuss business.'

He sighed.

'I know, I know! I don't stand a chance with you, do I? But at least let me enjoy the illusion for one night . . . let me see all the other fellows envying me.'

The restaurant Tony had chosen was an exclusive and expensive one, attached to a large motel, and again Dayle felt a pang of guilt at allowing him to spend so much money on her. She had offered to pay her share, but he would not hear of it.

Over the prawn cocktails which preceded the main course, she pressed him to reveal the secret at which he had hinted.

'Obviously it has to do with the Country Park?'

'Yes.' He looked grave for a moment. 'You may have heard that Councils generally have been making a lot of cut-backs, due to the recession . . . even in the educational field, which covers Barnet Country Park. It *is* basically educational, what with the museum and the visits from agricultural students and so on.'

Dayle nodded.

'They felt . . . the County, that is . . . that the Park wasn't making enough profit to justify keeping on the livestock. The feeding bill alone is pretty enormous, and if they'd axed the Home Farm, it would have meant pretty severe cuts in staff too.'

'But the Home Farm's important,' Dayle protested. 'It's not just a question of education . . . it's conservation too. Its whole purpose is to preserve the type of animal that's virtually dying out with modern farming methods.'

'Hold your horses . . . oh, excuse the pun! . . . You haven't heard everything. You wouldn't have been the only ardent conservationist up in arms. Just imagine Miss Wilson's face when she heard her precious garden had to go.'

Dayle could indeed picture the elderly head gardener's anguish. The walled garden, apart from being an extremely picturesque area, also housed many rare strains of vegetable, not now in common production. She waited until the main course of steak had been served, then asked:

'I take it, as you're speaking in the past tense, that the County has changed its policy?'

'Not the policy, no. They still couldn't afford to run the Park as a viable proposition, but . . .' he leant forward impressively 'they *have* found a private buyer, someone who's prepared to take on the whole thing, lock, stock and barrel.'

'But it will still be open to the public?' she enquired anxiously, thinking of the hundreds of people who daily derived so much pleasure from the amenities.

'Yes . . . and the existing staff will be kept on. In fact, I fancy the new owner may even extend and improve, which will mean more jobs eventually.'

'That's great,' Dayle murmured, wondering if she would be there to derive the obvious benefits. A wealthy man might even raise their wages.

'Isn't it?' Tony enthused. 'So you see why I felt a little celebration was in order? But keep it under your hat for the time being, until it's all officially signed, sealed and delivered.'

Dayle promised and they were silent for a while, doing justice to the excellent meal. Then, over coffee, Tony lit up a cigarette and continued with his account.

'It seems that the chap who's buying the property is a real human dynamo, a whizz kid, but himself a very keen conservationist. He reckons he can make the Park pay, while allowing it to fulfil its main function.'

'I hope he won't introduce anything ghastly . . . like a funfair, or railways rattling round,' said Dayle. 'That would spoil the whole atmosphere.'

'Doubtless there will be changes,' Tony pointed out.

'I'm not sure that I like changes,' Dayle said with a sigh. 'I love the Park just the way it is. If he makes too many alterations, I might just move on, rather than stay to see it spoilt.'

Tony looked and sounded dismayed.

'Oh, heck, Dayle! You can't do that!'

Looking at his anxious expression, Dayle thought it might be a good idea if she moved on anyway.

'At least stay for a while and see how it all works out,' Tony pleaded. 'You're good at your job and you know you like the work.'

'I do, yes, but . . . well, frankly, Tony, I think the time has come for me to get my personal life sorted out. Jenny thinks I should . . . and I suppose she's right.'

'Fine! Why not? Get your private affairs settled by all means. But that doesn't mean you have to leave.'

'It might do. I really ought to think seriously about getting a job with better pay . . .'

'Why not hang on?' Tony repeated. 'If this chap's got big ideas, he may be prepared to pay higher salaries. But that's enough shop talk. We came here to enjoy ourselves. Let's dance, shall we? And promise me you won't do anything rash?'

Dayle accepted his invitation to dance, but she did not want Tony to think he had persuaded her around to his way of thinking.

'I'm not making any promises,' she said firmly.

Inevitably, the conversation continued on the dance floor.

'I'm told the prospective buyer is coming to look around the place in a day or two. I'll get the staff together tomorrow and brief them. We'll have some extra spit and polish.

Once the first step had been taken, it was easy to accept a second invitation from Tony; after all, Dayle argued with her conscience, he *did* know the position about her marriage, so it was not as if she was misleading him. Moreover, he was good company and an accomplished dancer; so when he invited her to accompany him to a dinner dance, on the following Saturday evening, at the nearby Country Club, she accepted; it was a far more pleasant way of spending the evening than sitting all alone at the cottage with no one to talk to; and they discussed a varied range of subjects from the new prospects for the Park, music, literature and even speculated on how Jenny was enjoying her break.

'That's an interesting-looking couple just come in,' Tony remarked. His seat commanded a clear view of the room, but Dayle had to turn and look over her shoulder to see the man and woman who had caught his eye.

After one appalled glance, she turned away, glad that Tony's attention was now with the wine waiter. But that swift look had imprinted an indelible image upon her brain.

It was Mac . . . but dressed as she had never seen him,

immaculate in evening wear, the impeccable tailoring emphasising his height, his breadth of shoulder. Above the well-
remembered, bronzed face, the coppery hair was well groomed
and gleaming. But who was the woman? Dayle felt sick with
jealousy as she recalled the chic, petite figure of his companion.
Never before had Dayle felt any selfconsciousness about her
height, her proportions. But now she knew . . . this was the type
of woman Mac preferred, given his own choice.

Urgently, she leant forward.

'Tony, do we have to eat here? Couldn't we go somewhere
else?'

He looked at her incredulously.

'But, Dayle, we can't possibly leave! Our tickets are paid for
and our meal is ordered . . . and the wine. What's wrong with
this place?'

'Nothing,' she said tensely. 'It's not the place. It . . . it's the
people. Tony, that man who just came in . . . the one with the
tiny brunette. He . . . he's my husband.'

'Good lord!' It was Tony's turn to look stunned. 'What a
ghastly coincidence!'

'I don't think it is a coincidence,' Dayle told him grimly. 'I
think he's in this area, looking for me.' She related the content of
her father's letter.

'So you think he's come down here especially to look for you?'
Tony was beginning to look a little apprehensive. 'Is he the
jealous type, likely to make a scene?'

'Because I'm with you? Do you know, I've no idea. You see, I
don't know what was in his letter . . . I didn't read it. He may be
here to talk about a divorce.' She swallowed. The idea was very
unpalatable; but it was more than likely, since he had already
found himself a girl-friend. 'Can . . . can you see where he's
sitting?' she asked. 'I don't want to turn round again.'

Tony craned his neck.

'He's at a small table for two, in a window embrasure, right
across the other side of the room. I don't think he can have
spotted us, do you?'

'No. But as soon as we've had our meal, I'd like to go. I'm
sorry to spoil your evening, Tony, but I daren't risk getting up on
the dance floor. You *do* understand?'

He nodded glumly.

'He *would* choose tonight to come here. Still, can't be helped.'
He grinned. 'Anyway, I've no desire to be punched on the nose.

We'll eat up, then make ourselves scarce. We can always go dancing another night.'

There might not be another opportunity, Dayle thought fatalistically. She had an idea her days at Barnet Country Park were numbered now that Mac had discovered her whereabouts. She would give in her notice, she decided, before the new owner took charge. That would give her a month to look around for another job, as far away from here as possible. She would just have to hope she didn't encounter any more of her father's busybody friends. Maybe Jenny's suggestion had been a good one . . . that she should work abroad. Mac could divorce her for desertion. She need not appear in court . . .

'You're not eating,' Tony reproached her, and indeed she had only been toying with the food on her plate, not even aware of what it was that had been set before her.

'I'm sorry, I . . . I think food would choke me right now,' she apologised. 'But you eat your meal. Don't take any notice of me.'

'Why did that swine have to show up?' Tony said furiously. 'You were enjoying yourself until he walked in. I know you were.'

He finished the rest of his own meal hurriedly, pushed his plate aside and stood up.

'Come on, then.' His tone was almost savage. 'Let's get out of here.'

'Could . . . could you make sure it's safe, before I stand up?' Dayle begged. She wasn't even sure that when she *did* stand up her legs would hold her; they were trembling so much at the idea that Mac might see and recognise her. It would be mortifying if he made a scene here, in a public place.

'Their table's empty. They must have gone. Perhaps they were just passing through and stopped in for a meal?'

Dayle shook her head.

'No . . . they were formally dressed.'

'Well, they're nowhere in sight. You're quite safe.'

'You're sure they're not dancing?'

Tony swore under his breath, but he scanned the room again. 'No sign of them.'

It was unlikely he could miss Mac's distinctive height and build, so Dayle allowed herself to be urged out of her seat.

'Of course, if they've gone, we *could* stay and dance?' Tony said hopefully, but she shook her head.

'I wouldn't be very good company, Tony. It . . . it was a shock, seeing him suddenly like that.'

'I believe you're still in love with the fellow,' he accused as they crossed the room. 'I don't know the full story, of course, but . . .'

'No, you don't!' Dayle interrupted sharply. Not averse to denigrating Mac herself, she felt oddly resentful when anyone else attempted to criticise him.

She was a little nervous of going into the cloakroom to collect her coat, in case she should encounter Mac's petite brunette, but there was only the check-out girl in attendance and she breathed a sigh of relief. Tony had been right; they must have eaten their meal, then left. Feeling considerably better, she hurried back to the foyer, where Tony awaited her.

But she did not reach his side. Coming down the stair from the residential part of the Country Club was the person she least desired to meet, and that he had seen her was evident in the sudden arrogant lift of his strong chin, the slight pause in his long stride.

Her brain so paralysed by shock that she seemed unable to remember how to put one foot before another, Dayle stopped, her eyes held mesmerically by flashing green ones, as Mac closed the space between them. She parted her mouth in an effort to speak, but only the merest croak emerged from between suddenly parched lips and she licked them nervously.

Mac stood looking down at her, and with a tremendous effort she broke the spell that held their gaze fast locked, lowering her head, so that now she could only see a pair of long, muscular legs and thrusting hips in impeccably tailored trousers, the black, shining toes of his shoes. What would he say? What would he do? she wondered frantically, while the silence seemed to extend, as if time had stopped as irrevocably as her trembling legs.

'Well, Dayle?' he said at last, the deep, quiet voice she remembered so well very controlled. 'Have you nothing to say to me after all this time?'

'No,' she mumbled. 'Nothing . . . nothing at all.'

'I see.' His voice was still quiet, his tone considering. 'Well, there's a considerable amount I wish to say to *you*. You received my letter?'

She contemplated denying it, but she abhorred lies.

'Yes.' Defiantly, she raised her head once more. 'But I didn't read it.'

The line of his strong jaw tightened and she thought she saw a gleam of anger in the green, emerald depths of his eyes.

'I see. Then it is even more necessary that we should talk. Where can we go?'

'Nowhere! I'm not going anywhere with you. I'm here with . . . with a friend. He's waiting for me over there. We're just leaving.' Somehow she found the strength to walk to Tony's side. She slipped a hand through his arm. 'Sorry to keep you waiting, Tony darling, but I just bumped into an old acquaintance.'

If Tony's eyebrows had lifted at the deliberate endearment, the words had the opposite effect upon Mac's, for he was glowering at the pair of them and she noted that his hands were bunched into fists at his side. Apparently Tony had noticed it too, for he began to edge away, drawing Dayle with him.

She had to admire the control with which Mac mastered himself.

'So nice to have seen you again.' His tone faintly sarcastic. 'It won't be so long next time.' There was an unmistakable message in his eyes, before he turned away and strode towards the bar.

Dayle could not drag Tony out of the Club fast enough. She was shaking with a combination of fear and anger as she waited for him to unlock the passenger door of his car.

'Phew! That was a tricky moment!' Tony exclaimed, as they pulled away. 'Think you managed to discourage him?'

'No such luck. You don't know Mac. We haven't seen the last of him.'

Was it fear or anticipation that sent a cold frisson down her spine?

Dayle did not sleep at all that night. As soon as Tony had seen her to the cottage door, she locked and bolted herself in, then went to bed, extinguishing the lights immediately. She had no idea if Mac knew exactly where she lived, but she was taking no chances. She lay in bed, still trembling at the memory of their encounter and the other inevitable memories the sight of him had awakened. With no photograph of him, she had had to rely on recollection alone, when she wanted to picture his face, and she had believed that these imaginings had been very vivid. But they could not approach the impact of the reality. Nor could memory alone do justice to the vitality of him, his aura of potent masculinity. Oh God! Why had she been fated to see him again . . . a faded image was bad enough, but this had been unendurable. She writhed on her bed in an agony of frustration, all her

senses crying out for Mac's warmth, his nearness, his possession; and there was more agony to endure. Mac would not go
tamely away. Her rejection of him tonight would have whetted
his appetite for another confrontation. He would not rest until
he'd had his say.

She began to rehearse in her mind the things *she* would say to
him, the arguments she would put forward against his attempts
at self-justification.

But perhaps he would not seek to clear himself in her eyes.
How could he, without lying blatantly? Perhaps he meant to
accept her refusal to have anything more to do with him . . . to
notify her of his intention to divorce her. The vision of the
beautiful brunette rose to haunt her and she groaned, rolling
over to press her face into her pillow, trying to stifle the treacher-
ous, demanding throb of her body.

She was white-faced and hollow-eyed next morning, when she
reported for duty. She found Tony in a flurry of activity.

'The buyer's coming to look round today. Dayle, will you do
the tours . . . you're our best guide. I want this chap to be
impressed.'

She had wanted to discuss last night with Tony, to beg for a
few days off, during which she could disappear from the environs
of the Country Park, postpone that final confrontation with Mac
. . . but Tony was far too agitated about the impending visit to
pay attention to *her* problems and obviously, in the circumstances, leave was out of the question.

She took up her position in the entrance hall, awaiting the first
batch of sightseers, and she could only pray that she would do
justice to her work, since Tony was relying on her. The sleepless
night had left its ravages upon her mind as well as upon her face
and her brain felt fogged and disorientated.

'The country estates of Victorian and Edwardian times were
regarded by those to whom they gave home and livelihood as a
complete way of life;' Dayle began her talk. 'They had no doubt
that this would go on for ever, and there is much evidence here of
life as it was lived a hundred years ago. The mansion has
upwards of two hundred rooms, for as well as the family and
their servants, the building often had to house streams of guests
and *their* servants . . .'

It was at this point that Dayle realised there had been an
addition to her party, and she faltered in mid-sentence. It was

Mac! Oh! How dared he persecute her like this, coming here
when she was working and putting her off! Today of all days,
when it was important that they should all make a good impression. Trembling with a mixture of nerves and indignation, she
managed to complete her tour, concluding with the words:

'Large house parties often took place, during which guests
could indulge in leisurely pursuits; tennis, shooting, a visit to the
kennels or a stroll in the walled garden, which still exists today
and which you will shortly be visiting. Enjoy the rest of your
tour, ladies and gentlemen.'

As the members of her party drifted away, her sense of
injustice giving her false courage, she turned upon Mac in a
spirited condemnation.

'What do you think you're doing here? I'm working, and I
thought I made it quite clear that I have nothing to say to you.'

She was not to discover what Mac's reply would have been, for
a portly man who had been hovering now stepped forward,
snapping out a reproof.

'Miss . . . er . . . whatever your name is, you will apologise
immediately! Mr MacAlastair is here with a view to purchasing
this property. If you wish to keep your job here, I suggest you
mend your manners!'

CHAPTER TWELVE

It was unfortunate that Mac's companion had been the Chairman of the County Council, Dayle thought that evening, as she drank her bedtime cocoa; and it had taken considerable charm on Mac's part and the explanation that they were old friends and sparring partners to prevent her losing her job on the spot. It was galling to think that she owed her reprieve to him; but at least he hadn't humiliated her to the extent of publicly claiming her as his wife.

Dayle could not decide which had given her the greater shock, Mac's unheralded appearance in her tour party or the news that he was the prospective buyer of Barnet Country Park; but she did know that both added up to one thing; she must get away from here. She could almost wish she *had* been given the sack for her aggressive behaviour.

She had spent the rest of the day and all of this evening in a state of trepidation, expecting at any moment to hear the knock on her door that would herald Mac's arrival; for, as she turned away, after the embarrassing scene with the Chairman, Mac had placed a restraining hand on her arm, the warmth of his fingers through her thin uniform overall disturbing to her senses.

'I'll see you later, Dayle, when the business discussions are finished.'

'Don't bother,' she said shortly.

His fingers tightened.

'I said I'll see you later, and I meant it.'

So why hadn't he turned up? Perhaps he'd changed his mind? But that wasn't like Mac; he was as tenacious of an idea as a bulldog of its grip.

Dayle had vowed that she would not make any special preparations against the possiblity . . . or rather the certainty . . . of Mac's visit. But she always had a shower every evening after work and it would have been silly to put on the same clothes she had worn all day; yet it was surprisingly difficult to decide just what she should wear. Apart from their wedding day, Mac had

never seen her in anything except jeans and sweaters . . . and the
official overall she had worn today, of course. So she had put on a
dress, one which she knew was eminently becoming to her. But it
had been a wasted effort . . . not that she had made an effort, of
course; she had felt like wearing a dress for a change . . . because
Mac had not turned up to see her in it; and now it was late, far
too late for him to be calling on her. It was a relief, of course it
was . . . but all the same, she felt curiously deflated . . . like a
fighter who, his adrenalin charging his veins ready for battle, is
deprived of his opponent.

So she had prepared for bed and, as was her normal custom,
come downstairs in nightdress and dressing gown to make and
drink her cocoa.

The mug was empty now and she was on her way to the
kitchen to wash it, when the doorbell rang. The mug fell from
suddenly nerveless fingers, smashing on the tiled floor. He was
here! He'd come after all . . . and she couldn't pretend to be in
bed asleep, because all the ground floor lights were on. The
doorbell's summons was repeated impatiently and heart thud-
ding in her throat, she went to open the door.

'Oh!' she gasped. 'Tony! It's *you*!' She didn't know whether to
laugh or cry with relief or anti climax. 'What on earth are you
doing here at this time of night?'

Surely he wasn't intending to pursue his courtship of her at
this unpropitious moment?

'Can I come in?' he asked urgently. 'Dayle, it's important, or I
wouldn't be here.'

'All right. But make it snappy, will you? I was just going to
bed.'

He followed her through into the cottage's only living room.

'You'd better sit down, Dayle. I've got some bad news for you.
I thought I ought to tell you right away. I'm afraid there's been
an accident.'

Dayle could not have stood up anyway, even if she had been
paid to do so. It was Mac! Something had happened to him.
That was why he hadn't turned up. Was he . . .?

'It was a car crash,' Tony continued. 'The . . . the brakes
failed.'

She could scarcely frame the words.

'How . . . how bad was it? Is he . . . is he . . .?'

Tony stared at her.

'*He*? I'm talking about Jenny. I always told you two that

beat-up old car would get you into trouble some day.'

For a moment his words did not register on her panic-stricken brain; then fear and subsequent relief were swamped in a rush of shame at the gladness she felt . . . he was not referring to Mac. But Jenny was her friend, and her lower lip trembled, as she stared up at Tony.

'Jenny? She . . . she's not . . .?'

'Lord, no! I'm a clumsy brute!' Tony came to sit beside her, putting a reassuring arm about her shoulders. 'I was trying, in my own stupid way, to break the news gently, but I've only succeeded in putting my foot in it. Jenny's badly shaken up and the car's a write-off, but . . .'

Dayle gave a great sob and buried her face in Tony's shoulder.

'Oh, Tony, thank heaven! First I thought you meant Mac . . . that he'd been killed or something . . . and then, when you said it was Jenny . . . Oh, Tony, are you sure she's all right?'

'Quite sure.' He gave her a comforting hug, then, with an embarassed laugh, he added, 'You know, when I took the message . . . her father phoned to say she wouldn't be back next week because of the accident . . . I thought the same as you at first. My heart was in my mouth.' He hesitated, then continued more strongly. 'Something strange happened to me, Dayle. It was as if the fright shook my brains up, but sorted them out at the same time. I suddenly realised what a good sort Jenny is . . . how ghastly it would have been, if something *had* happened to her. I . . . I must be fonder of her than I thought. You must think me a fickle sort of chap, but . . .'

Dayle sat up and gazed at him, her tear-drowned eyes sparkling.

'Tony!' she breathed. 'That . . . that's marvellous, because I'm certain Jenny feels the same way about you. She's never actually said anything and you must never tell her I . . . Oh, Tony! I'm so happy for you!' Impulsively, she flung her arms about his neck and kissed him, not questioning the reason for this wild exuberance in her spirits, just knowing that in the last few moments she had touched the depths, that an intolerable burden had first threatened and then as swiftly been removed from her.

Tony smiled shyly as she sat back and looked at him, her hand still on his shoulders.

'And *I* think I must be in love . . . for real this time,' he said.

'How touching . . . how *very* touching!'

Startled, they turned towards the door. Dayle had been aware for the last few minutes of a draught, had guessed that, in his haste, Tony had left the front door ajar. Now Mac filled the living room doorway. Dayle had never seen him really angry before . . . irritated, yes, even heated, but not this freezing anger that turned his green eyes to chips of emerald ice, stirring a flutter of panic in her.

'Mac, I . . . we . . .'

About to explain the compromising situation in which she had been discovered, Dayle stopped. Wasn't this what she had wanted? To give Mac the impression that she was interested in someone else?

At the sight of Mac, Tony had moved away from her with unflattering haste and now he was on his feet.

'Well,' he said a trifle nervously, 'I'd better be on my way, now that I've told you about . . .'

'Yes, you had!' said Mac, his tone as frosty as his eyes, 'before I chuck you out!'

'Look here, old man,' Tony protested. 'Things aren't quite what they seem. We . . .'

'*Out!*'

It was only one word, but it contained so much venom that Tony decided not to press his argument. If Dayle had been in any mood to be amused, she must have had difficulty in repressing a giggle at the cautious way in which Tony edged past Mac and out of the door. But she was feeling anything but humorous, and the sound of the front door slamming behind Tony was like the closing of prison bars. She was trapped, alone here with Mac.

'You're too late!' she said defiantly, not realising the construction which could be put upon her words.

'Too late for what?' he snapped, green eyes raking her informal attire. 'Have you and that . . .?'

'I mean it's too late to call on anyone,' she interrupted hastily. 'I was just going to bed.'

'I don't mind continuing this discussion there,' he said grimly.

Dayle gasped at the sheer effrontery of this remark, the disturbing sensuality of its implication.

'You're . . . you're not coming anywhere near my bed!'

'Why not? I *am* your husband.'

'Only . . . only in name.'

At that he raised a sardonic brow.

'I know we haven't seen each other for some considerable

ime, but if my memory serves me correctly I believe we *did* consummate our relationship?'

Dayle could feel herself flushing scarlet. Worse, she could feel he beginning of an aching void in her stomach.

'You know damned well we did, but that won't happen again,' she assured him.'

'I wouldn't be too certain about that.' Mac had moved away from the door now to stand over her, hands thrust aggressively into his pants pocket, drawing the material tight across the thrust of his hips, on a level with her mesmerised eyes. Licking her lips nervously, Dayle averted her gaze.

But he was determined she should not evade him. Iron fingers gripped her shoulders, dragging her to her feet to face him.

'There are two ways we can settle this impasse, Dayle. The quick way is for us to go upstairs together, where we belong . . . agree to forget the past, start again. Or we can talk this thing through. Which is it going to be?'

'Neither!' she said with a tortured gasp at the images he had evoked. She tried to free herself from his disturbing hold. 'I'll never share a bed with you again . . . and I've nothing to say to you, except that you can start your proceedings for a divorce as soon as you like.'

'A divorce?' His voice was hard. 'So that you can marry that . . . that cowardly twit who just left here with his tail between his legs?'

Dayle hesitated. But she would not stoop to lies. She despised all liars . . . of whom Mac was one, she reminded herself . . . and her father.

'No,' she said. 'Tony happens to be in love with Jenny . . . my best friend. He only realised it tonight, when he heard she'd been in an accident.'

'I see,' he said slowly, releasing her shoulders. 'So that little scene . . .?'

'Was perfectly innocent . . . not that it's any of your business.'

'I don't agree. Until we are actually divorced, you are still my wife.'

So he did intend to divorce her. Dayle sat down again rather suddenly. She felt sick and she must have blanched, for he sat beside her, his hand going out to lift her chin.

'Are you all right?' he asked abruptly.

'Yes.' Her voice was tremulous; then, more firmly: 'And I'll be even better when you go away and leave me alone.'

'Let's get this straight, Dayle.' Mac's deep voice was quiet, yet unshakably firm. 'I'm not leaving. You are going to explain your unpardonable behaviour to me, if I have to make you sit there all night.'

'*My* behaviour? *My* unpardonable behaviour! What the hell are you talking about? What about *your* behaviour?' Dayle was glad of the anger that surged through her, banning the weak longing to be in his arms.

'I'm talking about the way you lied to me . . . pretended to be in love with me. Pretty drastic wasn't it, Dayle? To marry me . . . in the fullest sense of the word too . . . just to get to the mainland, in order to run away from me. Pretty cheap behaviour!'

Dayle was silent for a moment. Was that really what he thought had happened? How could he imagine that she would stoop to such low trickery, that she would demean herself . . . sell herself in effect, to obtain her freedom? It only proved what she knew already. He had never loved her, or he could not believe such a thing of her.

'I've told you, I have nothing to say to you. You can sit here all night if you like, but it won't make any difference.'

He rose abruptly and prowled about the room; then he swung round to face her, his lips tight, his jaw thrusting belligerently.

'You think a lot of this Country Park . . . and your friends here, don't you?'

Puzzled at this change of subject, she nodded.

'Presumably you wouldn't like to see it sold up for building plots, the livestock dispersed, your friends out of work?' He did not wait for her reply, but issued his ultimatum. 'Either you behave like an adult and agree to hold a reasonable discussion, or I shall tell the local County Council the deal is off . . . that they'd better go ahead with their original plan, to sell the land in small lots.'

Dayle jumped up, thoroughly incensed.

'You wouldn't! Even *you* couldn't be such a swine!'

'Why not?' he asked calmly. 'What does the fate of these few acres mean to me? I could acquire several such places, all equally suitable for my purpose.'

'Then why offer for it in the first place?' she challenged. 'If you don't care one way or the other?'

'That's another story,' he said curtly. 'Which isn't relevant, if I decide not to purchase.'

'You really mean it, don't you?' she said incredulously.

'I always mean what I say . . . and say what I mean . . . unlike some people.'

'It's blackmail!'

'Yes,' he agreed. 'So now it's up to you. Do we talk, or not? Do I get that apology?'

'We'll talk if you like,' she said dully, 'but it won't get us anywhere, and I'm certainly not apologising for something that circumstances forced me to do. Anyway, you haven't apologised to me for kidnapping me.'

'No,' he said, 'because I'm not sorry I did it . . . or I wasn't until . . .'

'Until you found yourself another lady-friend,' she said coldly, 'and realised what a silly mistake you'd made, agreeing to marry *me*.'

'Lady-friend?' He looked puzzled. 'Oh, you mean last night, I suppose . . . at the Country Club. That for your information, was Councillor Roberts' wife. He had an important meeting and wasn't able to entertain me on my first evening here, so his wife kindly deputised for him.'

'That gorgeous brunette is married to that awful fat man?'

'Yes. But then we know there's no accounting for tastes.' His tone was insulting.

'Then why do you want a divorce?'

He gave a short bark of unamused laughter.

'Would you want to stay married to someone who had lied to you . . . walked out on you the morning after the wedding? Anyway, who said I wanted a divorce?'

'You did! And no, I wouldn't want to stay married to a liar, which is why I walked out on you. When I heard those men calling you by your full name, I realised what a fool you'd made of me . . . you . . . and my father.'

'*You* were the one who introduced the subject of divorce,' he insisted. 'But let's get this matter of the name straight. I can't see why that should bug you so much. O.K., so I didn't tell you my middle name was Callum. So what? I only use it for business purposes anyway. As you yourself observed, "Alastair Mac-Alastair" is somewhat of a mouthful. Besides, most people know me as Mac.'

'My father didn't . . . and you didn't tell me your name was Callum because you knew I'd recognise it,' she accused. 'Recognise it as the name of the man my father had decided I should marry.'

'*What?*'

His look of outraged bewilderment was almost convincing.

'Oh, don't pretend. Ever since my eighteenth birthday, my father has been thrusting suitable men down my throat. You were just the latest in a long line. Only this time you both decided to make certain his plans succeeded. I don't know what inducement he offered you to abduct me . . . to marry me, but . . .'

'What the hell are you on about now?' he demanded. 'Inducement? To marry *you*?'

'Oh, don't give me that innocent look! It's true what they say, that lies beget more lies.'

'The only lie I have ever told you,' Mac said forcefully, 'was to pretend that your father was being held to ransom for your good behaviour, and that was agreed between us, as being the only way to bring you to heel . . .'

'Bring me to heel!' she seethed. 'What do you think I am? A dog?'

'More of a bitch, actually,' he said, then gripped her arm as she hit out at him. 'And don't try violence with me. It won't get you anywhere.'

'No, that's the touble with you . . . you know you're stronger than I am, but just because I've less muscle than you, it doesn't mean I've less brain . . .'

'Then use it!' he snapped.

'I *am* using it. You say you agreed one lie with my father . . . Maybe! But you also agreed between you to arrange my future . . . arranged that you should have control of me *and* my money, by marrying me.'

Mac flicked contemptuous fingers under her nose.

'I don't give *that* for your money. I've told you all along, there are other things in life besides wealth.'

'Don't do that!' Dayle jumped up. 'And I don't believe you. You can't argue against documentary evidence. Perhaps you didn't realise that my father had put it all down in writing? Well, I'll just show you! Stay right there!'

She ran upstairs to her bedroom and went down on her knees, to rummage in the bottom drawer where she had eventually thrust her father's letter and Mac's. She retrieved them both. Mac could have his letter back. That way she wouldn't be tempted to read it. She wouldn't keep anything that would remind her of him.

The creak of a floorboard startled her and she stood up and turned around to see Mac close behind her.

'I told you to wait downstairs. How dare you come up here?'

'I thought it would save time,' he said airily, 'because we shall end up in here eventually.'

Oh, the conceit, the arrogance . . . the presumption of him! He was so certain he was going to get her into bed with him before the night was out. Well, he would see that she could resist his blatant masculinity. If only he would move a little further away; if only he would stop looking at her in that challenging, provocative manner.

She thrust the two letters towards him.

'Here, you can have yours back . . . and you can read my father's. Then you'll see how useless it is to go on denying your schemes.'

'So you didn't read mine?' He turned it over in his hands.

'I told you I didn't!'

'It would have saved a lot of time if you had. Sure you wouldn't like to read it now?' he offered.

'Certainly not! Now, if you'll excuse me, I'm going downstairs.'

'No, you're not.' He strolled casually towards the door, blocking her way, turned the key in the lock and put it in his pants' pocket.

'Give me that key. You've no right . . .' Dayle glared helplessly at him, as he sat down on the edge of her bed, just as if he had every right that she denied him.

He took his time reading her father's letter.

'Nowhere here does it mention the fact that I agreed to marry you,' he pointed out, as he returned the sheets of paper to their envelope. 'You father says, with some truth, that it's just as easy to fall in love with a rich man as with a poor one . . . but there is no mention of any agreement between us.'

Dayle knew the letter by heart.

'He also says that he knew I'd be safe with you, that you'd promised to give me a taste of the kind of life I'd never experienced. Well, I certainly hadn't experienced your brand of seduction before. You even . . .' her breath caught on a sob . . . 'you even told me you . . . you loved me.'

'As I remember, you told me the same thing.'

'But you said it first, you . . .' She couldn't go on; if she did she would burst into ignominious tears and he might think she cared;

and she didn't ... she *didn't*. She turned away and moved towards the window, staring out through the open curtains, even though there was nothing to see but a thin sliver of moon in a midnight sky.

She heard that betraying floorboard creak again and knew that Mac was behind her. She stiffened, closing her eyes tightly, as she prayed that he would not touch her. It was a forlorn hope. His hands were on her shoulders, pulling her back towards him, his hands moving down over the fullness of her breasts, slowly, caressingly, his face buried in the silver silkiness of her hair.

'Poor little rich girl,' he murmured.

She tried to fight off the insidious ache that was beginning somewhere low down within her.

'Not any more.' She managed to instil a note of triumph into her voice. 'I'm not going to make any claims on my father. I don't want his money. I shall live by what I can earn. So you see, you're not married to an heiress after all ... and if he tries to leave it to me I ... I shall give it all to charity.'

'Do you really think that worries me?' he said softly; his fingers were at her waist now, moving across to knead the tenseness of her stomach, making her body leap with erotic sensation. 'Haven't you seen for yourself that I could exist on a shoestring if I had to? But I don't have to. By the time I'm your father's age, I expect to be three times as rich as he is ... by my own efforts. I don't need a bride with a dowry ... no self-respecting man would.'

'No self-respecting man would agree to do what you've done,' she argued, trying desperately to pry his trespassing fingers away from her body. 'Abducting me .. forcing me into marriage...'

'I didn't force you ... you agreed to marry me.' His hands were still continuing their intimate exploration and all her senses were screaming their desire.

'Mac, please, let me go.' The words came on a sobbing breath. 'I ... I can't think straight when you do that.'

'There's no need to think,' he murmured persuasively. 'Your body is telling you, quite adequately, what you should do.'

'No, no ... it isn't fair ...'

'Everything is fair ... in love.'

'But it *isn't* love! What you're talking about, what you're doing to me, is lust, and I won't ... I won't ...'

Her words ended on an outraged gasp as Mac spun her round,

moulding her to him, increasing her pulsating need, making her aware of his own.

'There's a time for talking, and there's a time for action,' he said, 'and we've done the talking . . . too much of it, for too little result.'

With one hand he held her crushed against him, while the other took her chin in an imprisoning grip, forcing her head up so that he could possess her quivering lips. It was not a gentle kiss, but filled with a punishing passion, and made warm, intimate demands of her that his hard, muscular body was reinforcing.

Fists clenched between them, so that only their small bulk prevented her breasts from being pressed to his hard ribcage, she tried to push him from her; but as she had feared, she was no match for his superior strength. He went on kissing her, until her resistance began to waver and she lay helplessly, tremulously against him. Only then did his iron hold relax, his hands cease to be her jailers, becoming loving, caressing, pushing aside her dressing gown, so that, somehow, it fell from her shoulders to the floor; and now there was only the thin silk of her nightdress to hinder him.

She was fighting for breath, and he released her mouth for an instant to allow a life-giving gasp of air.

'Mac . . . all right, I give in . . . we'll talk. I'll listen to what you have to say, if you'll only let go of me . . .'

'We don't need to talk any more,' he said, his low-pitched voice husky, his fingers already dealing with the intricacies of the nightdress. 'You know you want me to make love to you, as much as I want to love you.'

It was true. But she wasn't going to admit it to him.

'You may know how to make a woman's body respond to yours, but you haven't convinced me . . . mentally . . . that you're not a liar, a . . . a 'bought' husband.'

'Damn you, Dayle! You'd try the patience of a saint . . . and I'm no saint!' With a violence that betrayed the strength of his physical distress, Mac threw her on to the bed. 'What do you want to know . . . and make it brief, because I don't intend to waste much more time on these preliminaries.'

'I don't need to know anything. I already know that you had an arrangement with my father . . . that you would get me to marry you, by fair means or foul.'

He took a deep breath and with a very obvious effort at

self-control, he sat down, as far away from her as the width of a
small single bed would allow.

'Right, listen to this . . . and listen carefully, because I don't
intend to repeat myself, now, or ever again. Your father is a very
good friend and colleague of mine. He came to me, in some
agitation, I may add, to ask my advice. He told me that he had a
young, headstrong, wilful daughter, who was bent on ruining
her whole life for one moment of pigheadedness; and he was at
his wits' end as to how to prevent it. It's not easy for a widower to
be father and mother to a spoilt brat.'

Dayle opened her mouth to protest at these ungallant, un
called for epithets, but one large hand came out and clamped
over her mouth.

'I *said* listen . . . and listen you will, right to the bitter end
whether you like what you hear or not . . . and the truth *is* always
painful. After your father had told me the whole story, we talked
his problem over and we came to the conclusion that the best
thing was for you to be taken right out of your normal environ-
ment, away from the toadying friends who applauded and
encouraged your rebellion.'

Dayle *had* to speak, and the only way was to free her mouth
of his obnoxious hand. So she bit him; and as he swore and
inspected the broken flesh, she lashed him with her tongue.

'Who do you think you are to decry my friends, to decide
what's best for me . . . what the hell did it have to do with you
how I chose to spend my life . . .?'

Mac didn't bother to answer her question. Instead, he exacted
retribution for the injury she had inflicted. With a speed that
surprised her, she was dragged across his knees and one large
hand bestowed a punishment upon her which she had not
experienced since nursery days. His hand was hard and heavy
and he did not chastise her lightly. Dayle felt very real pain.
Only when she began to sob convulsively did he release her, and
she was too choked to speak; able only to stare at him, as the
tears coursed down her cheeks.

'That's something your father should have done regularly
every week of your life,' he told her grimly. 'And now you'd
better listen without any further interruption, unless you want
another dose of the same.'

He paused, as if daring her to speak, and when she did not, he
nodded as though satisfied, before continuing.

'I'd only recently purchased Haa Island, with the idea of

turning it into an official bird sanctuary. Believe it or not, I really am interested in conserving some of Britain's heritage. There were some jobs that needed doing there and I'd already arranged to take some time off from my various business interests . . . a sort of working holiday. So I suggested that I take Angus's troublesome daughter along with me, keep her occupied and out of mischief. He said you wouldn't go willingly, so we devised the idea of kidnapping you. I didn't realise just what I was letting myself in for.'

Dayle continued to stare at him miserably, her pride in rags, the flow of her tears unabated, and with an irritated exclamation, he reached out for her, and after an instant's resistance she collapsed against him, seeking only comfort.

He sighed and almost absently began to caress the soft hair that spread across his chest.

'When I came to your house that night, I was expecting to carry off a gangling teenager, straight out of the schoolroom. When I saw you, I nearly cried off . . . but I'd given Angus my offer of help and I don't like to break a promise. You'll never know what a shock you gave me . . .' his grasp tightened, '. . . in that clinging, skin-tight outfit you were wearing. It was only the fact that you were such a prickly, annoying, recalcitrant creature that cooled my blood . . . for a while.'

Dayle felt the first faint stirrings of renewed desire, as he spoke, as unconsciously his clasp tightened still more. So he *had* been attracted to her right from the first. Her tears had ceased and only the occasional tearing sob remained of her former distress.

'After the first few days . . . when you began to pull your weight . . . grudgingly perhaps . . . when I began to see that you had something going for you other than a fantastic body and a beautiful face, I started to realise just what I'd taken on. Have you any conception of what I went through . . . virtually marooned on an island with a very desirable woman? There were times when I didn't know how to keep my hands off you. Remember the night I caught you in the bath?' he asked huskily. 'I was going down with a cold . . . but that was nothing to the fever in my blood . . . and you locked your door!'

A quiver ran through Dayle at the remembrance . . . of how she had felt when he'd tried that door. What would have happened if she hadn't used the bolt he'd provided?

'I knew then that I was falling in love with you.'

She stirred restlessly and looked up at him as though she were about to speak, but he shook his head.

'Hear me out . . . I knew I was falling in love with you, but I didn't want to take advantage, betray the trust your father had placed in me. So, as soon as it was safe to use the boat, I decided we'd go to Slu-Voe . . . and I telephone him. Frankly, I was pretty scared, even at that distance, having to tell him I wanted to marry his daughter. I thought he'd blast me off the face of the earth, for using the advantage I'd had. But he was delighted. He . . .'

'He would be!' Dayle couldn't restrain herself. 'Considering that was what he was angling for all along . . . the reason you were invited to dinner at our house!'

Mac set her away from him, looking her straight in the eyes, his own gaze steady.

'I swear to you, Dayle, that I knew nothing of that. I fell in love with you without any prompting from your father. But unless you're prepared to believe me . . .'

Did she believe him? Dared she? Should she risk being hurt again? She wanted to believe him . . . oh, *how* she wanted to . . . and he'd said he loved her. She wanted to believe that too. He was still looking at her, green eyes unfaltering, and she thought of all the other people who loved and respected him. He couldn't deceive everyone. Of course her father would be cock-a-hoop, if she capitulated. But did that really matter? What did *his* triumph weigh in the balance against *her* happiness, her love for Mac? So what if Angus had got his own way, if he *had* been right? At least she'd discovered her love for Mac herself, when she had not known who he really was. A great sigh welled up in her . . . a sigh of relief and longing.

'I . . . I believe you,' she whispered.

'And you'll come back to me, with no reservations . . . go where I go, live as I live?'

'Anywhere!' She breathed. 'Even a tiny rock in the ocean . . .'

She longed now to be taken into his arms, to be given practical evidence of his love for her, but he made no move towards her.

'We may as well get all the talking over.' A whimsical, captivating smile twisted his mouth. 'For I don't intend that there should be much talking for the rest of the night . . .'

Dayle trembled at the implication of his words and swayed towards him, but he stood up and slowly paced the tiny room.

'About Haa Island . . . I don't really intend that we should

spend our entire life there, you know? Just the summer season.'
Mac looked at her expectantly.

She stared up at him, injecting all that she felt for him into her
expression, the tender softness of her blue eyes.

'I don't mind where we live, so long as we're together.'

He took an impulsive, half step towards her, then checked
himself.

'How would you feel,' he said, 'if we made this our home?'

'Here? The Country Park? But . . .'

'Yes.' His expression became eager, boyish. 'I've looked at the
flats over the mansion. Knocked into one, it's large enough to
make a splendid family home . . . there will be a family?'

She flushed.

'I . . . I hope so.' The thought of bearing Mac's children
wrenched her inside with exquisite agony. 'But what about
Tony? He lives in one of the flats?'

'We'll provide accommodation for our staff, of course . . . but
in the grounds. I understand there's more land adjacent to the
Park. I intend to purchase that too. But enough of business. Just
tell me, would *you* be happy with that arrangement? I only
contemplated the purchase in the first place, because I thought it
might appeal to you.'

Dayle nodded her agreement. Now she was longing for the
talking to be done, for him to come to her. But still Mac held
back.

'Isn't there anything you want to say, before . . .' His eyes
moved irresistibly towards the bed.

She knew he was still insisting on his right to an apology, but
she didn't mind. She could never be happy with a man who
allowed her to walk all over him.

'Only . . . only that I . . . I love you, and I'm sorry I ever
doubted you,' she whispered, her arms going out instinctively, in
an inviting welcoming gesture.

His eyes holding hers, Mac undressed before he accepted her
invitation, the inevitable delay rousing her to a fever pitch of
anticipation. Then long, sensitive fingers removed her nightdress and she heard the sharp intake of his breath as her lovely
curves were revealed to him, before he pulled her down on to the
bed.

Knowing the urgency, the need that possessed them both, she
had expected his lovemaking to be perfunctory, his possession of
her swift; but Mac had more experience than that. He did not

hurry her . . . even though they had made love before . . . even though she was no longer an untutored girl, he did not deny her any of the sensual pleasures of arousal.

As he kissed her, his hands stroked her, renewing their acquaintance with places only he had ever touched before. Ecstasy rippled through her as his touch lingered upon the soft mounds of her breasts, the flatness of her stomach, moving to the well of her hips. Then, as she responded fiercely, he pulled her tightly against him, controlling his own rising passion as she moaned in a fever of wanting. At last, when they had both reached intolerable heights of desire, his movements intensified and their union was an inevitable, earth-shattering climax.

They lay quietly, still fast in each other's embrace.

'Where,' murmured Mac, between gentle kisses that barely brushed her bruised, moist lips, 'shall we spend the rest of our delayed honeymoon?'

Inevitably, behind her closed eyes rose a picture of that dear green isle where she had first realised her love for him. She curved against him, already longing for a repetition of his lovemaking.

'I think,' she whispered against his suddenly eager mouth, 'that you know very well where I would like to go . . . Somewhere where we can be quite alone, for a long, long time.'

'Except for a few thousand birds?' he teased gently, but her reply was lost in a moan of pure ecstasy, as their physical oneness was renewed.

A WORD ABOUT THE AUTHOR

Annabel Murray was born in Hertfordshire, England, and now lives in Liverpool with her two teenage daughters and her husband, who is a college teacher. He has always actively encouraged her in pursuing her hobbies, which have been legion, with writing foremost among them. Annabel had ambitions to be an author from the time she was in school.

In the interim, other hobbies captured her attention and energy. Involvement in arts and crafts led to her participation in the foundation of a local arts group. Drama, too, intrigues her, and she has appeared in many plays, produced others and even won an award for a historical play she wrote. Hiking and gardening allow her to enjoy outdoor beauty and healthful air.

None of her interests, though, is truly separate from her writing activity, for she uses all her experiences to flesh out her heroines' backgrounds. Not even her holidays are exempt. Like every serious writer, she keeps her eyes open for the unusual detail that can be transplanted into fiction from the life around her. Annabel's several novels attest to the acuteness of her observation.

Coming Next Month in Harlequin Romance!

2629 A GIRL CALLED ANDY   Rosemary Badger
A tempestuous romance about a young teacher trying to
forge a life for herself and her younger siblings in
Tasmania—without the interference of her autocratic
neighbor, a handsome novelist.

2630 MAELSTROM   Ann Cooper
An arrogant oil executive believes that Samantha, a British
engineer, has no place in Saudi Arabia—except perhaps in
his bed! Samantha tries heroically to resist his charm and
prove him wrong.

2631 THE CHEQUERED SILENCE   Jacqueline Gilbert
A young actress deserts her man—a famous director—for
reasons she fears to divulge. When they meet again years
later, he still cannot forgive her—nor can she reveal her
secret....

2632 DESERT FLOWER   Dana James
Two British doctors, one an opinionated male and the other
a beautiful woman, fight for their different points of view—
and fight against their mutual attraction—in an Egyptian
oasis clinic.

2633 ONCE MORE WITH FEELING   Natalie Spark
Life becomes unbearably complicated for a young English
actress when she performs in a play directed by her one-time
idol, a man who years before humiliated her—and betrayed
her actress mother!

2634 ALMOST A STRANGER   Margaret Way
Sydney, Australia, is the setting for this intriguing love story
of a young woman caught in a family feud—and caught in
the throes of desire for a man she finds just too disturbing....

Harlequin Celebrates

Thirty-Five
Years
of
Excellence

...and our commitment to excellence continues. Indulge in the pleasure of superb romance reading by choosing the most popular love stories in the world.

Harlequin Presents®

Exciting romance novels for the woman of today—a rare blend of passion and dramatic realism.

Harlequin Romance™

Tender, captivating stories that sweep to faraway places and delight with the magic of love.

HARLEQUIN SUPERROMANCE™

Longer, more absorbing love stories for the connoisseur of romantic fiction.

Harlequin Temptation™

Sensual and romantic stories about choices, dilemmas, resolutions, and above all, the fulfillment of love.

Harlequin American Romance™

Contemporary romances—uniquely North American in flavor and appeal.

Code: 35-1